WHOM THE SON SETS FREE

"MY SON'S WIFE" SERIES
BOOK THIRTEEN

SHELIA E. BELL

"Perfect Stories About Imperfect People Like You...and Me"

WHOM THE SON SETS FREE

Book 13
"My Son's Wife" series

Shelia Writes Books

Perfect Stories About Imperfect People Like You...and Me!

NATIONAL BESTSELLING AUTHOR
Shelia E. Bell

Holy Rock Chronicles Shorts 4-6
Christian Black, Esq.
If Your Price Is Right
Love Shoulda Brought You Home

"Holy Rock Chronicles" is a spinoff series of short stories that take you on an addictive journey into the intriguing lives of the notorious members of the Graham and McCoy families from the national bestselling "My Son's Wife" series. These shorts are specially crafted to provide an exclusive, behind-the-scenes look at the characters' lives. I suggest you read the following shorts *before* reading "Whom the Son Sets Free," but *it is not* required.

To all literary supporters who have made this series, these characters, and these stories come alive and stay alive.

1

THE THRESHOLD

"Though it may be painful, embrace the endings, for they often mean the arrival of new beginnings." Shelia E. Bell

Hezekiah unfortunately spent his 55th birthday in the confines of prison. He was deep in his feelings, overwhelmed by his circumstances. Here he was, another year around the sun, and he was distraught and depressed about how his life was playing out.

"Ahh," he bellowed, his voice rumbling through the cell-blocks. A man once skilled at manipulating both hearts and pockets dropped to his knees and onto the filthy, grimy cell floor.

"God, help me! Get me outta this hell hole!" he cried. Each word, a desperate plea for mercy. Okay, so he'd done his share of wrong. The weight of his past pressed upon him like an unforgiving burden intensified by the reality of where he had been the last three years. The chilling echo of cell doors slamming shut and other inmates' screams and turmoil was a cruel and constant reminder of his fate. He'd been low-down and dirty to a lot of folks, but only if they deserved it. But this time, he was innocent.

He removed his phone from the hidden compartment inside the walls of his cell. He looked around, ensuring no one approached his door, and caught him. To get himself out of his foul mood, he called Stiles, his one trusted connection to his family and what was going on in the free world.

"When you get out of that place, don't worry, we're going to celebrate number fifty-five right." Stiles said, trying to sound positive and lift his brother's spirit.

"Thanks, but when I get out of this place, celebrating a birthday will be the last thing on my mind. Forget my birthday, tell me, what's the latest on Black's wife? It's been a minute since I talked to him."

"She's doing good, considering what happened," Stiles said.

"Yeah, man, I hated to hear that," Hezekiah said.

Christian Black had been and remained an answered prayer for Hezekiah. The former New York powerhouse attorney was quickly establishing a name for himself in the Memphis legal arena. Black was highly confident that he would get Hezekiah released from prison, and Hezekiah believed that if anyone could make it happen, it would be Christian Black.

"Yeah, He is. Anyway, physically, she's healing. But emotionally and mentally? Let's say I think she still has a ways to go. They haven't been back to church since it happened. When I leave here, I'm going to go see them. You know, say a prayer and see if there's anything me or the church can do for them."

"Good, good. They come from New York. All kinds of outrageous crimes occur there, yet they were safe there." Hezekiah sighed, shaking his head. "Memphis has to do better."

"I agree. But I thank the good Lord that they found her alive."

"I know that's right. Now tell me...what about my son? Any word on his whereabouts?"

"No more than what you already know. He's still MIA, and now his phone is off."

"Yeah, it was going to voicemail. Now I get that message you hear when your phone is disconnected," Hezekiah said. "I still can't imagine where he is, and what could have made him leave his family, especially the boys?"

"That's the million-dollar question."

"I pray to God he's not out there hurt somewhere or worse..." Hezekiah sighed as his voice trailed off.

"That's unlikely. I told you he told Pepper he was leaving because he needed time to sort some things out. Sounds like he may have had this planned."

"I don't understand, man. What can my son be thinking? He wants to be a punk that bad?"

"See, that's probably why he felt he had to leave. He feels judged by his own family. You and Fancy have never accepted him for who he is. I've heard him say that on more than one occasion."

"I won't go against what the Good Book says. If he has a problem with that, that's between him and the Lord. I don't see what's so hard about that."

"I understand what you're saying, but what I'm saying is the kid has a lot on his shoulders, Hezekiah. I can only imagine how difficult it must be for him to deal with his issues and everything happening around him."

"A lot on his shoulders? Like what?"

"You're his father. You should know what I mean. The guy

is struggling with his self-identity while trying to be a good father and husband, and you and I know Xavier worked his tail off for New Holy Rock. If it wasn't for his help in the office, not to mention he's the financial administrator, I don't know what I would have done."

With Stiles in control of New Holy Rock Ministries while he served his time, Hezekiah couldn't be more grateful for his son and brother's help. It was one less thing for him to be concerned about while he petitioned God for Christian Black to get him released, but today, he was not in the frame of mind to be all cheery and positive, not today. His hand trembled as he ran it over his balding scalp.

"I need to get out of this place," he seethed, hitting the wall with an open palm. "I have to get out!"

"Chill, bruh," Stiles told him when he heard his brother's outburst. "What will getting yourself upset solve? Absolutely nothing."

"Look, Stiles, that boy has issues, and so does that conniving brother of his."

"Come on, now. Don't you think it's time to work things out with Khalil? Especially with Xavier missing. You should try to draw closer rather than continue this bitter father-son rivalry."

"If he wants to talk like a man, I'll listen."

"He's young, Hezekiah. You and I—we've both been young, stupid, and irresponsible—until we learned better."

"But to steal from me? You know he's wrong. I guess you forgot he also tried to lock me up for embezzlement. But let's not stop there. He stole Holy Rock from under me, Stiles."

"Need I remind you that you were once a thief? Out of your own mouth, you said you and Fancy served time in prison back in the day for embezzling church funds in Chicago. Am I right?"

Hezekiah emitted a grunt.

"And you say he stole Holy Rock from under you? I beg to differ. You served as senior pastor after I left for Houston. When you had a stroke, your health became the priority. Khalil stepped up and filled your shoes. Overall, he's doing a good job at Holy Rock. All I'm saying is that you messed up badly when you were younger. Believe it or not, you and Khalil have more in common than you may realize. When you got out of prison in Chicago, you said that's when you turned your life around and answered God's call to preach. Khalil has done the same. He went from stealing cars and purses to serving God. Even now, you've made mistakes along the way. You being in prison again is proof of that."

"So, you're saying I should just let Khalil slide? Give him a pass because he's a young cat?"

"Yeah, that's exactly what I'm saying. The young man is still learning. He's still fumbling the ball. The same is true for Xavier."

"I don't care how you want to explain his actions by saying Khalil is young and doesn't understand some things. I'm telling you, he's not a kid anymore. He's a grown man. He knows the kind of game he's playing. Come on, now. What's wrong with you? He got you on his little payroll or something?" Hezekiah checked.

"You know what, I'm not going down that path with you. Not today. I'm about to head out here to see Black and his wife. I'll call Pepper on my way home and see what's the latest she's heard, if anything, about Xavier."

"Thanks. I'll try to call her again later this week. Man, I can't get over this one. Where could he be?" Hezekiah's voice dropped.

"He's going to turn up. And he's going to be fine. I know it," Stiles said.

"Yep, you're right. God's protecting him wherever he is."

"Right, well, we'll talk later. Oh, before we hang up, what's the latest on your situation? I know Christian's mind is on his wife's well-being right now, but you said he felt positive about your release the last time you two spoke."

"Yeah, he did. We're still playing the waiting game. Black seems to think a decision could be coming down at any time. I'm telling you now if they don't let me out of this place, I don't know if I'm going to make it. There's so much happening on the outside that I need to be helping you and my family with. My son has disappeared. Nobody knows where he is...if he's safe or even alive. God, I need out," he cried.

"Hey, what did I say? It's going to be all right. Everything is going to work out. Xavier's going to be good. Your relationship with Khalil is going to be restored. And you're going to get out of prison. You'll see. God's been taking care of you and our family all this time. He's not about to forsake you, me, or any of us now."

"I gotta go," Hezekiah said after a few seconds of silence. "I'll try to call tomorrow."

"Okay, but tell me you're going to be straight," Stiles said.

"What choice do I have?"

Hezekiah ended the call and returned the phone to its safe place. He laid back on his bunk, rested both hands behind his head, and stared at the concrete ceiling.

†

On the drive to see Christian and Luna, Stiles turned up the volume when he heard the song by gospel artist LeAndria Johnson. The words resonated in his spirit as she sang, *"Better days are coming. It's only a season..."*

Stiles swayed his head in tune with the music as the words

ushered him into a place where it was just him and God. He thought about all he had experienced in his life. All that God had brought him through. He felt for his brother being behind bars and feeling helpless and hopeless. He prayed that Xavier was safe and would return home soon and that better days *were* coming. Stiles did not want anyone to experience the indescribable pain that came with losing a child. He still lived with the painful memory of the death of his little girl. Her senseless death made him think about her mother, Detria. Seeing her walk around with only a damaged arm from the accident caused by her jealousy while his baby girl lost her life was still hard for him sometimes. He had found it hard to forgive her and the others who had hurt him. Yet, God had not given up on him. God would not give up on Hezekiah either.

As he continued the drive and the song faded, his thoughts turned to Luna Black. He began praying for her mind to be healed and for God to give Christian the right amount of patience, understanding, and love for his wife during this difficult period.

2

SHATTERED

"Happiness in the present is only shattered by comparison with the past." Douglas Horton

The couple sat on the sofa facing Stiles in their spacious family room.

Luna's physical wounds had long since healed. However, she was still experiencing trauma from the abduction and assault and the knowledge that life for her and Christian was far different than the couple had expected.

"Are you sure you don't want something to drink? I can make you some coffee, and we have soda and bottled water in the fridge," Luna offered, looking much thinner than Stiles was used to seeing.

"No, thank you, I'm good," he said, raising a hand to stop her.

"I have some fresh baked oatmeal raisin cookies. Would you like some of those?"

"No, I'm good. Tell me, how are you doing? The last time I came by, you weren't feeling well."

"Oh, I'm all right," she said, looking away briefly and then back at him.

"She went back to work this week, something I was hoping she wouldn't have done. At least, not now. And especially under the circumstances," said Christian.

"Maybe going back to work will be good," Stiles said. "I mean, I'm not a doctor; I'm just saying maybe work can help you heal, take your mind off what happened."

Luna and Christian's eyes locked. Christian grabbed hold of her hand.

"There's something we haven't told you, something we've been praying about," said Luna humbly.

"And we're *still* praying about it," Christian said, squeezing his wife's hand tighter.

"What is it?" I want you to feel comfortable talking to me."

"We do, we trust you," said Christian.

"You're our pastor," said Luna. "But what happened to me," she paused and looked at her husband, "affected both of us. It's different from anything we've ever experienced."

Stiles sat silently, waiting patiently, not wanting to make Luna or Christian feel forced to talk.

When she learned she was pregnant from the brutal attack, the couple faced a huge decision—to keep the baby or not. Their staunch Christian beliefs, especially Luna's, forbade her from having an abortion. She could not justify that in her spirit. Was this a sign from God? Christian could not produce children, and Luna had longed to feel the love and warmth of carrying a child. The couple, before the assault, had accepted that would never be—until now.

"I'm pregnant," Luna said quickly, looking at her husband.

"Pregnant?" Stiles repeated and frowned. "But...I thought y'all couldn't...." Stiles shifted his eyes from Luna to Christian.

A hush fell over the room as Stiles leaned forward in the chair, resting his elbows on his thighs.

"I, uh, congratulations," he said, raising both hands happily in the air and replacing a look of confusion with a huge smile.

"That's all we'd like to say, other than the baby should make his or her arrival in early fall," said Christian.

A faint smile appeared on Luna's face, and then, as if she forced it, her mouth spread wider, and she looked at her husband. The couple kissed quickly and squeezed hands as if announcing their undying solidarity.

"God is good," said Stiles. "Sista Black, you've been through a lot these past months." He then looked at Christian. "And Brother Black, I don't have to tell you to ensure this woman is pampered and well cared for."

"No, you don't. This is the love of my life." He placed an arm around her waist and pulled her next to him, closing the gap between them.

"Well, I guess I'll get ready to go. I want to pray with you before I leave," Stiles said, "if that's okay."

"You know it is," Christian spoke up.

"Your prayers and those of people around us are what sustained me. When I was abducted, I was terrified. I was in a dark, filthy room with rodents and roaches everywhere. But I could feel people praying for me. I felt God's presence and protection protecting me. So yes, I know prayer works."

"Absolutely." Stiles nodded. Christian echoed the sentiment with a nod as well. The three gathered in a circle and held hands while Stiles prayed.

"Okay, I'm going to leave you to get some rest. I understand now why Brother Black didn't want you to go back to work just yet, but I'm staying out of that. Y'all take care, and God bless you."

"Thanks, Pastor," said Christian.

"Yes, thank you, Pastor," Luna said.

"Remember, if there's anything I or the church can do to help, let me know."

"I'm sorry, Pastor. We've been so wrapped up in our situation that we failed to ask how you and your family are doing. Any word from your nephew?"

Luna looped her arm inside of Christian's.

"Nothing yet, but we're holding out hope. God has the final say so. He brought you home, didn't he," Stiles said and smiled.

"That he did," said Christian, wrapping an arm even tighter around his wife.

Luna smiled.

Stiles hugged the couple and departed.

When the door closed, Luna fell into Christian's chest.

"I guess you made your final decision, huh," said Christian, resting his chin on the crown of her head.

Luna slowly looked up but remained silent as she stared into his eyes. Tears formed. "But what about you? Are *you* sure?"

"We're keeping the baby. Really, what choice do we have anyway? And with the new anti-abortion laws in effect, it will be harder if we choose to do something like that. Which we're not," Christian said.

"I just want you to be okay with this. I know it won't be easy. It's not going to be easy for me either. I'm carrying the child of my rapist," she cried. "But I can't see myself killing this baby." She rubbed her tummy. "I'm sorry, Christian."

Christian held her and pressed her head back against his

chest. "Shhh, everything will be all right. We'll get through this. You'll see." He rubbed her head of hair back and forth. Did he mean what he said? Could he handle seeing his wife's belly swell from the seed of another man? Would he be able to love the child unconditionally? He didn't know if he could.

3
SAY IT AIN'T SO

"No matter what may come my way, my life is in your hands."
God's Property

Hezekiah woke up in the wee hours of the morning, soaked in a clammy cold sweat. He was grateful he no longer shared his cramped space with a cellmate, but he was alone, lonely, and in deep despair. Sixty-five days had come and gone since Xavier took off without a trace. Grief surrounded him like a weighted blanket. The weight of unbearable sorrow bore down upon his weary shoulders as he grappled with the devastating news that had shattered his heart—Xavier had been found in a hotel in Oregon—deceased.

The day he received the news, he had just returned to his cell from holding his Sunday service. One of the correctional officers met him at his cell and told him the tragic news. Hezekiah called Stiles, who confirmed that Xavier had indeed succumbed to the darkness of his mind and taken his own life.

The tragic suicide of his son weighed on him like an immeasurable burden, magnified by the choppy history they shared. The cold bars that confined him mirrored the icy grip of grief that engulfed him. Tears flowed freely, tracing paths down his cheeks as he was shattered in what could only be described as a sea of despair. The dull gray cell walls seemed to be closing in around him.

The pencil-thin mattress made him stiff as a board. He got out of his bed, stretched, and sat on the cold steel toilet, leaning his head over the sink just an inch or two away, feeling like he was going to puke up his insides.

Tears flooded, and he heaved as a fresh round of hurt washed over him as if it would drown him. He replayed the days of old when Xavier was a kid in Chicago before life took a swirling turn for all of them. During that time, Xavier was a whiz kid in school but an introvert. Hezekiah and Fancy didn't find out until much later that their baby boy was gay.

Memories of happier times flashed before him like a slideshow, each image accompanied by the sting of regret. Their relationship had been riddled with struggles and misunderstandings, leaving scars that never healed. The agony of his loss was entangled with remorse for what could have been had their father/son bond found healing and reconciliation.

Added to his pain were fresh, horrid memories of him draped in handcuffs and shackles, standing and looking down on his son's pearl-white casket. Seeing Xavier in a casket was a pain he would never be able to describe, and he didn't know if it would ever go away.

He reached underneath his mattress without getting off the toilet. He pulled out a brown envelope. Hunched over, his eyes dripping heavy with sorrow, his hands trembled as he opened it. He clutched his son's obituary and began weeping as he leafed through it.

Next, he pulled out a copy of Xavier's suicide note. Pepper sent a copy to him and Fancy. It almost tore him apart reading it. He could only imagine what reading the letter did to Fancy.

My Beloved Family,

I have found myself at a crossroads filled with unbearable pain. Pain that has haunted me since the days of my youth. The weight of my past, my choices, and the emotional scars that have lingered in my heart have finally become more than I can bear. As I pen these words, please know that I am filled with a deep sense of shame, regret, and sorrow for the path I am about to embark upon.

From childhood, I have carried a burden that has grown heavier each year, casting shadows on moments that should have been filled with laughter and joy. I want you to know that my decision is not one made lightly but born out of a desperation to escape the relentless pain that has consumed me since I was that boy of nine who was so unfairly taken advantage of by someone older, someone way bigger. That someone who alluded a fate worse than mine because I was too afraid to tell? Orlando Foster. Yes, you may be shocked, but I can finally say his name. You trusted him. We all trusted him. Until I no longer did. I told myself that Orlando's pain ran deeper than mine.

Why else would he hurt me? As I take this step into whatever lies ahead, I pray once more for God to give me strength to forgive Orlando. Yet, forgiveness always seems to stay one step ahead of me. Enough of me riding the self-pity train. It is time to move on. I cannot find the words to express the ache that fills my heart at the thought of causing you so much anguish. The knowledge that my choice will hurt the ones who love me is a pain I can hardly bear, and I am profoundly sorry.

To my precious sons, my heart breaks as I think of the life you will lead without me by your side. But you deserve a father who can offer you love, guidance, and strength, a role I am not worthy of filling. Please know that my decision does not reflect my love for you, but it is my heart-wrenching attempt to escape the torment that has plagued my existence.

To my family, especially you, Mother, I am so sorry for the pain and confusion my departure will bring. I hope you can find it in your heart to forgive me for my choices and the burden I am about to place upon you.

Pepper, I hope you understand that my decision is one born from anguish and despair, a plea for release from a lifetime of suffering silently. When you look at our sons, I beg you to remember the moments of happiness we shared and the love that bound us.

And to God, whose mercy I seek in this darkest of moments, I ask for forgiveness for taking matters into my own hands. I pray that you will find it in your infinite wisdom to grant me solace and peace in the afterlife.

So, with a heavy heart and tears in my eyes, I bid you all farewell. May you find the strength to heal and carry on, and may my memory be one of love rather than pain.

Forever in your hearts,
Xavier

Hezekiah sobbed as the letter fell from his hands onto the concrete floor.

4
DOES JOY COME IN THE MORNING?

"Getting over a painful experience is much like crossing monkey bars. You have to let go at some point in order to move forward."
C.S. Lewis

F our months after the abduction, Christian was doing everything in his power to understand Luna's changed personality. He would never know what she experienced under the hands of the sick, evil bastard who assaulted her. They would forever be reminded of the nightmare of her abduction because Luna was carrying this demented man's kid.

"Are you sure you're good?" Christian asked as he and Luna got ready for work.

"Yes, I'm good. Going into the office has kept me busy and I think it helps with my mental recovery."

"Good, what about physically?"

"I haven't been sick this morning. Thank God," she said,

staring at her reflection. "I did get a little queasy at work yesterday, but it passed after I drank a ginger ale." She placed the last bit of mascara on and shifted toward her husband.

Christian walked up behind her and kissed her lightly on the side of her neck. He felt her stiffen, and he immediately stepped back.

"I'm sorry, babe," she apologized. "It's...."

"No need," he said somberly, straightening his tie. "You about ready?"

"Yes." Luna rubbed her belly.

He missed being intimate and showing bits of affection. She used to like his spontaneity, and now it was almost like she couldn't stand for him to be in the same bed with her, and she definitely did not want to make love. Ever since her assault, she'd turned away his advances. Adding to the marital pressure was learning seven weeks after the abduction that she was pregnant. This revelation caused an even bigger gap in their communication. He and Luna had always been able to have open and honest conversations until now. He couldn't tell how she really felt about carrying the seed of a rapist. As for him, he had no choice but to take it one day at a time.

The drive to their respective offices was silent. Christian wrestled with his thoughts. He wasn't sure how he would be a father to another man's child. This was far different from adoption. Adoption meant they made a choice, but this was not the case. Each time he saw his wife's belly growing or heard her having morning sickness, it was a cruel reminder that the kid she was carrying was not his. What was God up to? Why had he allowed such a terrible thing to happen?

"You're awfully quiet," Luna said when Christian pulled up and stopped at the traffic light.

"A lot on my mind. I have a full day at the office *and* court."

"Are you sure that's all?"

Christian looked at his wife. "Yep, that's all."

Luna didn't seem convinced. "Look, I'm sorry for how I've been acting lately," she said.

"There's nothing to apologize for," he said. "You've been through a lot, Luna. I understand that. Don't worry about me. I'm good."

"I know you, Christian, which means I know how difficult this has to be for you. I mean, it's difficult for me but for you....God, I'm so sorry." She looked down at her belly and touched it while holding back the tears cresting in the corner of her eyes.

Christian reached across the seat, frowned, and grabbed hold of her hand, squeezing it. "Why do you keep saying you're sorry? For what? What are you talking about?"

"For everything."

"Look, we've talked about this. Baby, what happened was not your fault. Please, don't do this to yourself. I love you, and I'm going to do whatever it takes to support you during this. We have to believe that God allowed this for a reason. We both wanted a child. We can't dictate how God wanted to bless us with one. His ways are not our ways."

"But are you going to be able to love this child knowing how it was conceived?"

The light changed, and he slowly accelerated into traffic, avoiding answering the question. Luna had asked a viable question. Could he, would he be able to give love to this child? He wasn't sure, and it scared him.

"I'll call you if I can get away for lunch," he told Luna when he pulled up outside her office building.

"Okay." She opened the door and got out before Christian could kiss her goodbye. Things like this made Christian pause about the future of his marriage. Was this the beginning of their doom?

He pulled away from the curb and headed toward his office. A few minutes later, his phone rang as he pulled into his assigned parking space. His mouth upturned when he saw the name.

"What is it, Lorie?"

"Here we go again. What's up with the attitude, brother-in-law? I thought you would be happy to hear from me this time."

"I don't know why you would think that. Look, I'm busy; I have a lot going on. What do you want?"

"Aww, now. That's no way to treat your sister-in-law." Lorie laughed. "Remember the last time we talked? I told you there's a real estate conference in Nashville coming up that I plan to attend. I'm still thinking about driving to Memphis while I'm there. I want to lay eyes on my sister. How is she doing anyway?"

"Your sister is good. Like I told you before, there's no need for you to come and disrupt her life. If you've kept up with the news, which I'm sure you have, you know what happened."

"Yes, I heard," Lorie said, sounding serious.

"But like I said, she's good. She's just got a lot on her mentally." Christian didn't divulge Luna's pregnancy. The less Lorie knew, the better. "You showing up here unannounced, after the two of you being estranged for years, won't make sense. You know it, and I know it. So what's the real deal?"

"I told you, I want to make amends with my sister. After what happened to her, I'm even more determined to see her. Why are you giving me such a hard time about this?"

"You know darn well why. You're not coming here to make peace; just the opposite. You're coming to stir up confusion and to bring up the past. I've repeatedly told you I'm sorry about what happened between us. God only knows how I wish I never cheated, especially with you."

Lorie laughed into the phone. "You can't be serious."

"Oh, I'm serious, all right. I made a huge mistake, but what's done is done, and what went down between us happened a long time ago. When you told me you were her sister, it was a shock, true enough, but it was over when we found that out. So let it go. Leave Luna alone and leave *me* alone!"

"Look, this is not about what happened between you and me. You weren't all that anyway," she retorted. "Like you said, that was ages ago. I was just messing with you when I was calling before. I'm serious now. This really is about Luna. My sister could have been murdered! But thank God she survived that horrid attack. What happened to her made me realize that life is too short and fragile to hold grudges. I want to make things right with Luna and my parents, and I intend to do it whether you like it or not," she growled, and the line went silent.

Christian pounded his fist against the steering wheel. "That...uhh," he muttered, climbing out of the car and slamming the door.

"Good morning," he mumbled to his administrative assistant as he strolled past her cubicle. Before she could respond, he abruptly closed his office door.

He plopped down in his chair and twirled around, facing the riverfront view. Resting an elbow on the arm of his chair, he thought about Lorie's call. This was at least the fourth or fifth time she'd called in the past few months. The woman was becoming like a nagging itch he couldn't get rid of.

He wished he could believe she wanted to patch up things with Luna. That would be a good thing. But Christian felt there was more to Lorie's motives. However, given the current circumstances in his and Luna's lives, he didn't have the time or energy to invest in Lorie and her shenanigans. He would handle her if she called again.

He picked up a pen from his desk and stared into space. His wife was pregnant by a dirty freaking rapist. A nervous chuckle escaped him.

"I don't think I can do this, God. I need your help to help my wife," he prayed aloud.

The whirlwind of thoughts filled him with self-disgust. Thoughts like: *What if she conveniently lost the baby? Would that be such a bad thing? What if she found someone and someplace where abortions were still performed without being scrutinized by anti-abortion people? What if they gave the kid away?*

He placed his head into his hands in shame. "God, forgive me for thinking like that. Just do whatever you will, but whatever you do, Lord, I need you to help me to accept."

5
BEYOND REPAIR

"My mouth says, "I'm ok." My fingers text, "I'm fine. My heart says, "I'm broken." Unknown

Fancy put away the last of the flyers she had presented to the ministry teams at Holy Rock to the side. A whirlwind of thoughts danced through her mind. Despite experiencing her share of ups and downs, she was grateful for God's goodness toward her and her family. She was a grandmother with three beautiful grandkids, financially secure, talented, and creative. She was in a good space for the first time in a long time—UNTIL her world came crashing down. Xavier's death was something she would never ever get over. Her baby was gone, taking a huge chunk of her heart with him.

†

She returned from the cemetery. She had not missed a day

visiting Xavier's grave since she had to witness her baby boy being lowered into the ground. Her heart was shattered into a million pieces that day. She had returned to attending church, but that was an even more difficult task. Everywhere she went, everything she did, something seemed to remind her of him.

The phone rang, startling her.

"Fancy, how are you?"

"I'm okay," she said low and slow.

Silence.

"Fancy?"

"Yes?"

"Is there anything I can do for you? I hate to hear you like this."

"Can you bring our son back? Can you do that, Hezekiah? If you can't, then no, you can do nothing for me!"

"Oh, Fancy, how I wish I could bring him back," he replied, his voice cracking. "Stiles told me you've been going to the gravesite every day. I don't think that's good for you."

"I don't think you're in any position to tell me what I can and cannot do or where I can or cannot go. My baby is gone, Hezekiah. Do you understand that?"

"Of course I do. Don't you think I'm hurting, too? I had to stand over his casket in shackles and handcuffs, Fancy. I couldn't do anything but look down at his body and stare at him. That hurt. It still hurts a heck of a lot."

"Not as much as you hurt him when he was alive!"

Hezekiah was stunned to silence. "Okay, I deserved that. I've been praying and asking God to forgive me for not being there for him like I should have been."

"What do you want me to say? Look, I'm tired, Hezekiah."

"Okay, I'll call and check on you again in a few days. That's okay, isn't it?"

"Sure, whatever."

Hezekiah returned his cell phone to its spot and reached for his Bible. He flipped through the thin, worn pages for a few seconds until he came upon the scripture he was searching for.

He read the words slowly and carefully as if allowing them to penetrate his spirit. *"For he will hide me in his shelter in the day of trouble; he will conceal me under the cover of his tent..."*

Closing the Bible and placing it underneath his pillow, he lay back on the bed and stared at the ceiling.

He sat upright when the tears rushed forward like something had pierced his heart, and he found himself sobbing. All the hurt, pain, and grief were released, not just from losing Xavier but also pain from senseless, stupid decisions he'd made that had destroyed other people's lives. How could he sit up and talk about Khalil when he was the one partially responsible for Khalil being the person he was today?

A heaviness like a boulder sitting on his chest engulfed him like nothing he'd felt before. He got out of his bed and stood at his cell door, holding one hand over his heart. He prayed he wasn't having another stroke or a heart attack.

He sucked in several deep breaths, releasing each one slowly until he felt himself calming down. He wiped the last tears away and walked out of his cell. Perhaps this grief enshrouding him would leave if he started moving around the space.

Men in the open area sat around steel tables talking; others played card games and dominos. Still, others like him were merely walking around. He stopped and interacted with a couple of them until this latest bout of sorrow seemed to leave.

Upon returning to his cell, he sat on the bed, pulled out a yellow notepad, and began writing.

"Xavier, son,

God knows how much I wish I had talked to you before you left this earth--before you left us. I wish I had one more chance to tell you how grateful I am that we made amends and that our relationship was going in a good direction. Son, I'm sorry for all the mess-ups. I'm sorry I failed you as a father. I'm sorry I didn't accept you for who you were. If anything, I made you ashamed for being you. Oh, how I wish I could turn back the hands of time. I also want you to know I'm sorry for hurting your mother and destroying our family. I want you to know I love you, Xavier. When you were alive, I didn't say those words enough. I know that now. But what do words mean now when you're gone? They're nothing more than that...words written on a piece of paper. I'm sorry for that, too, son. It hurts knowing I will never talk to you again, see you again, or have the chance to make up for my mistakes. But I promise when I get out from behind these bars, I am going to do everything I can to be a better man. I promise to watch out for my grandsons and Pepper. To be better to them than I ever was to you—and to Khalil..."

When he wrote Khalil's name, Hezekiah paused. Stiles was right. Why was he still blaming Khalil for something that happened years ago—if it happened at all? Like Stiles said,

Hezekiah had no solid proof that Khalil stole anything from him. But even if he did, it was time bygones be bygones. He didn't want to lose another son. Tearing the sheet off the pad, he held the letter while throwing the notepad to the side. He looked at the letter again before he balled it up and flung it against the cell wall. Holding his head in his hands, he began weeping again. He recalled something he used to say to his congregation. *Weeping may endure for a night, but joy comes with the morning light.* Hezekiah couldn't see an end to the darkness, and as for the light, he didn't know if his light would ever shine again.

†

He walked in a single-file line to the dining hall for the day's last meal. Toying over his tasteless food, he laughed and joked with some of the other inmates.

After eating, he carried his tray to the proper place and headed toward the exit when his eyes locked in on a familiar face—one that made him bite down on his bottom lip and clench his teeth in anger. Time seemed to stand still for a moment, and Hezekiah was like a statue.

Another inmate slightly pushed against him when he placed his tray in the catcher.

"My bad," the inmate said.

Hezekiah nodded. Seeing Jude's stepfather was unexpected. When did he get to Bledsoe? It must have been recently because last he'd heard, Clay was serving his time in Whiteville, Tennessee.

Knowing Vernon Clay was at Bledsoe awoke Hezekiah's desire for revenge. He wanted to do to Clay what Clay had tried to do to him. But he also didn't want to get in trouble and face the possibility of catching a charge in this god-forsaken place, not when he could be getting his conviction overturned any day now. But then again, he wanted to see him go down. The stakes couldn't be higher, making gaining his freedom a yearning desire and a necessity—right up there with his determination to return an eye for an eye.

Hezekiah returned to his cell. He dismissed the encounter, read his Bible, and called it a night. Sleep didn't come easily, and when it did, it was a troubled rest. He relived the day he learned of Xavier's death and the long, arduous road to Memphis to view his son's body for the final time.

He woke up in a cold sweat. Getting out of bed, he went to the sink, threw water on his face, and sat on the toilet. He closed his eyes and began reciting the Lord's Prayer.

6

THAT'S WHAT FRIENDS ARE FOR

"The saddest thing is when you are feeling real down...You look around and realize there is no shoulder for you." Broken Heart Quotes

Pepper found some days impossible to bear. Redefining her life without Xavier was hard. The boys were still whiny and asked about their daddy at least once daily.

"I want Daddy," Zavion cried while he played over his cereal.

"Me too," Davion followed. "When is he coming home?" Davion asked.

She closed her eyes and sucked in her breath. It was taking everything within her not to break down crying. That was the last thing she wanted to do in front of her boys.

"I told y'all, Daddy lives in Heaven now. He can't come back.

Heaven is his home. But one day, we'll see him again. Remember the story I told you about God returning one day to gather all the people who love him and take them to Heaven? Well, sometimes he takes people to live with him early, people like your daddy."

The boys seemed temporarily satisfied with her answer because they returned to eating cereal and being consumed by the kid show they watched on their blue animal-shaped tablets.

The doorbell rang. It was Rolonda with her two boys.

"What a surprise, come in, girl," Pepper said.

"How are you doing?"

Pepper shrugged. "Uh, okay. I guess."

"I know, sorry for not calling. I thought I'd take a chance and stop by after leaving Kroger's. Did you get any sleep?"

"Not until I took something. My mother spent the night again, and I didn't have to worry about the boys, but I still couldn't sleep. I tossed and turned until I couldn't stand it anymore. I took one of the pills my primary care doctor prescribed. It helps take the edge off my anxiety, and I can sleep—a little. It's like I keep expecting to see Xavier lying next to me. I keep hearing him tell me to turn over on my side because I'm snoring." Pepper giggled.

"Snoring? Now, that's funny," said Rolonda, happy to see her friend smiling.

"Yeah, it is." Her face turned solemn again.

"I understand, and I didn't come here to make you feel worse. I came to get you out of this house."

"*Nooo*, Rolonda. Not today."

"I'm not taking no for an answer," Rolonda insisted. "That's why I lied about why I didn't call. I didn't tell you I was coming because I knew you would try to back out. I'm going to get you and the boys good and tired and your bellies full, and then I'm bringing you back home, and you are going to fall out. Watch what I tell you."

Pepper broke into a smile. "*Ohh,kayyy*. Where are we going?"

Rolonda grabbed her by the arm and pulled her toward the mudroom where the boys' car seats were located.

"We're taking the kids to the Children's Museum. It's free today. After we get them exhausted, we'll have lunch somewhere."

Pepper dressed for the outing while Rolonda helped her get the boys ready. She was actually glad Rolonda popped up. She needed to focus on something other than her hurting heart.

"Come on boys, pile in," Rolonda orchestrated as they climbed inside the three-row SUV.

Forty-five minutes after Rolonda arrived to pick them up, they were at the museum.

"I'm glad I let you talk me into getting out. Look at the boys." Pepper smiled, watching them running about, excited and having fun.

"Hate to say I told you so. No, I don't," Rolonda said, laughing.

They sat on a bench where they could have a good view of their kids. "If I hadn't gotten you out of that house, you would have just sunk deeper and deeper into depression."

"It's hard. I mean really, really hard, Rolonda."

"God only knows what I would do if something happened to Marlon. I can't imagine it, and I don't want to imagine it. You may not see it now, but I'm telling you what I see in you. I see a strong woman and a mother who will not let her kids see her crumble."

"Sometimes I do think I'm going to have a breakdown. I mean, I can't stop thinking about him. I wake up thinking about him. During the day, I think about him. I watch the boys playing, and I see Xavier on their faces and in some of their mannerisms. I'm mad, Rolonda! I'm mad at Xavier for checking out on us. I'm mad at God for allowing it to happen. And I'm mad at the devil because he's evil and low down, and he did this to my family."

Rolonda wrapped an arm around Pepper. "I'm so sorry. You didn't deserve it, and the boys didn't deserve it. But I will tell you this: you'll smile again one day, Pepper. One day, you're not going to spend every waking moment grieving. One day, you'll be able to think about Xavier, and instead of crying, you'll be able to laugh at all the precious memories you shared. One day, you'll see the light again. I know it." She squeezed Pepper and hugged her.

"Momma," Zavion said, rushing up to Pepper. "Did you see me? Did you see me climb high?"

"Yes, I saw you, sweetie. You're such a big boy!" Pepper chuckled and embraced her son before he moved out of her arms and headed back to the play tube. For that moment in time, life felt normal.

†

"It was nice of Rolonda to get you and the boys out of the house," said Victoria, standing at the kitchen island emptying a cloth bag filled with groceries.

Pepper stood on the other side. She began putting some of the items away. "Yeah, it was. I was glad she talked me into it. The boys had a blast. Afterward, we ate at the Cheesecake Factory. I brought a slice home if you want some."

"Thanks, but not right now."

Victoria put the last of the grocery items away. She hugged Pepper before stepping back, grabbing the cloth bag, and putting it inside the cabinet drawer.

"I'm proud of you. I know it's tough, but you're doing good, Pepper. It takes time for life to get back to normal. You've lost your husband; the kids lost their father. And to know he took his own life, well, again, it will take you some time to heal. Rolonda has been a blessing."

"Yep, she has. And Eliana, too. It feels good to know I have people who care about me. I'm grateful for my friends...and for you."

"You know I'll always be here for you, sweetheart."

"I know, Momma, and I love you for that. When I went through that terrible postpartum psychosis, you were right by my side. I don't know how I would have made it through that without you, and I don't know how I can make it without you now." She rested her head on her mother's shoulder.

Victoria patted the side of Pepper's head and kissed her hair. "I'll bathe the boys tonight, so don't worry about that."

"Are you sure, Mom?" Pepper smiled and pecked her mom on the cheek.

"Yes, those are my grandbabies. I love you guys." Victoria smiled.

"We love you too, Momma." Pepper poured herself a glass of fruit punch. "You want a glass?" she asked, standing with the fridge door open.

"No, thanks."

"How's Fancy? I haven't talked to her this week," said Pepper.

"She's struggling. Same as you. It's hard enough to lose a child, but to lose a child that took his own life? That's harder than anything I can imagine. She's been going to his grave every day. And no one can stop her. It's only keeping her down. That's why I was glad Rolonda got you out of this house. You closed yourself up in here and refused to come out. But you have to force yourself to take this thing one day at a time. For your sake and the boys. They've lost their father. They can't lose you, too. I know you don't want to hear me say it, but honey, life goes on. It can't stop for the dead."

"I know, Mom. I know. And believe me, I'm trying," Pepper cried.

"I know you are, baby. I didn't mean to upset you. Come on, we're done in here. I'm going to go start the boys' bath water."

"Okay, I'm going to my room. I'm tired." Pepper yawned.

"Are you still taking those pills?"

Pepper arched an eyebrow and squinted slightly as her gaze met her mother's.

"What?"

"You heard me. Are you still on those pills the doctor prescribed?"

"Yes. Why?"

"Be careful, Pepper. I've heard folks say how hard it is to get off that stuff."

"Momma, it's not stuff, and I don't intend to make it a habit, but the truth is, I need something to calm my anxiety. My mind is always racing and thinking about Xavier."

"Don't misunderstand me. I know it's tough, but try other alternatives rather than relying on a pill. That's all I'm saying, baby."

"For now, I'm not going to stop taking them. I can only imagine how much worse I'd be if I didn't have something to take the edge off my emotions."

Victoria raised an eyebrow. "Just be careful."

†

Today, Pepper and Rolonda were going to the grand opening of the new downtown open-air mall.

Victoria appeared from around the corner. "Remember, if you come home and we're not here, I'm taking the boys to spend the night at my house. I'm going to try to persuade Fancy to come hang out with us. I think it'll do her some good to spend time with them. As for you, I hope you have fun."

"I'm going to try." Pepper smiled. "Thanks for taking care of the boys."

"I told you I don't want you to worry about the boys. You need this time for yourself. I'm so glad Rolonda is forcing you to get back to experiencing life again," Victoria rambled. "You can't sit up in this house and grieve forever. You're young, smart, pretty, and you have to go on with your life."

"Momma, okay, okay, not this morning. I don't want to hear it."

Victoria shrugged. "I know, I'm just saying."

Pepper was glad when she heard the horn blowing. She peeped out the kitchen window and saw Rolonda's SUV.

"Mom, Rolonda's here. I'm leaving."

Victoria hugged her daughter. "Have a good time."

On the way downtown, Pepper's mind wandered. Passing businesses, turning down different streets, and seeing people going about made her think about her mother's words. *Whether we like it or not, life does go on.* For the first time since Xavier's death, she exhaled deeply and took in the beauty of life surrounding her.

The friends spent the first half of the day going from one store to the next. She and Rolonda laughed, joked, and had a good time. They brought several outfits and items for them-selves and their kids. Rolonda even found her husband a hoodie with his favorite team logo. Without the boys under-foot and scurrying about, they were carefree. They dined at one of the restaurants in the mall.

Pepper's text notifier chimed at the end of the all-day excursion as Rolonda pulled into her driveway.

Stiles: HRU and my nephews, young lady?

Pepper: Good

Stiles: Need anything?

Pepper: No. Mom has the boys.

Stiles: OK. I'll check on you later. Call if you need me.

Pepper: I will. Thanks, Stiles. TTYL.

"Thanks for a fun day, Rolonda."

"Yes, it was so much fun."

The friends embraced, and Pepper walked inside an empty house. She stood in the hallway, not bothering to turn on the lights or move forward. She stood with the darkness surrounding her for several minutes like a thick winter coat. The deep anguish of her loss and not knowing how life would be from this time forward terrified her. She remained still. There was no sound, only the silence of her falling tears.

7
FAMILY MATTERS

"I can be changed by what happens to me, but I refuse to be reduced by it." Maya Angelou

S tiles shook his head after reading Pepper's text, feeling a painful longing in his heart for her and the boys. He thought of his nephew. When he initially heard the news about Xavier, it did something to him. It still did.

He and Xavier worked together. He was a delightful young man and an awesome nephew. He was always meticulous about his responsibilities. His financial wizardry kept New Holy Rock afloat when Hezekiah was sent to prison. During that initial period, membership fell off, and finances were slim. The upkeep of New Holy Rock was in jeopardy. Xavier found ways to keep money flowing through grants and other funding sources.

Stiles knew about Xavier's homosexual tendencies, but even with that, he didn't think Xavier was troubled about it enough to kill himself. A bright light had now been extinguished. *May you find rest and peace, nephew.*

When it happened, Stiles relayed Xavier's death to Pastor. Pastor's dementia had worsened over the past couple of years, and he was practically nonverbal. When he did speak, he only said the words *hungry* and his longsuffering wife Josie's name. Pastor had long since forgotten most of his family members. If he recognized Stiles, he would point to the Bible on the coffee table in their family room. Stiles would pick up the Bible and read Psalm 1, Pastor's favorite passage.

There were times, especially lately, when Stiles visited that Pastor stared blankly, looking at Stiles like he was a stranger. It hurt Stiles to see the man he'd known as his father since he was a five-year-old kid reduced to a silent, frail shell of a man. Pastor used to be a bold, fiery, outspoken preacher. Sometimes, Stiles couldn't understand the hand life dealt.

Stiles called Josie.

"Hello."

Hi, Josie. I'm heading your way. Do you need me to pick up anything?"

"Um." There was hesitation.

"Josie?"

"Uh, well, no, we're okay."

"Come on, Josie. You know I don't mind stopping wherever you want me to. Are you hungry? Have you eaten?"

"I ate breakfast. You know your father keeps me busy when he comes home from adult daycare. I have to watch him like a hawk unless it's his sitter's day to be here."

"I told you to let me get someone to work more hours and days, Josie. Whatever it takes to make it easier for you. I know you insist on not putting him in a long-term care facility, but we may have to reconsider that. I don't want you wearing yourself down. Pastor can be a handful. We'll talk more about it when I get there. So, tell me, what do you want to eat?"

"Can you get me a barbeque plate from that place on South Third?"

"Yep, I sure can."

When he arrived at Pastor and Josie's, the visit went better than expected. Pastor seemed to be having a good day because he pointed at the Bible almost as soon as Stiles entered the family room.

Stiles visited with them until he received a text from Mya.

> Mya: Son went with his dad. You hungry? My treat.

> Stiles: I could eat a bushel of potatoes. 😊 .

He liked Mya. The past months with her had been the best he'd spent with a woman in quite some time. She was carefree, nonjudgmental, open-minded, and adventurous. She made no fuss about his busy schedule. In addition to her talents, smarts, and sweet personality, she was just as beautiful on the outside. Her deep ebony complexion and short black natural hair framed her face in a captivating manner. Her thin lips stretched into an inviting curve when she smiled. Her natural allure, combined with her looks and personality, fascinated him.

Later that evening, they enjoyed some delicious comfort food at a downtown restaurant. Stiles was feeling good and relaxed as they shared conversation.

"I'm glad to see you laughing and in good spirits. I know the past few months have been rough."

"Yep, they have. But I think it's especially difficult for my brother. Him being in prison, dealing with Xavier's death, and, on top of that, not being able to be present for his daughter-in-law and grandsons. Not to mention not being here for Fancy either." Stiles looked down at his food.

Mya extended her arm across the table and gently massaged his hand. "You're discussing your family's pain but neglecting your own feelings. I know you draw strength from your faith and trust in God, but that doesn't mean you aren't allowed to feel hurt and grief. I want you to know confiding in me and expressing your feelings is okay." Her fingers softly traced patterns on his hand.

Their eyes met as he leaned in effortlessly, placing a tender kiss on her lips.

After dinner, they went on a romantic stroll through downtown Tom Lee Park, stopping to take in the beauty of the crisp, clear evening. The Memphis-Arkansas bridge lit up the night with a warm, colorful glow, creating a perfect backdrop against the dark sky. The shimmering reflections danced on the river's surface, adding a touch of magic to the scene.

Stiles held her hand as they strolled. It was a great night. Mya made him feel relaxed. With her, he could momentarily forget about the stresses in his life.

After they went on a walk, he drove her home. She invited him inside. It didn't take very long for things to get heated between them. But he took a step back, moving her out of his arms. His kisses, her body, were the perfect recipe for what he wanted but couldn't allow—not yet. His physical body said it was the perfect time, but his spirit said differently.

"I don't want this...us...to be just physical. Not that I'm not attracted to you, because I am," he acknowledged, briefly looking at himself and back at her. "You're beautiful, you're sexy, and you smell like...like Sista Mavis' famous peach cobbler."

They started laughing, and she playfully tapped his chest.

"Seriously though, what I'm saying is, I like you. I like you a lot, Mya. But as a man of God, I want to practice what I preach. My past relationships," he paused, "and marriages were based a lot on physical attraction. I don't want to do it like that anymore. I'm past casual dating. I want someone I can get serious with. I'm ready for a first lady in my life. If I allow us to become physical, it could blind me and you," he said, pointing at her.

"I feel the same. I want companionship, openness, and acceptance. The physical part will come later. That's what I believe. I knew I liked you for a reason." She giggled and blushed.

Mya's reaction made him like her that much more.

"That's not all. I should have told you that I'm celibate."

Mya's eyebrows arched. "Uh, uh." She exhaled. "But hey, that takes a lot of pressure off."

"I'm not sure I know what you mean," Stiles said.

"I'm not saying I'm celibate, but I haven't been intimate with anyone since my divorce. I like you, but I don't think I'm quite ready for...what I'm saying is we're still getting to know each other."

"Right. So, Mya, on that note, I will bid you farewell, pretty lady. Goodnight." He smiled, kissed her, and turned to the door. "I'll call you tomorrow. Have a sweet sleep."

8

THAT'S WHAT ENEMIES DO

"May God have mercy upon my enemies because I won't." G. S. Patton

At his weekly Sunday service, Hezekiah, still grief-stricken, ministered with watered-down enthusiasm to a roomful of inmates. While his prison ministry thrived, Hezekiah's fervent passion when speaking about God had waned, resembling the flicker of a candle's flame. Perhaps because, on the outside, in the free world, his family was falling apart.

At the end of the thirty-five-minute gathering, Hezekiah was retreating to his cell when he heard his name.

"Hey, McCoy...McCoy!" the voice roared.

Hezekiah looked over his shoulder. Time seemed to warp, slowing down as he saw a hand rising and tightly gripping a long, sharp shank. A searing pain tore through his right side as his gaze locked onto Clay, who wore a malicious grin as he swiftly retreated in the opposite direction.

Hezekiah's reaction was as if he were frozen in place. Bending over and clutching his side, his eyes widened in shock when he withdrew a handful of blood and began to understand the harsh reality of what had happened. He felt himself becoming weak; his vision blurred, and then he collapsed.

Immediately, correction officers raced toward him as most of the inmates took off toward their pods, choosing not to be involved. Blood oozed onto the floor as they helped him to his feet.

In the infirmary, he was stitched up. The pain was excruciating.

Hezekiah chastised himself for not keeping a more watchful eye when he first learned Vernon Clay had been transferred to Bledsoe. He should have kept his head on a swivel, prepared for anything to happen. However, consumed by thoughts of Xavier's death and anxiously awaiting updates from Black, who was grappling with his own personal troubles, Clay had become a distant concern in Hezekiah's preoccupied mind. That distant concern placed Hezekiah in a vulnerable state, which is why Clay had been able to get up on him.

†

The following morning, on the drive to Bledsoe, Christian went into deep thought mode—some thoughts were good, some were not so good, and others were in between.

The *good*? He was about to deliver the best news his client could hope for. The evening before, he had received notice that Hezekiah's conviction had been overturned.

The *not-so-good* thoughts surrounded Luna's pregnancy.

She had returned to work, which seemed to help her mood, but things at home were still awkward. No matter how hard he tried to put on a happy face, he could barely contain his discontent when he saw her rubbing her belly or talking about fixing up a nursery.

The *in-between* thoughts that consumed him surrounded the need to know his biological father. He had put the search for him out of his mind until a few days ago. He missed his adopted father—God *rest his soul*. But Christian needed to know the man responsible for him being in the world. Whether the man cared to know him or cared about his mom back in the day or not didn't matter. Maybe the guy didn't know he had a kid out here. Perhaps he was dead. Maybe, maybe, maybe. Whatever the case, Christian needed to find him. Only then could he be free.

The next heavy thing on his mind was Luna's pregnancy and the fact she was still considering adoption.

"What about the adoption?" Luna asked the night before he drove to Bledsoe.

"What do you mean? Are we still considering that?"

"I don't know. Are we?" Luna replied. "You told the attorney we would get back with her weeks ago."

"And you?"

"Me what?"

"What do *you* want, Luna? I mean, you're already carrying a kid. I thought that was what you always wanted." He immediately knew he had messed up when he saw Luna turn a shade of deep crimson and her lips upturned.

"Are you saying I wanted to be pregnant by any means necessary, including being raped and impregnated by a vicious monster? How dare you, Christian," she shouted, threw a pillow from the sofa at his head, and jumped up.

He dodged the pillow and instead caught it in his hand.

"Wait, don't go, Luna. That's not what I meant. You know I didn't want something like this to happen, not to you or any woman, but I also know God works in mysterious ways. You've said that so many times when we found ourselves in precarious situations."

She looked at him and slowly sat back down.

"We had our sights set on adopting, but God used one of the most horrific crimes that could happen to a person to bring us a child. I won't lie, Luna, I've been grappling with understanding that, but you know I would never accuse you of being okay with what happened. Never."

Christian stood, walked over to the sofa, and knelt before Luna. He rested his head on her lap like he was a kid. "I'm sorry, baby."

She rubbed his head gently, leaning down and kissing him lightly.

He looked up at his wife, smiled, and then looked at her belly. He kissed it tenderly and rubbed it in a circular motion.

Luna's eyes poured over with tears at her husband's display of affection. She couldn't imagine what he was experiencing. She had been too wrapped up in her thoughts about what this child would mean to her to think about how it affected him.

†

The next day, arriving at Bledsoe, Christian was surprised when he was told Hezekiah could not receive visitors, including visitors from his counsel. He couldn't understand why Hezekiah or anyone in Hezekiah's family, especially Stiles, had not informed him. Something didn't seem right. No information would be given to anyone other than the listed emergency contact. He hoped Hezekiah hadn't gotten in trouble.

Christian exited the prison and sat in his car. Right away, he called Stiles. No answer. He left a message asking him to call him back ASAP.

Minutes later, as he exited the prison lot and pulled onto the highway, his phone rang.

"Hey, Stiles."

"Hey, sorry I missed your call. I'm just stepping back into my office. What's up?"

"I'm about to leave Bledsoe. They wouldn't let me see him."

"Wouldn't let you see him? Why?"

"I don't know, and they wouldn't say. That's why I hit you up."

"I have no idea," replied Stiles. I hope he hasn't gotten in trouble. But I remember him saying that his baby boy's step-dad, Vernon Clay, had been transferred to Bledsoe. I hope nothing went down between those two."

"That doesn't sound good. Are you his emergency contact?"

"Not that I know of. I'm not sure who he has listed. Maybe they're on another lockdown. You know how that goes, man. He'll probably be calling soon."

"Yeah, but I need to see him. It's important. I just thought about it. He made Trevor Price his POA, remember? It stands to reason that Hezekiah has him listed as his emergency contact."

"Oh, yeah, I didn't think of him. You're probably right. I'll call him. I'll call you back after I talk to him," Stiles said.

"Okay, I'm headed back to Memphis. I'll talk to you in a minute."

Stiles called Trevor Price. No answer. The phone went immediately to voicemail. *The mailbox you reached is not accepting messages at this time. The mailbox is full,* the recording stated.

Was Price still out of the country? Surely not. Price's wedding had occurred weeks before Xavier was found dead, meaning he should have long returned from his honeymoon. Stiles called the listing for his office.

"I'm sorry, Attorney Price is out of the office," a pleasant-sounding woman told Stiles.

"Do you know what time he's expected back?"

The woman hesitated before speaking up. "Uh, no, Attorney Price is on extended leave. Is there something one of our other attorneys can assist you with?"

"Uh, no, thanks. One more thing. Do you know if he's still on his honeymoon?"

"No, as I said, he's on leave—indefinitely," she emphasized. "But I'll be glad to connect you with another attorney."

"No, that won't be necessary. Thank you," Stiles said, confused. He ended the call.

"On leave? Indefinitely?" Stiles said aloud. "Where the heck are you, Price?" Just for the sake of it, he called Trevor's cell phone again and received the same automated reply as before. He called Christian and told him what the woman said.

"Hmm, and you didn't know anything about it?" asked Christian.

"Nope, not a thing. Which is strange now that I think about it, but so much has gone on these past months that Price has been the last person on my mind," Stiles remarked.

"I know that's right," Christian agreed. "I tell you what, I'll check with some of the fellows downtown. Maybe someone can tell me what's going on at Bledsoe."

"Okay, let me know if and when you hear something."

"Most definitely," Christian replied.

9
CHANGE IS GONNA COME

"When you have exhausted all possibilities, remember this—you haven't." Edison

Two weeks following Hezekiah's stabbing, a foul-smelling fluid began seeping from the half-treated wound, leading to his transfer from the prison's infirmary to the hospital in Pikeville, Tennessee.

He began to feel better over the next few days with intravenous antibiotics and daily wound flushing. He could sit up without as much pain as he had initially. But being handcuffed to the bed still made movement difficult.

The hospital door slowly opened. A nurse appeared, pushing her rolling desk and positioning it beside his bed.

"Morning," she said politely, entering data into the computer.

"Good morning. Can you tell me if anybody contacted my

family to let them know I'm here? I've been asking ever since they brought me here."

The woman didn't look at him. Instead, she tapped a few keys and said, "The person listed as your emergency contact, a uhh, Trevor Price, is unreachable."

"Unreachable?"

"Yes," the nurse sighed, her eyes narrowing as she observed Hezekiah. A subtle crease formed on her forehead, revealing her obvious irritation.

"Which did you call? His office or his cell phone? What about an email?"

She looked at something on the computer again. "All of the above," the nurse said, beginning to frown and cocking her head to the side.

"Do me a favor, please. Will you try calling him again? I need to bring him up to speed on what happened to me."

The nurse looked at her monitor again, then up at him, and told him she would. She proceeded to take his vitals. Afterward, she steered the rolling desk toward the open door and into the hallway.

An hour or more passed before she returned to Hezekiah's room. "He's not in his office. They said he's on extended leave."

"Extended leave? And his cell? Did you try that?"

"Yep, the mailbox is full."

"Thanks. I appreciate it," Hezekiah said.

"Sure," she said, shedding her brazen exterior for a softer tone.

"Uh, one more thing. Could you, uh, call my brother? Just let him know I'm okay and where I am."

The nurse nodded. "Yes, what's his name and number?"

"God bless you," Hezekiah said and gave her Stiles's information.

†

"I've been praying for you, man, and I told Fancy what happened," Stiles said, sitting in the stiff, upright chair beside Hezekiah's hospital bed.

"I wish you hadn't told her. She's going through enough already," Hezekiah admonished. "I *am* curious about what she said, though."

"You know, Fancy. She said she'd pray for you."

Hezekiah chuckled. "Yeah, I imagine she will," he said sarcastically. "How is she, really?"

"She's getting better, I think. I keep an eye out for her, and so does Victoria. She still needs someone to take her pain out on."

"No one better than me," Hezekiah said. "I can't say that she would be wrong. I wasn't there when he needed me the most. I failed him as a father on so many levels," Hezekiah lamented.

"Don't beat yourself up. You can't turn back the hands of time. The good thing is you and Xavier were in a good place before he died. I know you had issues with his preferred lifestyle, but that doesn't make what he did your fault. Xavier had issues with himself that no one could solve but him and God."

"I hear you. I hope Pepper will let me be a part of my grandsons' lives whenever I do get out of this hellhole," he growled. In the meantime, keep me in the loop. You're my only connection to family, you know."

"You know I will."

"Good."

"And you say Clay did this to you?" Stiles asked, still in disbelief that the man would set himself up for another charge. He was already serving seven years for Hezekiah's attempted murder. Now, he had tried to kill Hezekiah again? What deep hatred he must have for Hezekiah.

"I guess he got worked up after Mariah was granted a divorce weeks after he was sentenced to prison. That had to have hurt the man, but hey, I feel no pity whatsoever for the guy. The idea of him no longer having a say over Jude's life is a victory for me, even though it almost cost me *my* life."

"Do they know he's the one who stuck you?"

"Maybe they do, maybe they don't. You know how things go behind those steel bars, man. No one is going to say a thing, including me, and I saw him with my own eyes. I'm just trying to get out of that place. This will heal," he said, pointing to his bandaged side. "And don't worry, Clay will get what's coming to him sooner than he thinks," Hezekiah said, looking determined.

"I'll still see what Black can find out. He's been trying to find out what's been going on with you ever since he drove up here the other day and was turned away. That's when we knew something was up. We tried to reach Price to see what he could tell us, but he's MIA. I can't find the guy anywhere. You heard from him?"

"No. That's another thing that's got me worried. I haven't heard from him in a minute. Not since before Xavier's death. I think it was when he was leaving for his honeymoon. Dang, that's been a while ago!" Hezekiah said, chastising himself.

"Yep, over three months," Stiles corrected.

"What? Three months! *Jeez*, I guess I've been so consumed with Xavier's death that I've been unable to think about Price. But I need to find him, especially now. I need to see what's up with my money."

"I know that's right, bruh."

"And you say Black came up here?"

"That's what he said."

"Can you reach him for me?"

"Here, you can call for yourself." Stiles gave his phone to Hezekiah.

"Thanks."

When Christian heard Hezekiah on the phone, he was elated. "What? You were stabbed?" Christian bellowed from the other end.

"Yeah. Ain't that a bunch of crap? I was leaving the cafeteria after chow, headed back to my cell. He caught me by surprise. Stuck me on my side, real good. It's a nasty, painful wound. It got infected, but thank God it's better now, and I'm still around."

"I'm glad you are too. I can't believe no one contacted the family."

"I know. I finally got this nurse to call Stiles to let him know I was in the hospital. They said they tried to reach Price, but that wasn't successful. I don't know where he is. But, yeah, I was stuck pretty badly. The dude tried to take me out—again. It barely missed my vital organs. I almost bled out, but God had his angels at my side."

"Thank goodness," Christian remarked. "I'm glad Stiles is up there, and I'm glad to hear you're going to be straight."

"Thanks, me too. Speaking of being straight, how's your wife?"

"She's good. It's still hard for her to shake what happened, but I have to give it to her, she's a strong woman. She has faith like Daniel!" Christian lightly chuckled. He didn't tell Hezekiah about her being pregnant. He didn't want to get into it and didn't feel like answering suspecting questions. Heck, he was still asking himself questions that he couldn't answer. "Thanks for asking."

"Sure. So, you said you drove up here, and they wouldn't let you in, huh?"

"Right. I had some news to share, and I didn't think you'd want me to wait. But when I arrived, I was told you couldn't receive visitors. No one told me you had been assaulted."

"That's how they are in that place. The only relief I'm getting is from being laid up in this hospital. That's why I got to get out of there, man." Hezekiah's frustration was evident in the tone of his voice.

"Well, let's see what we can do to make that happen," Christian said.

"What? What did you say? Make *what* happen?"

"I might as well tell you on the phone."

"Tell me what? Come on, Black. What is it?"

"I heard from the court."

"You did? What did they rule?"

"I don't know how to tell you this, but, well –"

Hezekiah's heart dropped, ready to hear the distressing news. "Just say it."

"The court is overturning your conviction. You're going to be a free man soon. Real soon. I'm just waiting to receive the final court documents. That should be in the next week or two." Christian exclaimed.

Hezekiah was overcome with unspeakable joy. Tears gushed from his eyes. He looked at Stiles.

Stiles gestured and mouthed, "What?"

"Hol' up, repeat that, Black." Hezekiah put the phone on speaker.

"I said the court overturned your conviction. You're about to be a free man."

Stiles yelped, rose from his chair, lifted his hands, and openly thanked God.

"Did you hear that, brother?" Hezekiah screamed, "I'm *freeee!*"

10

SO IT GOES

"We don't know how strong we are until we are forced to bring that hidden strength forward." Isabel Allende

Sebastian let out a resounding meow and then affectionately nuzzled and rubbed against Fancy's ankles.

"Okay, okay, I'm going to get your breakfast. Give me a second. You're just like a man, so darn demanding." She leaned down, patted his head, and headed to the kitchen pantry.

While Sebastian gobbled his food, she sat at the counter, sipping a cup of matcha tea and scrolling through social media.

The phone rang, startling her. Her phone showed 8:23 a.m. It was the guard gate. Who would want to come to see her at this time of the morning? She wasn't expecting anyone.

"Good morning, Ms. McCoy. Pastor Stiles is here to see you."

"Ok, thanks. Let him through." Fancy bounced up from the kitchen stool and headed to the door.

"Hey, what's going on? Is everything all right?" she said minutes later, stepping aside and allowing him to enter the house.

Stiles walked into the foyer, stood, and then turned to look at a disheveled Fancy. He pushed thoughts of how she looked aside and went straight into telling her why he was visiting. "I don't know if you heard, but Hezekiah was attacked. He's in the hospital up in Pikeville."

Fancy's hand flew up and over her mouth. "Oh, my God. Attacked? What do you mean?"

"The same fellow who shot him, Vernon Clay, caught him off guard a couple of weeks ago. Stabbed him real good."

"A couple of weeks ago? And you're just saying something?"

"I just learned about it myself."

"How is he?"

"It was a serious wound; it got infected, but he's doing better. I drove up there to see him yesterday. He was doing good."

"Good for him." Fancy moved ahead of Stiles and went back into the kitchen. Stiles followed.

"Sit down," she offered. "You want a cup of coffee or tea? I have some pineapple juice, too."

"I'll have a glass of juice."

Fancy passed the glass to Stiles and sat at the kitchen island.

"That man is out for Hezekiah's blood. He's already serving time for trying to kill him. And he tried to do it again?" Fancy shook her head. "How stupid. Or is it? I mean, he's angry. That's evident. But Hezekiah also put himself in this mess. He cheated on me with that man's wife, got her pregnant, and...

and he's surprised her husband reacted the way he did? Anyway, I don't want to talk about that. I'm mad, too, Stiles. I'm mad that my baby boy is gone. I know I shouldn't say this, but I will say it anyway. Maybe if Hezekiah had spent more time at home with the boys and me instead of screwing this woman and that one, then so much of this wouldn't have happened. I might still have my baby, Stiles. Xavier wouldn't be lying in a cold grave." Fancy began to cry.

Stiles rose and stood beside her, wrapping a comforting arm around her.

Fancy rested her head against his shoulder and let her tears flow freely.

Stiles didn't move. He kept his arm around her, pulling her in as close as possible. "Let it out. Let it all out, Fancy."

Fancy wept. Her heart was shattered, irretrievably broken, and she didn't know if she would ever feel like living again.

"I want my son back," she wept.

"I know. I know." Tears formed in his eyes, hearing her sobs and seeing her so distraught. Unlike Fancy, he held them back and concentrated on comforting her.

"I...I'm sorry," Fancy said, looking up, wiping her nose with the back of her hand.

Stiles walked over to the other side of the kitchen, pulled a paper towel off the rack, and brought it to Fancy.

"Thank you," she whispered as her tears ceased.

"That's what friends are for. To be there for one another."

She looked at him and smiled slightly.

"I have something else I wanted to tell you, but I don't know if I should wait until you feel better."

"No, tell me. I'm fine. I have these crying spells and don't know how to stop them. I miss him so much."

"I know you do. And I'm so sorry. I wish I could do something to make you feel better."

She took a deep breath, released it, and said, "Okay, let me stop." She sniffled, took a deep breath, and slowly released it. "Okay, I'm ready. What is it?"

"Hezekiah's conviction was overturned. He could be released any day."

Fancy stared like she'd seen a ghost. "Are you serious?"

"Yep. Black told him yesterday."

"His conviction was overturned?" Fancy repeated.

"Yes. Black said he would be released when the courts send the final paperwork. He says that can take a week, two weeks at the most."

"I don't know what to say. I mean, I'm happy for him, but it won't bring my baby back."

Stiles shook his head. "I know. Nothing can do that, Fancy. You have to learn to move forward one step at a time. Xavier would want that. As for Hezekiah, if you don't want him back in your life, that's understandable. The man has put you through a lot, but even with that, you must find it in your heart to forgive him. That's what God wants us to be able to do."

"Don't start preaching at me," Fancy cautioned, looking sternly at Stiles while wiping away a loose tear. "You're the last person who can talk to me about forgiveness."

Stiles raised his palms. "I'm sorry, you're right. I didn't mean anything hurtful."

"I'm just saying I *have* forgiven him. But I don't think I can be around him right now."

"Understood." He gathered Fancy into his arms and hugged her tight.

Sebastian came up and circled round and round both of their ankles.

When they separated, Stiles kissed her on the forehead. "I better get going. I have a staff meeting at the university this morning. That's where I'm heading. But I wanted to see you. I'm sorry for popping up unannounced."

"No worries. You're among the few people with that privilege," she said, smiling. "I was glad to see you. I needed my friend," she said softly as they approached the front door.

"I'm just a phone call away. You know that," Stiles reminded her.

"Yes, I know. And if I sounded unhappy about Hezekiah, it's not that. It's not that at all. I wish him the best whenever he gets out."

Stiles gave her another hug. "I'll check on you later." He leaned down and stroked Sebastian underneath his chin. "See you later, Sebastian. Take care of your momma."

11

REVENGE IN MOTION

"Life is to be lived, not controlled, and humanity is won by continuing to play in the face of certain defeat." Ralph Ellison

A few days after Stiles's visit, Hezekiah was discharged and sent back to Bledsoe. Since his return, no one at the prison officially told him the news of his overturned conviction, but if Black said it was so, then it was so.

One of the correction officers that Hezekiah was cool with told him Clay had been placed in solitary confinement and was facing another attempted murder charge on top of the one he was already serving time for. It gave Hezekiah a sense of relief. He didn't want any good to come to the likes of that guy.

He lay back on his bunk and removed his hidden phone. He called Trevor again. Another automated message. Next, he called Trevor's office.

"This is his client, Hezekiah McCoy. When do you expect

him to return?" he asked the pleasant-sounding woman on the other end.

"Sir, Attorney Price is on extended leave. I'm not sure when he will return. I can send you to the attorney filtering his cases. Would you like that?"

"No," a frustrated Hezekiah replied. This was getting ridiculous. Where the heck could Price be?

"Ma'am, you don't understand," he continued, "I need to talk to him. It's urgent. Is there any way you can reach him? Did he leave a number in case of emergencies? I mean, the guy is my POA. I need to get ahold of him," Hezekiah demanded.

This time, the woman sounded like she was becoming irritated. "Sir, as I *said*," she emphasized, "Attorney Price is out of the office for an undetermined amount of time. He left no forwarding number other than his cell. You said you have that number. I wish I could tell you more, but that's all I know."

"So you mean to tell me that no one in his office has heard from him since he left for his honeymoon? Doesn't that sound a little off?"

The woman sighed heavily. "Sir, Attorney Price took an extended leave," she repeated. "We do not know when *or* even if he will return."

"*Ohhh*, you didn't say that before— that he may *not* return. That's strange. If he calls or returns to the office, I need you to tell him I need to talk to him immediately. Like I said, this is urgent."

"Yes, Mr. McCoy, I sure will."

Next, Hezekiah called Christian Black.

"Hold on, Mr. McCoy. I'll get him on the line," Black's admin informed him.

"Hello, Hezekiah," Christian said when he came to the line moments later. "How are you?"

"I'm back at Bledsoe."

"Oh. When did that happen?"

"A couple of days ago. They have Clay in solitary. He's picked up another charge for attempted murder. Looks like he's going to be in here a long, long time," Hezekiah said, chuckling.

Christian chuckled as well. "I don't know what he expected, but he's going to have a lot of time to marinate on it. Now that you're back at Bledsoe, I'll drive up the day after tomorrow."

"That's why I need to get in touch with Price. I called his office today, and his admin said she doesn't know if he's coming back. Said he's on extended leave. I've tried his cell phone, too. An automated message keeps coming through. I should have known something was up when he didn't call or extend his condolences about Xavier. Xavier was supposed to be part of his wedding. The two of them were friends. I don't know. I pray that nothing foul has happened to him. Price is a good guy."

"The good thing is you can revoke the POA at any time. I'll print out the form you need to fill out. In the meantime, we need to start preparing for your move. The papers should be coming down any day."

"That's good to know. Get that form to me as quickly as you can. I need to do that anyway now that I'm getting out of this place."

"Right," Christian agreed. "So, don't worry about a thing. Just continue to heal. How's that wound looking?"

"I went to the infirmary yesterday for a follow-up. They said it looked good—no signs of infection. Good color. The area around the wound is still tender, but the nurse said that's normal."

"Good to hear you're on the mend. I'll see you later this week. Get some rest. Everything is working out."

Hezekiah massaged his temples, then rose to his feet, pacing the cramped six-by-eight-foot cell. Sitting on the toilet, thoughts of his imminent freedom occupied his mind.

†

Months had passed, and Rianna still had not heard from Tiny. She'd occasionally gone by the pharmacy in the guise of shopping, but Tiny was never there. Earlier today, she stopped by the pharmacy again. This time, one of their co-workers told her Tiny had quit a few weeks ago.

"Where did she go?" Rianna asked the rough-looking woman.

The blond-haired woman hunched her shoulders, placed a stick of gum in her mouth, and began chewing furiously while looking at her phone. "I heard she got a better job at the CVS. *Shooot*, I'm gonna go check 'em out too. You know this place don't pay me enough," she complained. "But Tiny was so dang snooty. She ain't gonna help nobody. I'm glad she's gone." She looked up and gave Rianna a rough stare. "Dang, girl, ever since that preacher dumped yo behind, you look like crap," the woman said, shaking her head and laughing.

"Thanks for nothing," Rianna snapped and walked out of the store. "To hell with you, Tiny," she said, mumbling and getting into her car. She couldn't understand why Tiny called herself still mad. The vandalism incident was over. Neither ended up being charged, so what was the big deal? Yet, Tiny had gotten all bent out of shape and ended their friendship. She drove by the CVS up the street from where she and Tiny used to work. She didn't see Tiny's car. Next, she drove past her house. Tiny's car was not on the street or in her driveway.

"If that's how you wanna play this game, suit yourself. I don't need you," she said, cursing and speeding off. She stopped by the liquor store and bought a bottle of rosé before heading home.

Inside Apartment 3D, Rianna crossed her shapely legs at the ankles as she relaxed on the sofa channel surfing before she got up and prepared a bowl of soup and a pre-made grilled cheese sandwich.

After she had a glass of wine, she was in an upbeat mood. A month ago, she received approval to receive Social Security Disability benefits. However, the limited amount took her back to square one, before she was First Lady Rianna McCoy. If only for a brief stint, she still enjoyed that role. That's when she had access to spending Hezekiah's money frivolously, maxing out charge cards, and enjoying a different life. A life far better than this. But she told herself she wouldn't be down always. Somehow, she was going to turn her lemons into lemonade.

The good thing was that her disability check was enough to keep the rent paid on Apartment 3D. Additionally, she had a reliable car she had bought after the accident. Her monthly expenses were minimal, and the check would cover everything, leaving her with enough to buy gas and her occasional bottle of wine.

She had a meager sixty-eight hundred dollars in her savings, money left from the accident settlement. Hezekiah's cheap behind made sure she didn't get much, although he denied having anything to do with the amount his insurance paid out. She didn't believe one word of what he said, Christian Black said, or Trevor Price said. All of them were nothing but hustlers and manipulators.

Now that she was living on a fixed income, she could receive food stamps. She took advantage of the monthly stamps, mostly ordering groceries online. She'd gained at least fifteen pounds since the accident.

She returned to the living space with her food and drink,

sat back on the sofa, and picked up the remote. She was about to turn from the news that had popped on but stopped when she saw a news report about a pastor's conviction being over-turned. She laughed.

"Hezekiah, I bet you wish that was you," she said aloud. Immediately after the words came from her mouth, it dropped open when a news clip appeared of Christian Black talking to ever-popular news reporter Jeremy Parker.

"Pastor Hezekiah McCoy proclaimed his innocence from the very beginning. I initially wasn't involved in this case, but upon taking it over, I wholeheartedly dedicated myself to securing his release. I was able to find and introduce fresh evidence to the courts, conclusively demonstrating my client's innocence. The courts couldn't help but make the decision they did," Black said proudly, as an image of Hezekiah was shown.

Her temples were visibly throbbing, and the remote slipped from her hand while Rianna clenched her fist and slammed her other hand onto the sofa.

"Well, I'll be darn. You lucky son of uh...."

12

HARD HEAD – SOFT BEHIND

"You cannot expect victory and plan for defeat." Joel Osteen

Khalil watched the local news from his church office. Reporter Jeremy Parker was interviewing his father's attorney, Christian Black. He didn't know what his emotions amounted to when he heard Black say his father's conviction had been overturned and that he could be released any day.

"Elaina, did you see the news?"

"No. What happened now?" she said, frustrated by all the crime and violence in her city. "Please don't tell me another one of our church members was on the news."

"No, not that. It's about my father. It looks like Black pulled it off. He got Dad's conviction overturned. Can you believe it?"

"Good for him. Now, he can be a free man and get to hold his grandkids. With Xavier's death, Pepper raising the boys all alone, and your mother hurting like she is, so much damage has been done to this family. I'm just saying maybe things can change for the better. Maybe your father has changed. Who knows, maybe the two of you can let the past be in the past. That's what Xavier was trying to do."

"Right, and where is *he*?"

Eliana gasped. "Khalil, what the heck's wrong with you? Xavier killed himself! Where is your empathy, your compassion? He was your brother. Now is the time for you to step up and be a part of your nephews' lives. You've said you wished you had done things differently when he was alive. Well, this may be your chance to do just that."

"Nothing will change my father, not for the good anyway. I don't see it."

"God can do anything," she assured him. "You're talking about him needing to change; you need to practice what you preach! Look, I've got to go. I know you hear Khaliyah making a fuss," she said, frustrated.

"Put her on the phone."

"Hey, Daddy."

"Hey, sweetpea."

"I miss you."

"Miss you," Khaliyah said in return. Her baby voice sweet and innocent.

"Daddy will be home soon. Okay?"

"Okay, Daddy."

"Bye-bye, baby."

"Okay," Eliana said, returning to the phone. "Bye."

"Uh, okay," he said, annoyed. He sprang from his chair, swiftly put on his suit coat, collected his phone and laptop, and exited his office.

As he passed the front office area, Sista Mavis called him.

"Pastor? Pastor Khalil, you leaving?" She got up from

behind her desk and swished to the door, her wide hips swinging from side to side like a pendulum.

"Uh, yes. I don't have any appointments, right?"

'No, your calendar's clear. Are you okay?"

"Yes. Just one of those days, Sista Mavis."

"I know you're still grieving over Xavier. Honey, I am, too. And then to hear that your father is getting out of prison, my sweet child, you have so much on you." She walked up to him and laid a hand on his shoulder.

"Yeah, it's definitely a lot. Sometimes I can't see my way, Sista Mavis." He found Sista Mavis easy to talk to. She was a gossip, but he knew she had a special place in her heart for him. She treated him like a son and often told him that's how she saw him.

"So, you heard about my father's release, huh?"

"Yes, I saw it a while ago...on my phone. I got that news app, you know," she said, half giggling. "It tells me everything going on around this city."

"I heard that." He smiled and kissed Sista Mavis on the cheek. "I'll see you tomorrow."

"Pastor K."

"Yes, Sista Mavis."

"God knows what He's doing. You may not always see it, but He's in charge. And whether you choose to admit it or not, you know your brother had problems beyond what any of us could solve. He needed the good Lord but chose to do things his way." Sista Mavis shook her head, looking sternly at him. "I loved your brother just as much as I love you. I looked at y'all like my boys. I'm telling you to make it your business to be there for those babies. You're their uncle. Now that their daddy's gone, it's your responsibility to do what you can to help his poor wife with them. As for Pastor Hezekiah, God is giving him another chance. He better take it."

"Thank you, Sista Mavis. God bless you." Khalil smiled, gave her another peck, and exited the church. He got into his car and right away made a call.

"Hey, I'm headed your way."

†

"I don't know what it is, Mama. I still love him, I think. But I don't feel the way I used to. I can't explain it."

"Honey, you're not going to feel butterflies every day of your marriage. Some days, you're not going to like each other. On other days, you can't get enough of one another. You should know that by now."

"I do. You've told me that many times, and you are absolutely correct; there are days and times like that, but I still don't think you understand what I'm saying. Becoming a mother changed me. I'm focused on raising my daughter. Sometimes, it seems like I'm doing it by myself. Khalil is always busy," she said, throwing up hand quotes. He's at church, some days, from morning to night, and then he has to prepare his message to preach every Sunday and again during the week. Between that time, he visits his so-called sick members. Or should I say, more like his mistress? Mama, I'm not cut out to be a First Lady anymore." Eliana flinched like she'd been startled at the words that came from her mouth. She slowly walked around the family room, stopping and staring out the wide window showcasing their backyard oasis.

Her mother responded in the exact manner Eliana knew she would. She didn't understand why she even bothered to open up to her. It never did any good.

"Don't you ever mention to anyone, and I do mean anyone, that your husband has a mistress. Do you hear me?" her mother fussed.

"Mama, you can't be serious? I know you're not saying my daddy cheated."

"You didn't hear such a thing come from me. Listen to me, Eliana, you just said it; you're a first lady, a mother, and a wife. You are obligated to your husband. You're supposed to be his helpmate. Act like it. Stop listening to the gossip and hearsay. I've told you this and I'm going to tell you again, he doesn't cater to you. You cater to him. How do you think me and your father have stayed together all these years? I learned how to be submissive—decided not to let stuff bother me. He took good care of his family. It wasn't easy at first, but God guided me along the way."

Eliana was glad her mother couldn't see her vast frown and roll of the eyes through the phone. She couldn't believe how antiquated her mama's thinking about marriage and relationships. Then again, yes, she could. Her mother had always been this way.

When Eliana got in trouble and went to jail because of an old ex-boyfriend, her mother blamed her and didn't do anything to help her through that terrible period. If it hadn't been for her father and Ian, Eliana didn't know what she would have done or if she would have survived prison. But thank God those foolish days were behind her, and she had moved forward. She learned from that situation not to be a fool for a man ever again. Yet, here she was. She thought things would be different between her and Khalil, especially with him being a preacher. Yet, Khalil was no better than the player walking around.

She had allowed him to hang her past over her head too long. So what if she didn't tell him about her past prison stint before they were married? Everyone makes mistakes, and that happened when she was a young, stupid, in love, silly girl. That one mistake did not define her. She used that period in her life to better herself. She pursued her college degree while incarcerated, and when she was released, she continued school and graduated. Now, she was a mother and wife. Eliana was over feeling guilty about her past failures.

Another thing that had begun to annoy Eliana was being a first lady—there was no one she could fully trust and confidently confide in. Her friends, who were mostly single, drifted off when she married Khalil. It's not like she had a ton in the first place, but for those who remained in her circle, she didn't trust them with the secrets of her troubled and unhappy life. The one person she could trust, to a point, was her friend Jocelyne, who had also been her maid of honor. The only other person she felt comfortable talking to was Pepper, but Pepper wasn't in any frame of mind to listen to Eliana complain about her marriage—she was dealing with Xavier's death.

"Mother, I've got to go. The boys are waking up from their nap."

"I thought you said you just put them down for a nap."

"Uh, I did, and I hear them fussing. I need to see what's going on. Talk to you later."

"Well, just remember what I said, and call me—"

"Okay, gotta go, Ma." Sick of her mother's backward thinking and useless advice, she ended the call before her mother could say another word.

Eliana presented the perfect façade in public to coincide with her status as First Lady of Holy Rock, but she was nobody's fool. Probably like much of the congregation, she knew her husband was still going behind her back with Detria Graham. She was beginning not to care what he did one way or the other. She would tolerate a marriage where her husband did not reciprocate love because he was a good father and provided very well for her and Khaliyah.

She would stick it out until she decided not to.

13
THE OTHER SIDE

"Everybody's at war with different things...I'm at war with my own heart sometimes." Tupac Shakur

"I told you, I'm tired of you treating me like a yo-yo on your string, Khalil. You want to be in and out of my life. You tell me to back off one minute, and the next, you're over here pretending everything is peachy between us." Detria pouted and turned to walk away as he stood on the other side of the open front door.

"Hol' up, baby girl." He reached out and pulled her by the arm so she faced him. He stepped up on her and further into the house, closing the gap between them.

She barely had a chance to gasp when Khalil planted a deep, passionate kiss on her polished mouth.

She then relaxed in the comfort of his arms. She missed him. What it was about Khalil, she couldn't quite place her finger on it, but she felt what she felt, and Khalil McCoy was the beat of her heart.

"Khalil," she whispered hungrily.

"Where's Priscilla?" he asked, his voice low and husky.

"She's out of town."

"Good," he said, closing the door with a solid foot kick.

Next, he led her to the family room, where they sat on the sofa and made up for the time they'd spent apart.

Detria didn't protest. Instead, she made it her business to make sure Khalil knew precisely what he'd missed by avoiding her.

"Umm, so you missed me, huh?" Detria giggled as she lay underneath the weight of his perspiring body. "I can tell."

"Is that so?" He moved from over her and lay back, his long legs stretching the sofa's length.

She repositioned herself on top of him and looked down into his face.

"Yep, that's so," she said, giggling again and kissing him. Her expression grew serious. "I just wish I could see you more often, you know like we used to do. Why can't you just leave her already? We could be together. You already know money is no issue."

"You know the deal, Detria, and we will not do this today. I didn't come over here to hear you nag me about how long it's been since the last time I came over. *Jeesh*," he said, placing a hand on his forehead accompanied by a sigh of frustration.

"I'm not nagging you," she said, moving from on top of him and going to the end of the sofa.

"You sure sound like it." He eased up, sitting up on the sofa.

"No, baby, I'm not. And I also want to tell you how sorry I am about Xavier. I still can't believe he did something like that."

"Yeah, well, he did. It is what it is."

She rubbed her hand over his head of hair. "You don't have to act tough with me, Khalil," she said, easing back toward him and laying her head against his chest. "I know it has to be hurting you."

"Look, I don't want to be reminded of what a wimp my brother was. I mean, taking his own life? What was he thinking?" Khalil openly questioned for the first time since Xavier's death. He shook his head and bit down on his lip.

"It's going to be okay," Detria said, her voice soothing as she snuggled closer and wrapped her arm around him. Kissing him softly on the side of his face, neck, and ear, she continued to speak comforting words.

Khalil pushed her away. "No more. Not right now."

Detria moved away. She knew Khalil well enough to know he meant it when he said back off. She was thankful that he'd come over. It had been almost two months since he'd last been there.

When she heard the tragic news about Xavier, she was unable to attend his funeral. For her life, she didn't understand why they held a private ceremony when the McCoys were well known in the church community. Either way, she wished she could have been there for her man.

Eliana must not have been giving him the support he needed, or he wouldn't have run to her—again. She welcomed him no matter his reason for showing up like a wounded puppy on her doorstep. Detria would always welcome him, and nothing and nobody would change that.

†

Hours later, on the drive back from Detria's, Khalil was consumed with one thought after the other. He chastised himself for running back to her when he had vowed to himself and God to give his marriage a chance. More important than keeping his marriage intact, there was his daughter. He would do anything to be there for his little girl, even if that meant staying in a marriage that seemed to be going downhill fast without brakes.

He couldn't help it if Eliana was not his cup of tea. He thought he could love her and be the man and husband she deserved, but he felt mounting disdain for his situation. It wasn't all her fault, either. He knew in the beginning, before he said *I do*, that he wasn't in love. He chose her because he believed she would make a good first lady and a great mother —she was both. But being a good first lady to the public was not enough because, behind closed doors, Khalil was not a happy man. He thought about Xavier. Look at where being unhappy had landed his brother—an early grave. Xavier chose to end his life rather than remain in his relationship with Pepper. What a choice. Khalil could never see taking himself out, but he felt a sense of dread and longing to escape.

The crack of thunder brought him temporarily out of his scurrying thoughts. He quickly saw a flash of lightning as it darted across the sky.

"God, tell me what's going on. So much is happening in my family and life, and I don't know what to do. I have so many unanswered questions. Why did my brother take his life? Why did my family fall apart? What will it mean for my family and me when my father gets out of prison? Help me be open to reconciling with him if that's what he wants. Only you know, Lord, what this family is coming to."

The heavy downpour ushered in by the rain cracked open the sky as Khalil drove through the worsening storm, similar to the ferocity of the storm brewing within him.

14

RUNNING ON EMPTY

"There is little that can withstand a man who can conquer himself."
Louis XIV

Hezekiah lay in his bunk, his mind racing with endless thoughts of his upcoming freedom. It had been a day or two short of three weeks since Christian Black told him the news of his overturned conviction.

His stab wound was almost healed, and he was feeling fine. Vernon Clay had been transferred to another section of the prison, but Clay was the last person on Hezekiah's mind. True enough, Clay had a personal vendetta against him, but that would soon be a thing of the past. Hezekiah would be free, and Clay would be in prison for at least the next seven years. That didn't include the additional time he would likely face when he received his fate for the other charge against Hezekiah.

He removed his phone and called Trevor Price for the

umpteenth time. Hezekiah was beginning to feel some way, not being able to reach Price. He needed to get ahold of him. When he was released, he needed money to get a place to live, get a ride, and refresh his wardrobe. Once he was out of prison, he would remove Price as his POA. But like all the previous times, the automated message came on when he called Price's number.

"Dang, Price, where the heck are you?" He made another call. He was beginning to grow concerned. It wasn't like Trevor not to be in touch. The more he thought about the guy, the more Hezekiah realized how long it had been since he talked to Price. It was when Price came to Bledsoe to tell him he was getting ready for his honeymoon. Not a word had he heard since then, not even when Xavier killed himself. Something was up with Trevor, something that may not be too good. He called Christian Black, but that call went to Black's voicemail. He rested his head against the hard prison pillow.

"Price, wherever you are, you better have my money," he said aloud.

†

Trevor and Niesha strolled hand-in-hand through the bustling marketplace, filled with vendors selling crafts, aromatic spices, and colorful materials and textiles. Morocco's natural beauty was equally enchanting. They had settled on a spacious two-bedroom flat in the coastal city of Essaouira, with breathtaking picturesque beaches, modern elegance, and historic charm.

The beach hut business he planned to open was in the works. Life couldn't be better. He and his new bride's transition from the U.S. to Morocco had been relatively trouble-free.

However, his buddy, M. J., had called him the day before and told him about Hezekiah's impending release.

M.J. wasn't personally worried about Hezekiah's release. He knew Hezekiah had no idea about his identity, his association with Trevor, or their profitable house-flipping projects, which Hezekiah's money unknowingly financed. The substantial profits they had accrued from these real estate dealings were in their pockets. A nonprofit endeavor the two friends established also continued to flourish. M.J. had cleverly secured multiple grants to conceal its origin and erase any trace of the use of Hezekiah's money. As a result, the friends considerably bolstered their wealth and financial security while leaving Hezekiah in a state of economic poverty.

"You're going to have to do something, man. He's already looking for you, or should I say, for his money. He's about to be a free man walking, so I think you need to get your ducks lined up. We don't need to have any eyes on us."

"You said there's nothing to be concerned about. We have everything legit on paper if things did somehow backfire—which they won't," he said, somewhat cocky and self-assured.

"Man, we weren't expecting him to get his conviction thrown out. We thought the dude would be out of the way for at least another three or four years. This is messed up," M. J. complained.

"Chill, man. Any idea when he's getting out?"

"Nah, not really," said M. J. "From what I've heard, it could be any day."

"Okay, but that's why we kept that one account open in his name. It has over fifty thousand in it. As for anybody calling the law office looking for me, there's nothing anyone there can tell them except that I'm on extended leave. They don't know where I am or how to reach me, so that settles that. And like we talked about, there's not much, if anything, Hezekiah or his hotshot attorney can do to me. I handled his financial affairs and made decisions I thought were in my client's best interest. I can't help it if some of those investments fell through financially. I mean, you win some—"

"You lose some," M. J. finished.

"So, stay cool. I'll check back with you later in the week."

Trevor returned to his hammock while Niesha was inside their home preparing dinner. He watched the sky transform into deep orange, fiery red tones as the sun began to set. A soothing, gentle wind carried the scent of the sea past his nose. This was life. He would let nothing or no one mess up what he had going on. That included Pastor Hezekiah McCoy.

Trevor smiled, reached for his wife, and pulled her close when she appeared beside his hammock with a freshly made fruit drink.

"You're going to make me drop this," she giggled. She held the frozen margarita tightly in one hand while holding on to Trevor.

He removed the drink from her hand, took a sip, and made a slurping sound. "This is delicious. Maybe we can set up a small pub or bar along with the beach huts," he suggested.

"Uh, no way. I want to enjoy the sun and the beach and have fun meeting people. I don't want to be a bartender." She chuckled.

"I know, I know," he said. "I was just teasing. But for real, this is good." He kissed her on her lips.

"Thanks, babe." Niesha climbed out of the hammock. "Gotta go finish making dinner. I'll be back out soon."

"Okay." He playfully swatted her behind as she walked off. She looked back over her shoulder and laughed, and he winked.

He was not about to let M. J. get him nervous about Hezekiah. He was in Morocco, where he intended to stay. He had plenty of money to start his business and live off for a very long time. The properties in the States were thriving, and he and Niesha had purchased another property in Morocco that they planned to turn into a rental property. M. J. did an excellent job ensuring their businesses could not be traced or connected to Hezekiah McCoy and his money. All was well.

15

OPEN YOUR HEART

"Never be ashamed of a scar. It simply means you were stronger than whatever tried to hurt you." Unknown

Seated at a corner table in the steak restaurant, Christian and Luna's strained silence hung heavy in the air. Seeing his wife's burgeoning belly filled him with a quiet fury. He tried to conceal his emotions, not wanting to distress his beloved wife. Compounding his unease was that the low-life who attacked her, leaving her for dead, remained unknown, and the police had no reliable leads.

"I'm driving to Bledsoe in the morning. I have to talk to Hezekiah about our victory. This is what we've been waiting on. I fought hard for this," Christian said proudly after telling Luna about Hezekiah's overturned conviction.

"I'm so happy for you, honey." Luna beamed. "This dinner is the perfect time to celebrate."

"Thanks, baby. This is a significant win for me," he

continued to boast. "I got his conviction overturned. Yes!" he said under his breath so as not to cause a stir inside the restaurant. He raised his clenched fist triumphantly into the air, only to bring it down in a gesture of victory.

Luna shook her head and laughed with him. While he was still laughing, she reached into his plate with her fork, taking away a big forkful of his food.

"I couldn't resist," Luna remarked playfully, "your food always looks more appetizing than mine." A soft giggle escaped her as she spoke, and she covered her mouth with her hand while still chewing.

"Is that all you can come up with?" Christian shook his head and grinned. It felt good to let loose and share light conversation and laughter.

Lately, Luna had been moody and often expressed she was tired. Not to mention, they had not been intimate since her sexual assault. She would give him that look or come out and tell him she wasn't ready yet. He didn't want to pressure her into having sex, so he didn't, but it was hard to abstain.

They continued eating and chatting. "How was work?"

"It was a busy day, as usual. Meetings both in the office and virtual."

"You sure you're not doing too much?" Christian asked, concerned.

"I'm fine. I can take a power nap if I need to. That's the good thing about having that sofa in my office." Luna giggled.

"You can take maternity leave early. If you don't want to do that right now, maybe return to working from home," Christian suggested.

"Believe me, if it comes to that, I don't have a problem doing it. Thanks for looking out for me." She made a kissy face at him. "Seriously, I wasn't complaining. It does tire me out some days, but the company has been experiencing an uptick in pharmaceutical sales since opening our new location. If it keeps going like it is, my direct reports and I can expect a hefty bonus this year."

"Good for you, sweetheart." Rising from his chair, he leaned over and affectionately kissed her lips. He then settled back into his seat, enjoying his meal.

Luna spoke cautiously, not knowing how Christian would take hearing the news. "Uh, Attorney Nguyen called today."

Christian paused midway through his bite and looked at Luna. "What did she want?"

"Uh, the same thing she wanted two weeks ago," Luna said softly. "She wants to know, Christian, and we need to tell her. I don't want to keep her on hold if we don't plan on proceeding."

"Proceeding? Are you serious? Look at you," he said, his eyes pointing at her belly.

Luna turned crimson, stopped eating, and tears quickly formed.

"I'm sorry, babe. I didn't mean it like that. What I meant is, how can we even think about adopting now? We're going to have our hands full in a few months. I've been thinking about it. I don't see how we can consider another child," Christian said, his voice uncertain.

"That's exactly why we should let her continue matching us. This baby is going to need another sibling, and we always said we wanted to adopt more than one child. So, I don't want to call it off just because I'm—" She looked at her belly, rubbed it in a circular motion, and then looked up at Christian, "because I'm pregnant."

"As if I didn't know," he mouthed.

"Look, Christian, I know this is hard. I can't imagine what you're going through seeing me like this. But please, you don't have to make me feel bad about it."

"Stop, don't start," he said, frowning while placing his fork on the edge of his plate. "Don't ruin a lovely meal with your words of pity. I don't need it. I've told you before," he said, low but seething, "do what you want. Just like I have to deal with this, I'm sure I'll be able to deal with another kid. Tell her we're moving forward with adopting."

"I wasn't pitying you, Christian. I was just. Forget it. Are you done eating? I'm ready to leave. I'm tired," she said, pouting.

"Sure, I'm good," he said, just as irritated. He threw up a hand, calling for the server.

"I can't believe you can be so cruel, Christian," Luna's voice wavered, carrying a tremor of hurt as Christian drove them home.

"I'm sorry. Will you forgive me? Again?"

Luna nodded and gazed affectionately in his direction.

"I love you, Luna." He reached across the seat, grabbed her hand, and gently kneaded it.

She didn't resist. She loved this man. How could she stay mad at him? He was accepting her and another man's baby. She hoped adding to their family could help them and their marriage. They would be so busy being parents of little ones that they wouldn't have time to see that their marriage was on life support.

"I thank God for you. I can't do this without you, Christian. I can't," she said, squeezing his hand in return and using the other to wipe tears that had formed in the crest of her eyes.

He briefly looked at her. He used his hand to brush away her tears quickly. "We're going to get through this. You wait and see. I'm sorry if I sounded cold and callous. I *do* want another kid. You're right; we did say we wanted kids close in age. We should tell Attorney Nguyen to keep looking for a match." He smiled as he continued the drive.

"I love you," Luna said.

His phone rang just as he was about to say to her in return, "I love—"

The console identified the caller as NEW YORK OFFICES. He pushed IGNORE. It was Luna's sister. He had saved Lorie's number under the fictitious contact for times like this. *Why the heck is she calling me—again?* He was pissed. He felt his temples pounding.

"You okay?" Luna asked, frowning and looking at him.

"Yeah, I'm good."

"Didn't you need to answer that?"

"Nope, I know what they want."

"Okay."

"Okay, what?"

"Christian, don't play games. Who was that?"

"New York."

"New York. The New York law office?"

He nodded.

"What do they want?"

"They want me to take this big case. I already told them I couldn't. They don't seem to understand that I don't have time to go back and forth between Memphis and New York. I don't want to do that anymore. Especially now." He looked at Luna and smiled.

Seemingly satisfied with his answer, she said, "Thanks, babe." She rested her head against the headrest, placed a hand across her belly, and closed her eyes with a smile.

Christian drove in silence, his mind racing. He had to stop this foolishness with Lorie. He didn't know her motive for showing up and trying to disturb his life, but he sure would find out. As if Luna's assault and pregnancy hadn't been enough to drain him mentally, now her sister wanted to play games.

How quickly and drastically his life had changed. Christian

inwardly chastised himself for being selfish and only thinking of himself and not Luna or the innocent child she was carrying. His wife had endured a violent, life-threatening sexual assault. She had to live with the memory of what was done to her for the rest of her life.

God, forgive me for my selfishness. Help me to love and accept this child unconditionally. Help me to show more love and concern to my wife. Open our hearts to receive more children into our family if that is your will.

He turned into their driveway, pressed the overhead remote, and drove into the garage.

The sound of the garage door opening woke Luna. She raised her head and, with droopy eyes, looked around. "We're at home? Already?" she said, stretching and then opening the door.

"Yep, we're home," Christian said, chuckling, as he watched her walk to the front of the car. "Come on, sleepy-head." He encircled his arm around her, and she nestled her head onto his shoulder as they strolled into the house.

16

BETTA HAVE MY MONEY

"For there to be betrayal, there would have to have been trust first."
Suzanne Collins

"Where could he be? He has my money. I've reviewed the paperwork he's given me over the past eighteen months. I don't have anything with my correct account numbers on it, which was supposed to be for security purposes. Up in here, all it takes is one slip up," Hezekiah seethed, hitting his open palm on the table, causing papers to fly across the table and onto the floor.

The guard stationed at the door looked over his shoulder.

Christian threw up a hand. "Everything's good, Officer." He returned to talking to Hezekiah. "Don't worry; we'll find Price, but remember you'll be transported to Nashville for court next week. From there, the judge will officially announce your release. I have the form ready for your signature, releasing Trevor Price as your agent."

"That's great news. So, you're saying I'll be a free man after court?"

"Yep, you'll be a free man. All of this will be behind you."

Hezekiah looked like he'd seen Jesus. He joyfully applauded and exclaimed, "Oh my Lord, oh my Lord!"

"You still don't have a place to live?"

Hezekiah stopped rejoicing and looked at Christian. "Not yet, that's why I need Price. I need my money, man."

"Do you have a place in mind?" asked Christian.

"Not really. I'm sure Stiles can help me find a spot. Somebody at New Holy Rock has to be a realtor or know somebody who knows somebody. Know what I mean?"

"Sure, well, I'm still trying to locate Price. All leads stop in Morocco. I don't know if he returned after the honeymoon and relocated somewhere else. It's like he dropped off the face of the earth. I can't find family or anyone associated with him who knows his whereabouts. His wife's family has nothing to say or won't divulge anything. In the meantime, talk to Stiles and see what you can line up between now and next Thursday. If push comes to shove, we'll have to rent you an extended stay or Airbnb until you can find a spot."

"Gotcha," said Hezekiah, rising from the steel chair and walking around to embrace Christian. He hugged the at least half-foot shorter Christian Black for a few seconds before stepping back. "Thanks, thanks for everything, man,"

"Just keep your nose clean until you're out of here. Stay in your cell, do whatever you need to do to avoid trouble. Especially stay clear of Clay. Your day in court will be here before you know it. Good luck," said Christian, shaking Hezekiah's hand tightly.

†

"He doesn't have anywhere to live? Are you serious?" Fancy said, sitting on her sofa with Sebastian curled against her. "Something doesn't sound right. It's too bad the parsonage isn't available."

"For a minute, you know Rianna was living there. Hezekiah made sure she was kicked out, and shortly after that, we started leasing it since I had no plans to live in it," Stiles explained. "We're leasing it to a pastor and his family. They signed a three-year lease," Stiles said.

"Oooh," replied Fancy. "Well, I'm sure Hezekiah will find somewhere to lay his head. Knowing him like I do, he has something lined up. And you say he still doesn't know where his attorney is?"

"Nope. We've called his office and his cell. From what I understand, he returned after his honeymoon, but a week later, he cleaned out his office and told them he would be on an extended leave. He left instructions for any future cases that came across his desk to be distributed to the other attorneys in the firm. They haven't heard from him since. The admin said she thinks he went back overseas. She doesn't know that for sure, but she said he often talked about moving to Africa one day. Said he was tired of all the hoopla with the U.S."

"Do you think he was serious?" Fancy asked, stroking a purring Sebastian from his head to his tail.

"Maybe." He shrugged. "I can see him doing something like that. Think about it. He's young, just got married, they both have lucrative careers. No kids. I'm sure they could be successful overseas, depending on where they settled. But I don't understand why he would do that without telling Hezekiah. You said his office said he had settled his cases and reassigned any existing cases he had. Do you think one of them is Hezekiah's case?"

"Not hardly. Remember, he's Hezekiah's POA. That's different."

"Oh, yeah, that's right." Fancy stood, walked over to the enclosed space, slid the door back, and entered the sanctuary-like area. Standing and viewing her backyard, she smiled when she saw the casita she had recently built on her property after the arson. She intended to list the 675-square-foot, one-bedroom, one-bath for short-term rentals on a private site. The doors were intentionally designed with extra width, allowing easy wheelchair access with an expansive open living area into the kitchen.

"Fancy? You there?" Stiles asked.

"Yes, I'm here," she said as Stiles pulled her from her thoughts. She turned and walked back into the house.

"According to Black, his release hearing is scheduled for next Thursday. I haven't heard from Hezekiah yet, but I'm sure he'll call soon."

"You already know," said Fancy. "He's probably sitting on pins and needles in his cell right about now. He's ready to get out and do some damage."

"I hope not. I hope he's learned a lesson and see that this release is a blessing," said Stiles.

"Honestly, I don't care what he does when he gets out. I don't want to see him, at least not right now," she said, her words biting. "My baby is dead. Nothing can bring him back. But his cheating, lowdown daddy will be walking around a free man. Why couldn't it have been him instead of my Xavier? I know that may sound mean, Stiles, but it's the truth. It's how I feel. I don't get it. God knows I don't," Fancy uttered, her voice carrying emotional sorrow.

"You don't mean that."

"I *do* mean it. Don't you get it? Losing Xavier was the last straw. I can't forgive him for that."

"But he had nothing to do with Xavier's death, Fancy. You and I know Xavier chose to end his own life. I'm sorry that he did, but it's the truth. Hezekiah is not to blame. No one is. Maybe in your eyes, Hezekiah wasn't the best father he could have been, and I know he hurt you, but to say he's responsible for his son's death? That's a bit much, and it's unfair."

Fancy soaked up Stiles' words before speaking up. "I can't help what or how I feel. Maybe I'm wrong. And maybe my feelings will change—I don't know. But I do know this," she cried. I need someone to blame—someone other than Xavier."

17
REVENGE IS BITTER & SWEET

"Revenge is a powerful motivator." Marcus Luttrell

The week whizzed by. Tomorrow, Hezekiah would be transported to Nashville for court. He didn't expect to see the inside of these prison walls ever again.

He gave his personal belongings to a young inmate housed in the same cell block where he learned Clay had been transferred. The inmate had attended Hezekiah's Sunday service on a few occasions. He was serving a life sentence for murdering his girlfriend and the guy he caught her cheating with.

"I'll put the money on your books as soon as I'm on the other side of these walls," Hezekiah told the lifer. "In the meantime, I gave you everything that belongs to me. You straight for now?"

"Yeah," the inmate said.

"You know what I need, right? Nothing less."

"An eye for an eye. Nothing less. You got my word," the inmate swore.

"And you have mine," Hezekiah said as they dapped each other.

Later that night, laying back on his bunk, the main thing on his mind was his freedom. Tomorrow morning, he would stand before a judge and be granted a new start, a fresh opportunity, and the chance to right some wrongs on the outside. Out of nowhere, a scroungy, white, pimply-faced inmate appeared at his cell door, pulling him from his thoughts.

Hezekiah sat up but did not move from his bunk. "What is it?" he huffed. "I don't have nothing else to give away," thinking that the dude must have heard about his release and wanted to see what he could do to collect anything Hezekiah may have had left.

Instead, the inmate slowly and deliberately pushed a crinkled piece of paper through the cell and released it before he walked off.

Hezekiah got up, picked up the paper, and read the words *'an eye for an eye. It is done,'* scribbled on it in what looked like blood. He broke out in laughter, knowing it was a message from the lifer. Any worries about Clay were forever a thing of the past.

Hezekiah's mind went back to Trevor Price and his money. Without money, he could not secure a place to lay his head or do anything he needed to do as a free man.

Stiles had offered him a place to stay in his guest room. Hezekiah was grateful for the offer and accepted it, but he only expected to be with his brother for a few days. As soon as the judge announced his freedom, he was going to the bank to see what they could tell him about his money. From there, he planned to find a spot of his own.

He didn't want to think the way he was starting to think,

but if Price had run off with his money, Hezekiah was ready and willing to come back to prison because he would surely hunt him down and kill him.

†

Inside the courtroom, anticipation lingered in the air. Hezekiah stood next to Christian with a fresh jailhouse haircut and shave. He wore a black suit paired with a black and blue tie, complemented by a crisp white shirt. Black leather loafers completed his attire. The clothes were a gift from Christian Black.

The judge cleared his throat, capturing the attention of everyone present.

"Having thoroughly reviewed the facts and circumstances of this case," the judge began, his voice carrying a weight of authority, "and considering the new evidence presented, the court has reached a decision regarding your release."

A pause followed, allowing the significance of the moment to sink in. The judge's stern expression softened as he continued. "It is the court's ruling that your conviction is hereby overturned, and you shall be released from the state's custody immediately."

A strong feeling of relief seemed to sweep across the courtroom, but Hezekiah especially felt it. He took a deep breath, closed his eyes, and quietly mouthed a thank you to God and the judge.

"In your journey towards reintegration into the community," the judge's tone softened once again, "I encourage you to seek positive connections, gainful employment, and contribute to society in a meaningful manner. Mr. McCoy, this court wishes you success in rebuilding your life and hope you use this opportunity to grow, forgive, and make amends."

"Thank you, your honor," Hezekiah said, nodding with a big smile.

Accompanied by Christian, Hezekiah strolled outdoors and stood on the steps of the ancient, historic courthouse. A very light and misty rain began as the sun kept shining brightly. Christian and Stiles opened the umbrellas they had brought along.

Stiles stood on the opposite side with an arm draped around Hezekiah's shoulder. "How does it feel to breathe in this fresh air?"

"Divine," said Hezekiah, taking deep breaths and looking around at the hustle and bustle of life passing by.

"So what would you like to do now that you're a free man? We could go sit down in a restaurant and enjoy a hearty steak or whatever you'd like," Stiles suggested.

"You fellows, go ahead. I have to head back to Memphis. My day is far from over. Congratulations again, buddy," Christian said, extending his hand toward Hezekiah. "Call me if you need me."

Stiles and Hezekiah walked towards his car. "So, what do you have a taste for?"

"Honestly, man, I can't think about eating right now. I want to get to Memphis. I need to find my money."

"Sure thing."

†

Hezekiah's chest tightened when the bank officer told him there was only one account with his name on it that he had access to. This account had a little over fifty thousand dollars. The bank officer searched but found no other accounts under Hezekiah's or Trevor Price's name.

"Excuse me, madam. Can you check this account?" He

removed a piece of paper from his old, beat-up wallet and gave it to the officer.

She entered the account number into her computer. Shaking her head, she looked at Hezekiah. "I'm sorry. It shows that this account once had a significant amount of funds, but they were withdrawn, and it's been closed for over a year. That's all I can tell you. Do you have another one you want me to check?"

"No," Hezekiah replied, his face turning a deep shade of red. His anxiety peaked upon learning that he could only withdraw funds from the account bearing his name by providing proper documentation, such as a driver's license or state ID, to verify his identity. Storming out in anger, if he had any doubt before, it was now clear that Trevor had run off with his money.

Inside the car, Hezekiah repeatedly slammed a fist on the dashboard. "How could I have been so darn stupid? I trusted that guy," he yelled as Stiles pulled out of the parking lot and onto the busy street.

"I thought he was straight, a cool, trustworthy dude. I can't believe he did something like this. Maybe there's a viable explanation. We need to find him. He'll make sense of everything," Stiles said, not trusting his own words.

"I'm going to find him alright, and I swear, when I do, I'm going to kill 'em!"

"Wait a second. I know you're angry, but violence is not the answer. You can't risk going back to prison. We're going to tackle this the smart way. We'll contact Black, lay it all out for him, and get the authorities on our side. You've got your freedom now. Trust me. If he's anywhere in this city or the U.S., for that matter, we won't stop until we find him. In the meantime, we're going to get your ID processed, and then we can go back to the bank. You can withdraw your money and open a new account."

Hezekiah responded with silence, feeling completely unsettled. He had entrusted Price with overseeing almost half a million dollars, his life's savings, only to have the man vanish with every penny except the 50 thousand.

Hezekiah now suspected that Price was no longer in Tennessee. For Price's sake, he prayed that was the case because if he was still in or around the mid-south, Hezekiah had already determined that he would not rest until he found Price and made him face the piper.

18

THE TIME HAS COME

"The world breaks everyone, and afterward, some are strong at the broken places." Ernest Hemingway

Khalil walked around the backyard with his mother to the casita.

"I've always said your designs are phenomenal, Mama," Khalil complimented his mother when they entered the beautifully furnished space. "I don't know why you don't advertise more. You can have all kinds of clients just from Holy Rock alone."

"I know, but I don't want that. I like having an occasional client, but that's it. I used to think I wanted a full-time interior design business, but my life is just, well, I've got too many other things on my plate," she explained, holding Sebastian in her arms.

Khalil continued walking around inside the tiny house, taking in how tastefully decorated it was.

"Opening your own business could be a good thing. It can keep your mind off the past, and you can concentrate on living the life you deserve, Mama. You can also get good money from renting this space, even if it's only for a weekend or occasional holiday. Or this can be your office. There's enough room to reconfigure this space, store your design stuff, and have an office area. You know that, right?" In a 360 motion, he scanned the space.

"Yes, I know. That's one of the reasons I had it built. All the extra yard space was going to no real use. Even with the pool, hot tub, and outdoor kitchen, plenty of yard space remained. I always wanted a house with a casita in the back for my parents or in-laws when they got old, or my kids," she looked affectionately at Khalil, "if y'all ever needed to come home for whatever reason." She threw up a hand, almost dropping Sebastian, but quickly recovered. "But I do have it listed on a private Airbnb site. I had a couple of renters lined up, but then," her tone turned melancholy, "but you know, then your brother died."

She walked over and sat down on the decorative sofa, stroking a purring Sebastian.

Khalil sat beside her, wrapped an arm around her, and kissed her forehead.

"I miss him so much," she began to cry while cuddling Sebastian.

Khalil continued holding her. "Shhh, I know you do. I do, too. We all do. But you're going to be okay, Mama."

She looked up at him, wiping her tears with her hand. "Stiles called me. He said your father was released today."

He kept his arm around his mother. "I knew it was going to be soon. I didn't know it would be this soon, though." He shrugged. "Good for him."

"You mean that?"

"Sure, why wouldn't I?" he said, removing his arm and resting his back against the sofa. "It's not like I hate the guy. I mean, he's my dad. I don't like the dude; I admit that. And we don't see eye to eye on a lot of things. He's a jerk sometimes, but at the end of the day, he's still my dad. I do love him, Mama. Know what I mean?"

Fancy exhaled. "Yes, and that's good to hear, baby. I'm glad you've come to that point." She grabbed hold of his hand and held it in hers. Half-smiling, she confessed, "I wish I could say that I wish him well, and Lord forgive me for saying this, but I don't feel anything for your father but contempt right now. Stiles says he's not responsible for Xavier's death, but I feel like, in some way, he is, although I can't make sense of it."

"Mama, I feel ya. But Uncle Stiles is right; it's not Dad's fault. I can't believe I'm taking up for him, but I am. My brother had a lot of problems. He kept a lot to himself. I could blame myself, too, for not being there for him more, but what good would that do? I blame myself for not knowing what Orlando was doing to him. I didn't know he was like that. I swear I didn't."

"Honey, it's not your fault. None of us knew. Xavier was always a quiet and introverted boy. I didn't see anything that could have warned me that he was being," she paused and shook her head before continuing, "I didn't think someone, anyone, especially that Orlando boy, would hurt my baby. He was always so respectable when he came around. His parents were some wonderful Christian people. Why didn't Xavier tell us," she cried.

"I would have killed him had I known back then," Khalil said, looking disgusted.

"Then, thank God you didn't know."

"I do know that what was going on with him was too much for us to understand or deal with. We can't place the blame on anybody but the person responsible for abusing him, and he's good and dead. Orlando can never hurt anyone else."

Fancy looked at her son. Her eyes were still filled with fresh tears, but she nodded. "I know," she murmured, "but it makes me feel better to be able to blame someone, I guess. What better person than Hezekiah?"

He hugged her again and quickly leaned over to retrieve the box of tissue to wipe the tears streaming down her face.

"Thanks." She wiped her nose and stood. "You ready? Sebastian is getting antsy." She headed toward the door.

"Yes, come on, let's get out of here. Thanks for showing me this place again. I have a bishop and his first lady flying in next month for a week-long revival. I want to tell them about your place. That is if you think you're ready to rent it."

Fancy looked around the space again before answering. "Yes, I think I'm ready. Tell them to go on the website and put in this address. I'll work up the contract and email it to them when it comes up. It's just that simple."

"See, Mama, you're good at stuff like this." He kissed her on the cheek and hugged her as they left out of the casita.

Fancy laughed and blushed. "Come on. I know you're ready to eat."

"You know it. Especially since you made fried cabbage and meatloaf."

"Yes, I sure did. And mac 'n cheese and hot water cornbread, too."

"Dang," Khalil chuckled and patted his six-pack. "I can't wait. You should teach Eliana how to make your meatloaf. I haven't found another person who can make it like you."

Fancy giggled as they entered the house. "Speaking of Eliana, how is she? How is Khaliyah?"

"They're both good. I'm sorry we haven't been over. Things

have been hectic at church and home, and then, like you said, losing Xavier. Time gets away."

"I understand, but I do miss my sweet grandbaby. She's so precious."

Fancy made a hefty plate for Khalil and a smaller one for herself.

"Thanks," Khalil said when she put the food before him. "This looks so good!" He sniffed. "Ummm, smells delicious! Oh, Lord," he bowed his head, "bless this food I'm about to receive for the nourishment of my body. Amen." He quickly scooped up a forkful of cabbage and cornbread, popping it into his mouth.

"Boy, you sure said that fast. Don't hurt yourself," Fancy said, chuckling as she sat at the island beside him.

They enjoyed the savory taste of the food for a few minutes before Fancy started the conversation again.

"How are you and Eliana?"

Khalil stopped chewing momentarily and looked at his mother. "I already told you; she and Khaliyah are good."

"That's not what I asked. I said, how are *you* and Eliana? You know good and well what I mean."

She was right; Khail knew exactly what his mother was alluding to. He didn't want to get into the problems in his marriage. But knowing his mother like he did, she would not let him escape this conversation.

"Things could be better," he remarked, hunching his shoulders. Then he popped a forkful of food into his mouth.

"Better? Better how?"

"Ma, I don't know. Just better. I mean, she's a good mother. She keeps a clean house. She does her best to be a good first lady..."

"So, if she's all that, why do I detect you're unhappy?"

"I told you. I don't know. Sometimes, I think being married

isn't for me. I can't see myself tied down with one female for the rest of my life. It's going on three years since we got married, and every day, it doesn't seem to get better. The highlight, only highlight, is Khaliyah. I can't see her not being part of my life."

"I hear what you're saying, and now I'm going to tell you this. I'm going to tell you the truth because I'm your mother, and I wouldn't dare lie to you. You will never be happy with Eliana as long as you're tipping around on the outside."

Khalil stopped eating, looked at his mother, and grinned. "Are you serious? Tipping on the outside? What are you talking about?"

"Boy, please. You know darn well what I'm talking about and *who* I'm talking about. That tramp, Detria Graham. I don't understand you. You're just like your father in that instance. You have to have a li'l whore on the side. But it's wrong; I'm telling you something you already know."

"Mama, Detria knows her place, which means she knows she'll never be more to me than what she is—a convenient sidepiece."

"That's even worse. You're supposed to be a man of God, Khalil. You're held to a higher standard. Yet, here you are using women. It's not right. I'm telling you, and you hear me well. That woman is nothing but trouble. For goodness sake, Khalil, did you forget she slept with your daddy before she started sleeping with you? And before that, she was married to your uncle. She's nasty, just plain nasty."

Khalil shook his head, laying his fork on his plate. "No, Mama, I haven't forgotten."

"Then I don't know what's wrong with you. She and Rianna are two peas in a pod. I bet your daddy sees that now. As for you, if you love your daughter like you say you do, you'll try to make things work with her mother. Especially since you say Eliana is trying and that she's a good mother and first lady."

"That she is, but I still have needs, Mama, if you know what I mean." He pushed back his almost empty plate and swallowed his iced tea.

"Sex? Is that what you're talking about? Baby, that will fade, too, in time. You better get a woman who will be with you when things no longer work like they used to—somebody who has your back and will be by your side through the rough times. Now, do you know what *I* mean?" she emphasized and smiled.

Khalil half smiled. "But she's so closed-minded when it comes to sex. But look, Mama. I don't want to talk about this with you. It's too intimate." He rose from the stool and carried his plate to the sink.

"Intimate my foot. You better talk to somebody, or else you'll look up, and Eliana will be gone, and you best believe she'll take that little girl with her, too. So, if you love your wife, even just a little, I say I try to make it work. Heck, get you some sex games."

"Ma? Are you serious?" He turned red but chuckled.

"Yes, dead serious. Introduce some things in the bedroom, but do it subtly. Don't overwhelm the poor girl." Fancy quipped. "And seriously, please, leave Detria alone and any other woman who tries to come to you outside your marriage. Some hurts are avoidable, as well as some mistakes, baby. I wish your brother had realized that before he chose to take his life."

Khalil appeared genuinely attuned to his mother's words. Typically, he would let her advice slip past him, but today was different. Perhaps it was her tone. Whatever it was, he sensed the urging of the Holy Spirit compelling him to heed her wise counsel. Deep within, he did want the family life, yet his actions conveyed a different message. He was a young man who loved women, and the women loved him. The bachelor life seemed tailor-made for him, an existence that perfectly suited his vibrant spirit if he didn't wear the title of *pastor*. But the die had been cast, and there was no reversing his course now. He had committed himself to marriage and parenthood. His mother was right—as a man of God, the time had come for him to step up to the plate or gracefully step aside.

"Mama, you're right. I promise to try to do better. Okay?"

"I sure hope so. I'd hate to see you lose your family because you're thinking with the wrong body part."

19
FRESH STEPS

"The magic in new beginnings is truly the most powerful of them all." Josiyah Martin

"Make yourself at home. There's plenty of food and beverages in the fridge. Nothing's off limits," Stiles assured his brother.

Hezekiah opened the stainless steel double-door fridge. His eyes scanned the refrigerator filled with food containers, prepackaged meals, sodas, water, fresh produce, and fruit.

Chuckling and shaking his head, Hezekiah said, "Let me guess. From the Kitchen Ministry?"

"Yep, you got it. They keep a brother stocked, man."

"Some things never change," Hezekiah said. The brothers laughed.

After eating a hearty plate of food, Hezekiah retreated to the guest room, showered, and collapsed on the full-size bed. He had completely forgotten the blissful comfort a quality mattress could offer. As he yawned and stretched, he sprawled across the bed, gazing at the ceiling. He was free. The feeling was indescribable. He remained silent, soaking in the peace that covered him like a blanket.

He thought of Fancy and raised in the bed. Looking to the right of him, he spotted his small bag of clothing. On the way home, after he got his new license, Stiles drove him back to the bank. Hezekiah withdrew his money and set up a new account. He kept twenty-five hundred dollars in his pocket for personal use.

"I need to stop by the Criminal Justice Center. I need to pay a fine."

"A fine? If your conviction was overturned, why are they making you pay a fine?"

"It's something from when I was initially incarcerated. I want to take care of any outstanding debts. I want to make sure nothing comes up by surprise," Hezekiah quickly lied.

Once inside the CJC, he found the lobby kiosk and proceeded to deposit the maximum amount of money in the inmate's account, just as he promised him he would do.

After leaving the CJC, they stopped at a department store where he picked up a few essentials: underwear, toiletries, two pairs of slacks, three polo shirts, and a stylish pair of faux leather loafers.

This store was not his go-to place for shopping, but their choice of clothes was better than the bright orange jumpsuit he'd worn the past three years. He would have plenty of time to shop at finer stores after he found Trevor Price and got his money back.

The thought of Price infuriated him. *That conniving, sneaky thief...* He abruptly halted those thoughts and redirected his mind to thinking about Fancy.

The last time he attempted to talk to her was right after

Xavier died. That was a big mistake. He didn't know what gave him the idea that the two of them could grieve their son together, if only for the duration of a jailhouse call. But, boy, was he wrong. She blamed him for their son's death. She cried and lashed out at him like he was the devil himself.

He got up, retrieved the bag of clothing and other items, and returned to the bed. He pulled out the same phone he'd had in prison. He planned to get a more updated phone in the next day or so. In the meantime, he scrolled his CONTACTS until he got to Fancy's number. Should he take the chance and call her again? He scrolled past her number.

He came to Khalil's phone number. Paused—scrolled past.

Next, he saw Rianna's number. Laughed. Shook his head—scrolled past.

When he reached Xavier and Pepper's numbers, laughter turned to sadness. He dropped his head and scrolled past.

He came to Mariah's number. Clay had been found in his cell with his throat slashed the same morning of Hezekiah's scheduled release. He thought about calling her and offering his insincere condolences but decided against it. He would be in contact soon enough about making arrangements to see his son.

He sighed deeply, grateful to be free but worried about his money and Trevor Price's whereabouts. He placed his flip phone on the nightstand and knelt to pray.

†

The following morning, he accompanied Stiles to New Holy Rock. Entering the church for the first time in three years was surreal. His spirit lightened, and a broad smile consumed his weathered face.

Three staff members were in the office. They greeted him

with hugs and well wishes and announced their happiness over his release.

After talking to the staff for several minutes, he and Stiles walked along the church's corridors. Everything around him looked unfamiliar, but then he recalled the vandalism Stiles told him the church had experienced some months prior.

"This looks like a different church."

"I know. A lot had to be redone. We took advantage of the situation and invested in getting some other renovations done. Xavier made sure we received an ample insurance settlement, and we got a building grant on top of that. He was good at what he did." Stiles hung his head briefly.

"Yep, he was a genius when it came to keeping the books," Hezekiah agreed. "You still think Rianna had something to do with the vandalism?"

"Heck, yeah. My feelings about that haven't changed. The police couldn't gather enough evidence to tie her or her floozy friend, Tiny. I don't think it's high on their list of unsolved cases."

"You're probably right."

Opening the door leading to the sanctuary, Hezekiah stopped, inhaled deeply, and closed his eyes. He was in awe of the majestic beauty of the space.

"It feels like the presence of God is in this place," Hezekiah mouthed.

"That's because God *is* here," Stiles agreed. "It's one of the reasons I love spending so much time here, especially when there are no services, the office is closed, and it's just me. That's when I feel His presence the most. I can't explain it. I find myself being able to talk to Him, tell Him everything on my mind and in my heart."

"I feel you on that. I've only been here for a minute, and already, I told you, I can feel the spirit of the living God. This place is anointed. Thank you, man, for taking care of it. I don't know what would have happened had you not stepped up to the plate." He placed a hand on Stiles's shoulder as they trudged further inside the area.

"Do you mind?" He looked at his brother. "I'd like to spend a few minutes alone."

"Okay, I'll be in my office."

As Hezekiah approached the altar, he was drawn to a painting of the Last Supper hanging behind the choir stand. Next was another image depicting Jesus walking on water with his hand extended toward Peter.

After a moment, he knelt, clasped his hands, and lifted his head to pray.

As he prayed, he felt his cheeks become warm and was surprised to find tears rolling down his face. A heaviness filled him, and he fell prostrate, crying to God to help him. Grief took hold of him, wrapping around his heart like it was trying to strangle him. The tears that came down earlier were nothing compared to the release of a tsunami of fresh ones, streaming heavily down his face onto the purple-carpeted floor.

His prayers continued until moments later, he felt winded and exhausted. The weight was now lightened. He pulled himself to his knees, looking at the cross imprinted on the podium stand.

"Thank you. Thank you, dear God." He stood, wiped his tears, looked around a few more minutes, and then left.

He walked around the church until he arrived in front of the still engraved door: Senior Pastor Hezekiah McCoy. He smiled, seeing his name had not been removed. He turned the doorknob slightly but then halted. Instead, he turned and walked along the hall of the remaining offices. He came upon Stiles's office. His door was partially open. He saw him doing something on his computer with the phone to his ear.

Refraining from disturbing him, he headed back toward his office. He stood at the entrance for a few seconds before opening the door and entering.

Initially, the office felt empty and cold, but as he looked around, a sense of peace consumed him, and he felt mentally relaxed. Everything was basically as he remembered. The same office furniture, his pictures, plaques, Bible, and other desk items were all in the same place. It was as if he had never left.

He walked around the space and then stood at his desk before pulling out the chair and taking a seat. Everything felt different yet the same. He smiled again, suddenly feeling grateful at realizing he was free. He removed his cell phone from his pocket, looked up Christian Black's number, and called him from the church phone.

"How's it going, Pastor McCoy?" Christian said, sounding quite jovial.

"Enjoying this new opportunity, man. I wanted to call and say thank you again. This wouldn't have happened without you and the good Lord. I can't thank you enough."

"It's what I do," Christian said. "Oh, know this: Price's POA officially ended when you completed that revocation form."

"That's good to know. But I still have unfinished business. Wherever he is, he needs to show up and give me my money."

"I told you it may be hard to recoup that money, that is, if we find out what he did with it and if there's any left. You gave him durable power of attorney over your medical and finances. Making him your POA was understandable. At the time, you thought you would be in prison for at least eight or nine years. You didn't want your ex-wife to try to get her grubby hands on it, and well, you made the best decision for yourself at the time. You had no idea this Price guy was a con and a scammer. *Dang*, he's a lawyer and pulling this kind of crap."

"I don't know what he's trying to pull, but he's treading on dangerous ground, Black. I'm telling you. That's all I'm going to say. I'll talk to you later. Oh, how's your wife?"

"She's good. The baby's good. Everything is good."

"I'm glad to hear that," said Hezekiah, although Christian didn't sound convincing. Christian had recently told him about Luna's pregnancy, so Hezekiah knew the baby she was carrying was not Christian's kid. He didn't know how Christian could deal with that. Heck, Hezekiah didn't know how Christian's wife was dealing with it. Carrying a kid by the man who raped her had to be tough on both of them.

"Thanks. Have you seen any of your family besides Stiles?"

"Nah, not yet. I've had a lot of business to take care of since my release yesterday. I got a lot of stuff done after I left you, and I think that was only hours after my release. I wasn't messing around." He chuckled.

Christian laughed into the phone. "Good for you."

"But I'll get around to seeing everybody, at least everybody who wants to see me. My friend, I can tell you that the list is short, and I mean very short." Hezekiah kept chuckling.

"You might be surprised. Anyway, I'm about to walk into the office. If you need me, you can call me later."

Hezekiah relaxed back in his plush leather office chair. He twirled around slightly and, like he used to, placed his legs on top of his desk with his hands behind his head.

He suddenly popped out of his chair like he'd been stung. He left his office and headed to Xavier's office. Xavier's name was also still engraved on the door. He turned the knob. The door was unlocked. Slowly, he pushed it open and stood frozen for a few solid seconds before he walked inside.

He could smell the faint scent of his son's cologne as he approached his desk. Xavier's plaques, awards, commendations, and degrees, among other things, still lined the walls. On a sofa table, several pictures of him, Pepper, and the boys were still in place. There was another picture of Xavier and Fancy with Zavion and Davion. He walked around the small space, and tears filled his eyes. But just as quickly as they fell, he wiped them away.

He sat behind Xavier's desk and opened one of the file drawers filled with files and papers. He leafed through some of them before closing the file drawer. He turned on Xavier's computer, but he couldn't access it. Xavier had it password-protected.

He stood up as the sense of overwhelming grief began to consume him. He had to leave. At the door, he lingered momentarily, looking back over his shoulder before walking out and closing the door.

Returning to his office, his mind fell on Fancy again. He wanted to see her face to know how she was doing for himself. Xavier was her baby. He knew she had to have been hurting more than anyone knew.

A light knock on the door halted his thoughts.

"It's open."

Stiles walked into the office. "Hey, how long do you want to be here?"

"However long you need to be here, I'm in no hurry." Hezekiah hunched a shoulder. I don't have to punch anybody's time clock - at least, not yet." He laughed.

"I meant to tell you I would be here most of the day until around four or four-thirty this afternoon. I'm just saying, if you have somewhere you want to go, you can take my car."

"Thanks for the offer. I'll take you up on that, but not now. I'm going through some stuff and making some calls."

"Okay. Here are the keys." He tossed them toward Hezekiah, who promptly caught them.

"I'll let you know when I leave."

"Sure thing," said Stiles and turned to leave.

Hezekiah went through his phone again. This time, he stopped at Pepper's contact information. He called her.

Surprisingly, she sounded almost glad to hear from him. Something about her voice made him feel welcome. He silently thanked God, and the father and daughter-in-law continued to talk.

"The boys are running around. I'm about to make them a snack and take them to the neighborhood park."

"I hear them," Hezekiah said, laughing into the phone when he heard his grandsons in the background keeping up a ruckus.

"Uh, if you'd like, you're welcome to meet us there, or if you want to come to the house, we can go together."

"I...I'd love to come by the house. I'm at New Holy Rock right now, so I'll leave now. Are you still in the same spot?"

"No, we're in the same neighborhood, but Xavier and I moved to a bigger house right before the pandemic. I thought you knew."

"I don't recall him telling me about it. Maybe he did. So much happened in that place that I guess I lost track of things going on in the free world."

"I understand. I'll text you the address. You can put it in your GPS. A lot of rebuilding has happened since you were last on these Memphis streets. I wouldn't want you getting turned around."

"Okay, send it, and I'll be on my way."

Hezekiah couldn't be happier when Pepper pleasantly greeted him when he called. It was further proof that she didn't hold any anger against him about Xavier. That took a load off of him. Now, he could establish a relationship with his grandsons—another blessing.

"Hey," he said, stopping at Stiles's office. "I talked to

Pepper. She said I could come to see my grandsons. Do you want to come along?"

"No, you go ahead. It would be best if you had that one-on-one time with them. They haven't seen their grandpa since they were babies. They need to get to know you."

"Yeah, you're right. They don't know me, but you best believe I'm going to change all of that. I'll be back in a couple of hours."

"Okay. Enjoy yourself, bruh."

20
ACCEPTING CHANGE

"Life is like riding a bicycle. To keep your balance, you must keep moving." Albert Einstein

"Thanks for coming," Pepper said, giving Hezekiah a light hug as he prepared to leave. His grandsons stood behind her, sharing a pack of seaweed.

"The boys got used to you right away. I think it's because Xavier resembles you, and y'all have many of the same ways," she told Hezekiah.

Hezekiah chuckled. "I had a good time myself. I'm so glad you welcomed me into your home. I know it's been tough. Is there anything I can do to help you, Pepper? Anything you need? I can't offer you money right now, but that'll soon change. Not that you would care, but I think my POA ran off with my money. I can't be one hundred percent sure, but it's sure looking like that's the case. I can't find him anywhere."

"Oh, my gosh, I'm sorry to hear that. And thanks, but I

don't need money. I'm straight. Xavier had a substantial life insurance policy. Thank God the suicide clause was no longer in effect, and I could get paid. It should take care of the boys and me for quite a while until I decide when or if I want to return to work. But you're talking about Trevor, right? He ran off with your money?"

Hezekiah nodded.

"Wow, that's so messed up." She spotted the boys tussling over a toy. "Stop that fighting," she yelled, "or you're going in timeout."

Hezekiah watched and listened as she disciplined his grandsons. Immediately, they obeyed their mother and ran to another pile of toys like they hadn't been quarreling seconds before.

"You know, Xavier was supposed to be one of the groomsmen at Trevor's wedding, but Xavier had already left Memphis by the time Trevor's wedding day arrived. That's when I knew for sure something had happened. It was not like him to miss out on a friend's special day—not like him at all." She briefly looked at the boys who had run into the family room.

"Yeah, that definitely wasn't like Xavier. He was a man of his word and loyal to a fault. But look, I need to go. I need to get Stiles his car back. Are you sure you're straight?"

"Yes, I'm good. It's just a slow process. I still cry every day, sometimes several times a day. The pain is unbearable, Hezekiah. I don't know if I'll ever get over this," she said, wiping her eyes before tears fell.

He reached out and held her for a while as they stood at the front door.

"Look, I'm going to get this car back to Stiles. I'll call and check on y'all later. I'll come by again one day next week."

"Okay."

After leaving Pepper, he headed toward the Lion's Gate community as if on auto-pilot. Upon arriving outside the gates, he hesitated, uncertain of his purpose. Parking across the street, he observed cars coming and going.

He wondered if Fancy was at home. She hadn't responded the last few times he had called and texted her. He didn't blame her for not wanting to talk to him. He longed to explain that Xavier's suicide wasn't his fault. He knew within himself that he could have been a better father, husband, preacher, and overall man, but all of that was because of past mistakes and bad decisions. He wanted things to be different now that he had been set free. He need only settle a few scores, and then he would be ready to walk God's path.

He saw a car approaching the gate resembling Fancy's metallic gray Honda sedan. He closely examined the vehicle as it exited, and it was indeed Fancy's, with the "Holy Rock" specialized plate on the front.

He followed from a distance, ensuring she didn't notice him as she drove through the city and neighborhoods. After a while, she turned onto Khalil's street. He remained hidden from her view but could see her entering Khalil's driveway. He watched as she moved a tricycle blocking the walkway to Khalil's massive two-story mid-century modern home.

At the front door, Fancy conversed with a woman who opened the door before she disappeared into the house.

Hezekiah remained parked for about ten minutes before leaving and returning to New Holy Rock.

When he returned to the office, he refamiliarized himself with some old sermons he'd written and preached before incarceration. He printed out three sermons to take home to read and study. Whenever he decided to stand in the pulpit of New Holy Rock again, he wanted to be fully prepared. He was still nervous about returning to the pulpit after all this time. He held Sunday service in prison, but for some reason, he felt returning to his pulpit would be different. Yet, he was eager to return if that made sense. It was like a catch twenty-two. He hoped the members would accept his return as senior pastor. Would they remain with him, or would they flee?

Hezekiah sat in front of the computer and decided to go online. He needed to set up a new email address for himself. A bright red banner with the words " BREAKING NEWS " scrolling in white letters appeared on the screen, capturing his attention.

BREAKING NEWS...Over 2,500 people died when a powerful magnitude 6.8 earthquake struck Morocco. 7 Americans are among the dead. Most of the damage occurred in the town of Marrakech.

"Morocco? That's where Price went on his honeymoon," he mumbled, frowning at the horrific images of the extensive damage, fallen bricks, mountains of rubble, hot ash, and a mess of broken stuff lining the streets. Many of the structures in the marketplace had collapsed.

A video showed the City Square filling with people making pallets to sleep on the ground. Reporters stated people were afraid aftershocks could kill or severely injure them if they remained inside.

He reached for his phone and called Trevor's number again. There was no answer; not even his voicemail came on this time. He called Trevor's office. The person who answered told him the same thing he'd heard the last time he called —*Attorney Price is on extended leave.*

"I know he's glad that didn't happen while he was over there." Hezekiah shrugged, ignoring the possibility of Trevor still being in Morocco but quickly growing furious at the thought of Trevor running off with his money.

21

LET THE GAME BEGIN

"Deadly poisons are concealed under sweet honey." Ovid

The news about the earthquake overrode any concern M. J. may have had about Hezekiah's release. His anxiety deepened as he read reports of the extensive damage, loss of life, and widespread destruction in Marrakech, near where Trevor and Niesha had settled. He absorbed this distressing information and prayed for his friend's safety.

His heart sank as he gazed upon the harrowing images depicting the widespread destruction of the town. Among them were heart-wrenching photographs capturing the lives tragically lost, including a family from Utah who had been visiting relatives when the earthquake struck. Yet, despite the grim scenes that had already unfolded before him, nothing could have braced M. J. for the astonishing revelation that awaited.

Midway through eating his sandwich, he nearly spat it out

in disbelief when he saw an image resembling Trevor among the American casualties. He convinced himself he was mistaken, but it still left him shaken.

Quickly abandoning his meal, he abruptly left the table and hurried into his home office. Once there, he swiftly accessed his computer, rearranging files and conducting financial transactions to move funds as he and Trevor had discussed if something happened to one of them.

†

After a tiring week, the weekend had arrived. Christian relaxed in the comfort of their sunroom with a cold glass of Southern sweet iced tea and a deli sandwich.

Luna appeared, cradling her baby bump as she strolled past. "Honey, Attorney Nguyen just called," she exclaimed.

Christian found it increasingly difficult to pretend to be happy, but he forced a smile as he watched her sit on the edge of the hot tub.

"What'd she want?"

Luna turned and looked at him, her face glowing, her smile bright. "She may have a match for us."

Christian postured himself upright in the lounge chair.

"A little boy, biracial, thirteen months, born to teenage parents. He was placed in the system after being removed from the mother's custody for child neglect and abuse. When CPS got him, she said he was severely malnourished."

Christian listened, absorbing what she said. "What about the father? Where's he? Doesn't he want him? Or what about the grandparents?"

"No, sadly, they don't. The father already signed away his parental rights. So did the baby's mother, but only after they removed the poor thing."

Another child? They agreed to continue the adoption process, but he did not expect them to find a child this quickly. Still, the adoption would be a deliberate choice, unlike the baby his wife was carrying.

"Where is he?"

"Davidson County, in foster care. He's been there ever since they removed him from the home almost a year ago. Before you ask, the foster parents, according to Attorney Nguyen, have no desire to adopt."

Christian remained silent. He took a swallow of his tea.

"What are you thinking?" She really didn't have to ask because she knew him so well, but maybe he would surprise her by saying something opposite to what she thought he would say.

"I think we need to look into it some more before we make a decision. You said the kid was neglected and abused?"

Luna nodded.

"He could have long-term psychological problems or require extra care. Not that there's anything wrong with that, but we have full careers, Luna, and you're about to have the baby soon. It's going to be tough raising a newborn and a thirteen-month-old."

"I know, but we can do this, Christian," she said, her voice quivering with emotion. Her eyes met his, wide and glistening with unshed tears. "And before we agree to anything, we'll have a chance to meet him. As for psychological issues, I don't think that's anything we have to be overly concerned about. There's nothing that lots of love and affection can't cure in a child that young. I know it," she said, beaming. "So what do you say? Should I call her back and tell her we're interested in taking the next step?"

"Let me think about it. It's the weekend. I don't want to think about anything other than watching Coach Prime slay them boys tomorrow." He slightly chuckled and took a bite of his sandwich.

"Okay, that's fair. Come join me," she said, extending her hand toward him.

He walked over and sat beside her. She gently clasped his hand. That simple touch conveyed more than words ever could, a silent declaration that together, they could face whatever lay ahead.

Christian eased into the warm, bubbly water, then turned, grabbed her hand, and gently guided her into the tub beside him. Caressing her buttocks, he began kissing and squeezing her—his desire mounted as gasps and moans filtered from their mouths.

"I love you," she said hungrily as Christian's kisses deepened.

He was surprised but very pleased when she didn't push against him. Maybe she was beginning to move past what happened. God knows he'd prayed long and hard that she would. One thing about her was that before the assault, she never denied him. That was one reason he was even more disgusted with himself for cheating on her with Lorie.

"Come on, let's get out of here."

"Already?" she protested. "It's barely been ten minutes ago."

"I don't care. Shh, it's getting hot in this hot tub, girl, and I don't mean the water either. If we don't get out now, I can't be responsible for what I might do next."

Luna giggled when he grabbed her and started kissing her again.

†

Draped in his arms, Luna snuggled in her birthday suit

against her husband. The bed felt relaxed and welcoming, and their gentle lovemaking sealed the deal. This was the first time since the assault that she had allowed him to come this close to her, let alone make love. She didn't know what made this day different, but she felt relaxed, safe, and secure in her husband's arms. Desire rose in her, and she wanted him. When she closed her eyes, she no longer saw the monster who attacked her, she saw Christian, the love of her life, her husband. She gave in to her flesh, and it felt good.

Christian was gentle. He seemed to understand what a big deal this was for her, especially given that her burgeoning belly made it a bit difficult, yet it was satisfying.

He moaned and leaned in, kissing her on her forehead and wiping back the locks of her sweaty hair off her face. He began planting butterfly kisses all over her face as he caressed her. The more he lay against her nakedness, the less intimidated he felt about the baby in her belly.

His manly nature began to reactivate. He tenderly rolled her to her side, and again, they made love.

After their lovemaking, they showered, and Luna left for the kitchen to make them a snack.

"You change the bed to some fresh linen. I'll be back," she said, pecking him on his lips. "Do you want water or coffee with your sandwich?"

"Um, water will be fine."

While he gathered the clean linen, he turned on the television. The nine o'clock news was on.

He paused and listened to the reporter talk about a massive flood in Libya that killed 20,000 people. He shook his head. "My God, help this world." He continued making the bed but paused again when the story about the earthquake in Morrocco appeared. He was stunned to see an image of Trevor Price and his new bride in their wedding attire. He sat at the edge of the bed, his attention on the reporter.

"Parents of Memphis newlywed Niesha Price confirm their daughter and her husband, Attorney Trevor Price, also from Memphis, are among the casualties from a 6.8 magnitude quake that hit the town of Marrakech in Morocco. Price was a rising divorce attorney in the mid-south, well respected by his peers. The couple recently exchanged vows and honeymooned in Morocco. A bride's family member says the couple was making plans to live in Morocco permanently, which is why they were in the country when this tragedy occurred. This is Jeremy Parker, News Channel...."

Christian pushed OFF on the remote, stood up, retrieved his phone, and called Hezekiah.

"Hey, I don't know if you heard, but I just saw the news. Says Price and his new bride were killed in Morocco."

"I know. I heard about it earlier today. But who's to say he's dead? Did they find their bodies?"

"Come on, be for real. I just watched his distraught in-laws talking about their daughter and her amazing husband."

Hezekiah reclined on his bed, his hand gently massaging his throbbing temples as he shifted his head from side to side.

"I don't think either would be pulling a prank at a time such as this. No, you better face the facts—Trevor Price is dead. Let's hope and pray the whereabouts of your money didn't die with him."

22

RUNNING ON EMPTY

"Every new beginning comes from some other beginning's end."
Seneca

H ezekiah gazed at his reflection in the expansive office mirror, relieved to find his regal purple and black robe, though it draped loosely over his frame. This outcome came as no surprise; he had shed approximately thirty pounds during his prison stint. The food was terrible, so Hezekiah ate sparingly, only consuming what was necessary for sustenance. Other food came from the commissary, which was no better than the prison slop.

Scrutinizing his appearance, he opted for the suit. The robe would have to be altered, or he would have to gain weight so it would fit appropriately if he planned to wear it in the pulpit again. But that wasn't the case. Stiles still had the task of delivering today's message, the same as he'd done every Sunday while Hezekiah was incarcerated.

Hezekiah was eager for the day to come when he delivered a sermon again from the pulpit of New Holy Rock, the church he founded. But he also felt that he had too many irons in the fire that needed extinguishing before he felt ready to stand before God and His people again. In addition, he didn't know how the congregation would accept his return to the pulpit. He'd heard mixed rumors and whispers. Some people thought it was a blessing, while others thought it would be a slap in the face of God if he reclaimed his position and title.

In the vestibule, he met Stiles, dressed in a black and purple robe similar to his. He and two other ministers fell in line behind Stiles and proceeded to the sanctuary.

As they walked to the pulpit, the minister walking behind Hezekiah positioned himself in front of the glass podium. In contrast, the others continued to their designated spaces.

"God's grace is sufficient," the minister proclaimed.

"Amen," much of the congregation replied.

To Hezekiah's pleasant surprise, the sanctuary was packed. He noticed some people smiling and others looking bewildered. He didn't know if he should expect people to stay away now that he was back or if they would fill the pews.

"Thank you, God," he shouted, laughing joyously as he walked to his seat, clapping his hands and praising the Lord.

Still standing, he stomped his feet and lifted his hands as the first minister sat down, and the other one took his place and extended a prayer.

The New Holy Rock Praise Team, comprised of seven men and women, came forward after prayer and rendered two uplifting, soul-stirring songs. This time, Hezekiah popped up from his seat and broke into a 'holy dance' that could have been mistaken for a quick two-step or cha-cha.

Fancy was in attendance, seated three rows from the front, her hands folded in her lap. This was only her second time at

New Holy Rock since Xavier's passing. It still felt weird, knowing she would never again see him come parading through the sanctuary dressed like a magazine model. She half-smiled at the thought but then discreetly rolled her eyes as she observed her ex-husband enthusiastically buck-jumping around in the pulpit as if some spirit had possessed him. Only Fancy couldn't convince herself that the Holy Spirit was guiding his jerky movements; it seemed more like the devil's work to her. She quickly covered her mouth, stifling a laugh.

For some reason, seeing him prancing around like that made her think about when she and Hezekiah were young in the ministry in Chicago. They were invited to this out-of-the-way church for fellowship with a couple who proclaimed to be healing evangelists. Their names were Frances and Jim. That was one of the memories Fancy and Hezekiah used to laugh about when they were married. She smiled while thinking about that night so many years ago.

Frances and Jim had them and other church attendees gather in the small church's fellowship hall.

"We're going to teach you how to speak in tongues," Jim said. He then instructed everyone to raise their hands, pray out loud, and start saying words and syllables without thinking.

"Louder. Louder!" Frances barked at the screaming group of people.

"Hold your hands in the air until you lose control," the so-called healers continued to shout. "Dance, shout, that's it!" Jim said while Frances went around placing her hands on people's foreheads.

That went on for at least fifteen or twenty minutes until Fancy, Hezekiah, and some others realized that after all the instructions and yelling, they were no closer to speaking in tongues than before they went there.

Next, Frances called up a woman who wore a brace on one leg, which was also shorter than the other. Jim began praying, speaking in *tongue*, or that's what he called it, while tugging on the braced leg and telling the young lady to watch as her leg began to grow... "In three days, you'll be walking straight and without a brace."

Another person had pink eye. His eye was smacked with a glob of Jim's spit as he proclaimed, "You are healed." Grabbing hold of Frances' hand, they darted out the exit, leaving the young man with spit dripping from his eye.

Fancy said they saw that young man the next day, and his eye was closed shut and swollen as big as a golf ball!

Fancy laughed almost out loud at the thought of how naïve and gullible she and Hezekiah were early in their Christian walk, believing just about any self-proclaimed prophet that came along. It was funny now when she thought about it, but it wasn't funny back then. She wondered just how many people Frances and Jim had deceived. God's people at that! Talking about wolves! That they were.

She dismissed the thoughts of the past and focused back on the order of service. Hezekiah, done with his dance, sat down and started wiping his forehead with a handkerchief.

That man deserves an Oscar. Part of her yearned to get up and leave, yet she remained firmly planted in her seat, reminding herself she needed to become accustomed to encountering Hezekiah in shared venues and spaces. At the end of service, she darted toward the exit.

"Sista McCoy," Stiles called with Mya standing next to him.

Fancy stopped and turned around, smiling instead of showing her irritation, as she met Stiles mid-way.

"Hello, Pastor Stiles, Hello, Sista Mya," she said, seeing Hezekiah approaching in her peripheral vision.

"Hello, Sista McCoy," replied Mya.

"Mya and I were going to go grab a bite to eat. We thought you might like to join us. And before you try to call me out, yes, Hezekiah will be coming along."

"If that'll make you uncomfortable, I'll stay back," Hezekiah said, walking up and standing next to Stiles. "No problem."

He still exuded an irresistible rugged charm, and his gracefully balding head added to his appealing sexiness. The subtle salt and pepper stubble on his chin transformed him into an even more captivating version of his former self. He was a thinner version but still just as handsome. A sudden surge of warmth enveloped Fancy, leaving her breathless and tingling with attraction.

"You okay?" Mya asked, obviously noticing something was off.

"Uh, yes. You all go on without me. I'm not hungry. I had a bagel this morning and a cup of coffee."

"You look good, "Hezekiah said, not entertaining what Fancy had stated.

Nervous, she gripped both hands together. "Thanks." She paused. "You too, she mumbled, not giving him direct eye contact.

"Look, Stiles, on second thought, I'm going to sit this one out. Fancy, please, go with them. Hopefully, you and I can talk. Soon, I hope."

"No, please, you go, Hezekiah. I really do need to get home. I have some plans for later." She shifted her gaze to Stiles. "Thanks for the invite." She stepped to him and kissed his cheek while holding his hand. "You too, Mya." She repeated the warm gesture toward Mya, then turned and walked away.

As she walked away, she hoped her nervousness wasn't detected. At this point, she felt like she would collapse. When she finally reached her car, she let out a relieved sigh.

†

Fancy and Victoria were seated at the kitchen island, engaged in conversation.

"When you called, I didn't know what was going on. You sounded like you were about to explode." Victoria flung a hand up and shook her head.

"I couldn't help it. I was so mad at myself. I called you as soon as I got off of that parking lot. I'm sorry for getting you out of bed."

"I was already up. I kept on my lounger when I decided I wasn't going to church." She looked down at herself and grinned. "That's why I know I could never be anybody's first lady." Victoria laughed. "Although Stiles came awfully close to making me change my mind."

Both ladies erupted into laughter.

"But forget about me. Girl, did seeing Hezekiah in all his glory get you like this?" Victoria giggled.

"Seriously, Vicky. What happened to me? What happened to all the anger I felt toward him? What happened to all the things I was going to say to him? I was going to let him have it. You know I was, but then, when the opportunity presented itself, what did I do? I shriveled up and acted like some stupid little girl who was face-to-face with her first school crush. *Ughh*," she said, frowning and twisting her lips.

Walking up to the stove, Victoria removed the whistling tea kettle from the eye and filled each coffee cup.

"Here you go." She placed a cup in front of Fancy.

"Thanks." Fancy reached for condiments on the small tray before her, adding sweetener and cream.

"I don't know why you're being so hard on yourself. You knew the time would come when you would see him. The man has been home a week. It stands to reason that, being the official senior pastor of New Holy Rock, he would be at church today. You could easily have gone to Khalil's service to avoid him. You chose not to. How you reacted, well, there's no certain way you have to act or *react*. You haven't seen that man face to face in three years. And so much has happened in those three years, the most hurting thing—you all lost a son."

Fancy remained quiet, nodded, and sipped her coffee.

"And you know the church wasn't the place or time to let him *have it*," Victoria said, using air quotes. "You know better than that."

"Right...right," Fancy agreed.

"But I agree with Hezekiah. You do need to talk. If for no other reason than to honor Xavier and bring closure for both of you. After that, you can go off on him or do whatever to let go of those pinned-up feelings you've been holding in." Victoria sipped her coffee while Fancy twirled her spoon round and round in hers.

"Yeah, I guess it makes sense to talk to him. But I'm not looking forward to it."

23
FACE THE MUSIC

"Here's to the Future because I'm done with the Past." Anonymous

"I need my own crib," Hezekiah voiced in frustration.

"You'll get a spot. Give it some more time. You've barely been home two weeks, man, and seeing Fancy for the first time today, well, I could see that it stirred up a lot of feelings—in both of you."

"It did for me, I won't lie." Hezekiah walked around the perimeter of what Stiles had designated his mancave.

"Sit down, man. All that pacing isn't necessary. I'm trying to play the game."

Hezekiah took a seat in the other recliner. "I don't see how you sit there and play that game like that. For hours, too. I don't get it."

"It's how I relax." He paused the game and looked at Hezekiah. "What's going on?"

"I need to put that money to good use. I'm going to look into renting a place and getting a ride."

Stiles nodded. "Do what you feel you need to do, but I said you could stay here as long as you need to."

"I know, but I wouldn't be going through this crap if that crook, Price, hadn't run off with my money."

"I know, but Price is dead now."

"I know that, but I still need to see what he did with my money," he griped. "I read online that the families are holding a joint memorial service for him and his wife tomorrow. I plan on being there—do some people-watching. I may see something or somebody who could tell me what he was up to before he left the States."

"Okay. I'll go with you. You know what time?"

"One o'clock."

"One? Hol' up. Let me make sure I can go." Stiles looked at his phone calendar. "Yeah, I'm free."

"Cool. But man, flipping the script, my ex-wife looked so good. Talking about thick. Ooh wee." Hezekiah laughed, both feet flying in the air and back to the ground.

Stiles chuckled, quickly eyeing the game and then shutting it down.

"Hey, man, I didn't mean to make you get off the game."

"Yeah, sure you didn't. It looked like she was pleased with you, too, my man."

"I don't know about all that, but then again, we have never been able to deny our attraction to each other. I don't care how mad I've made her or how pissed she made me, we never had problems in, you know, in that area—"

Stiles raised a hand, chuckling slightly. "I know what you're saying," he said, pausing. "Hey, I just remembered something."

"What's that?"

"While you were away, Fancy had a tiny house built on her property, a casita, whatever you want to call it. Anyway, it's nice. She was planning to rent it as an Airbnb, but then, you know, she put things on hold after Xavier's death." Stiles's excitement turned somber as momentary silence filled the room.

"I'm going to his grave tomorrow." Hezekiah hung his head low.

Stiles reached across and petted him on his knee. "Hey, you want a beer?"

Hezekiah looked up. "Yeah, an ice-cold one sounds good right about now."

They both went into the kitchen. Stiles grabbed two bottles out of the fridge.

"So, you say she plans to rent it?" He popped the bottle top off and turned up the brew.

"Yep. I don't know how you would feel about living with your ex-wife, but it's a thought."

"More than that. I don't know how Fancy would feel about it. The woman hates me."

"She does not hate you." Stiles gulped his beer. "*Ahhh*," he growled in satisfaction. "Fancy isn't capable of hating. Is she angry, or does she want to take her grief out on you? That is highly possible, but she doesn't hate you. Like you said, you two need to talk."

"For sure. In the meantime, I need to handle my business and reach out to Khalil."

"Good, and what about Pastor? Do you plan on going to see him?"

Hezekiah stared at his brother and took another swallow of his beer. "I hadn't given it much thought, but now that you've brought it up, maybe I will."

"At least you're willing to entertain the idea. That's a start."

"I have a lot of starts to make."

"When do you plan on resuming your role as Senior Pastor? I'm not talking about sitting in the pulpit like you did today."

"I want to have myself together before I stand up there and deliver a word to the people."

"Have yourself together? If that's the case, you'll never get back up there. All of us are constantly evolving. None of us is perfect. As for preaching, you've never stopped. Just because you did it behind bars doesn't make your ministry any less effective. Anyway, what do you have to do?"

"A lot. On the inside and outside."

"How long do you think that will take?"

Hezekiah shrugged. "I can't say. But I'm in no hurry. You're doing great. You had the church on fire, my man. You even had me cutting a step." Hezekiah laughed.

"That you did," Stiles said, laughing as well.

†

He sat in the corner chair of the bedroom, contemplating how to approach Fancy. He had initially considered calling her, but he ultimately decided to reach out via text, given how uncomfortable she seemed when she saw him at church.

> Hezekiah: Fancy, it's Hezekiah. Would you be open to meeting up and talking?

After tapping SEND, he took a deep breath as fresh memories of her entrance into New Holy Rock took front and center in his mind.

Fancy walked into New Holy Rock. A black and white A-line midi swing dress complimented her radiant almond skin. Her natural hair was perfectly styled in a coiled updo. Shapely legs adorned with black pumps left him in awe.

Seeing her again brought back his deep longing for her and made him confront his regret. It was also a hurtful reminder of how he treated her. How could he have orchestrated her relationship with another man and taken advantage of her love? He couldn't blame her if she hated him. He had hurt her terribly and destroyed his family on so many levels. No wonder his sons despised him. His only solace was knowing he had somewhat mended the relationship between himself and Xavier before Xavier killed himself. Khalil was a different story. He would have to face his eldest son before he could move forward.

A profound sense of guilt came over him. Here he was, a representative of God, a preacher, and a pastor, yet he was as shameful as they come. He was a thief, a liar, and a cheat. The thought of all his mistakes and the wrong roads he'd chosen to travel burdened his soul. Rising from his chair, he knelt beside the bed, hoping to find solace through prayer. When he rose minutes later, he looked at his phone. Fancy had replied to his text.

> Fancy: I'm free Tuesday around noon.

Hezekiah smiled. Sitting on the edge of his bed.

> Hezekiah: Sounds good. See you Tuesday.

Ding.

> Fancy: I'll text you tomorrow and let you know where we can meet.

> Hezekiah: OK ☺

†

Stiles woke up early, brewed a pot of coffee, and recited affirmations as part of his daily routine.

"Morning," Hezekiah said, yawning and strolling into the kitchen just as Stiles recited his last affirmation.

"Good morning. There's coffee already made."

Hezekiah poured a cup and added heavy flavored cream and sugar.

"What do you have going on today?"

"I want to visit Xavier's gravesite. That is if I can use your car."

"Sure, you can. Just drop me off at church. Handle your business. I have a full day."

"Okay, after I leave the cemetery, I plan to look for a car. I don't want to keep using yours. I appreciate it, but I need my own."

"I know. I understand."

The brothers talked over coffee and then headed for New Holy Rock.

"Remember, take your time," Stiles told Hezekiah when they arrived at church. "We're still going to Trevor's memorial service, right?"

"Yes, that's a given. See ya, and thanks."

Hezekiah stopped along the way, filled the tank, and went to the cemetery.

Tears welled up in his eyes as he stood in front of Xavier's headstone, reading the engraved words. *"You left us quietly, your thoughts unknown. Thank you for precious memories we are proud to own. Here on earth, you were one of the best. We pray that you now have eternal rest."*

He knelt at the grave and began talking to his son. "I read your letter, your last words and thoughts. I am so sorry. I'm sorry for not being what you needed in a father. I'm sorry if I made you feel like you weren't worthy enough. Xavier, I'm sorry for all the wrongs and all the mistakes I made. For how I hurt my family and especially your mother," he said and began sobbing.

"I hope you can find the peace and love you longed for on earth. I miss you every day, son. And every day that I have breath in my body, I'm going to work on being a better person, a better father, a grandfather to your sons, and a better man overall. I promise."

He had been at the gravesite for almost half an hour before turning to leave. As he headed to his vehicle, he saw a car approaching. The vehicle pulled in behind his car. He paused and watched as a familiar figure exited.

As she neared, she said daringly, "What are you doing here?"

Hezekiah remained calm on the outside as he resumed his slow walk in her direction.

"I have just as much right to be here as you. I loved him too, Fancy. I loved him too," he repeated, head hung low, as he walked past her.

"Wait," she said in a softer tone.

He turned around steps from the car door.

"I'll see you tomorrow."

Hezekiah nodded, got in the car, and slowly drove off.

He spent the remainder of the morning visiting several car dealerships before deciding on a certified pre-owned Mercedes SUV. He wanted a spacious vehicle in which to easily transport his grandchildren.

Leaving the dealership, he smiled, thinking about how quickly his perspective had changed. He wondered if this was the new version of himself or just a temporary phase.

"I bought a car," Hezekiah told Stiles when he returned to New Holy Rock.

"Oh, you did?" Stiles rose from his chair and moved towards his brother.

"Yep. They're detailing it. They'll bring it to me when they're done later this afternoon."

"What'd you get?"

"Found a sweet little metallic gray Mercedes. An SUV, certified, pre-owned. Got a good deal on it. Small note. And my credit went through, too!" Hezekiah chuckled.

Stiles patted him on the back. "Good for you. I told you things were going to work out."

"That you did. I went to Xavier's grave," Hezekiah said, his voice weakening. "I tell you, man, it was hard. When I was leaving, Fancy showed up."

"Oh, yeah? How'd that go?"

"At first, she sounded a bit salty, but then I reminded her I had just as much right to be there as she did."

Stiles nodded. "True. How'd she take that?"

"She actually calmed down. We agreed to meet tomorrow for lunch and talk."

"That's a good first step. The two of you have endured a lot. I think it's time you make some amends."

"I know. I do, too. But I'm telling you, man, standing at that grave was tough. I still can't believe it." He started getting choked up as the words poured, and his voice trembled. "Oh, God, help me," he cried, exploding into tears and quickly wiping them away with the swift movement of his hand.

Stiles embraced his brother. He didn't share words of wisdom. He didn't quote scripture. He just held on to him, allowing him to release the emotions that he had held back for so long.

†

The memorial service failed to reveal anything more than two families grieving over the loss of their loved ones. Portrait displays of Trevor and his bride together and individual pictures of them filled the front of the space, surrounded by a bevy of funeral wreaths, flowers, and live plants.

Members of Niesha's family and people from the nursing profession spoke highly of her. The same held true for Trevor. Members of the law firm where he worked spoke of his integrity, sense of humor, and overall great personality.

Hezekiah learned that Trevor had a younger brother who lived in Switzerland. He spoke kind words about his brother, but they had not physically seen each other since before the pandemic.

M. J. also shared words. He talked about their long friendship, things they used to do as rowdy young teens, and how much he was going to miss him. Nothing he said raised red flags.

Stiles and Hezekiah interspersed with the crowd at the end of the service, hoping to glean some information that might tell them clues about Trevor's last steps, but there was nothing. They left the service with nothing more than an obituary.

24

A DOSE OF FORGIVENESS

"Nobody can go back and start a new beginning, but anyone can start today and make a new ending." Maria Robinson

Fancy and Hezekiah sat across from each other at a popular Mediterranean restaurant. Despite trying to avoid staring, Fancy couldn't help but notice how good Hezekiah looked for a fifty-five-year-old man who'd been incarcerated for the past three years. He still radiated handsomeness. His dark melanin skin, touched with a bit of ruggedness and graying stubble, ignited her passion. This was not what she wanted. She wanted to despise him, but instead, she was drawn to him like a moth to a flame. He'd always had that effect on her. Guess some things never changed.

"So, what are your plans now that you've been released?"

"Right now, I'm trying to find my POA. I need to know what he did with my money."

"Trevor Price?"

Hezekiah bit into his food and nodded.

"I thought he and his wife died in that earthquake in Africa."

"That's what they say, but almost five hundred thousand dollars of my money didn't die. That was every penny to my name."

Fancy looked away, took a bite of her food, and then looked back at him. "Five hundred thousand dollars? I never knew you had that much money put back. You barely left the boys and me with anything. You hid those assets quite well, I see," she fumed, angry at the thought of how he had once again used and manipulated her in their marriage.

"That's not exactly true, but I'm not here to debate what happened in our divorce. That was years ago. I made mistakes. You made mistakes. But no matter my financial situation, you aren't doing too bad either. And for your information, a lot of that money was made after our divorce. And look at you, you're still living in Lion's Gate. You still have a nice ride and dress like a fashionista. Those diamonds on your wrist, neck, and hands aren't fakes. So please don't act like I left you penniless. You're not working a standard nine-to-five, so I assume your bank account is also in pretty good shape."

"Okay, you're right. God *has* been good to me. I'm not here to argue with you about what did or didn't happen in the past. I'm here because you said you wanted us to talk. So, let's have it. What do you want to talk about?" She took a bite of food and a swallow of her beverage.

"I want to tell you face-to-face that I'm sorry, Fancy."

"Sorry? *Umph.*" She hunched her shoulders and nervously picked at her food. "Is that so?"

"Yes, I'm sorry for hurting you. I'm sorry for not being there when you needed me the most. I'm sorry that our son, our baby boy, decided dying was better than remaining on this earth. Being sent to prison, my son's death and this last attack in prison have shown me that my life needs to change. Especially now that I'm a free man. I'm sorry," he said again, reaching across the table to take her hand.

Fancy quickly pulled her hands back out of his reach.

"I guess you say I should have said a lot of this a long time ago." He paused. "I guess it takes some folks longer than others. I turned double nickels on my last birthday. I celebrated it in prison. I've had a lot of time to reflect on all the things I've done in life. And my biggest regret is losing you, tearing our family apart."

Fancy remained quiet, looking down at her plate of food and then glancing up at him. She didn't want to cry, but she was so close to the edge. Hezekiah hadn't been this vulnerable since they were a young couple and about to go to prison. He had cried and pleaded for her to forgive him all those years ago. She did. When they were released, Hezekiah did everything he could to make things right between them. But now it was many years later. They were not kids anymore.

"You *did* hurt me, especially when you set up that whole embarrassing relationship with Winston. To this day, I don't understand how you could be so cruel and insensitive. I don't know how you could sit back and allow another man to make a move on me, convince me to enter a relationship with him and go so far as to sleep with him. I thought he cared about me, and then it turned out you were behind it all."

"That's not exactly true. Did I arrange for him to meet you? I did, but it was not to take you to bed. He crossed the line with that. He was supposed to get your mind off me and some things I was trying to do behind the scenes. Needless to say, it all fell through. But anyway, he took it too far. I could have killed him when I learned you were all goo-goo-ga-ga over each other." He threw aside a hand, shook his head, and then took a bite of his food.

"You never said that."

"There are a lot of things I never said that I should have said. That's why I'm here now. I want to set things straight. I still love you, Fancy. Remember the night we spent together at the hotel? Our love for each other was evident. You know it, and I know it."

"I don't want to think about that. That happened three years ago—before you went to prison, Hezekiah. And it was a mistake. I shouldn't have slept with you. I don't blame Khalil for going off about it."

"Oh, so you regret it?"

"I said I don't want to talk about it."

"Ok, ok, sorry." He lifted both hands in a surrendering gesture.

Fancy diverted from the subject. "So, you got a car, huh?"

"Yeah, I did."

"That's good." She nodded. "What about a place to live? You're living with Stiles, right?"

"Yeah. I've been looking, mostly online. I have a tour scheduled for later this afternoon. It's a townhouse close to New Holy Rock. It's a new build. I've seen a lot of that since I've been home."

"Right, there are a lot of townhouses, condos, and apartments being built. But it still depends on the location. Crime is just so bad. But I guess it's bad everywhere."

"That's what I'm talking about. I want to find a decent neighborhood. I'm grateful to be back on the church payroll because I still have some financial obligations, including this new car note. I've factored rent into that, but again, I need it within my budget. I heard you built a casita on your property. How's that going for you?"

"I'm glad I had it built. I planned to rent it as an Airbnb. I still do, but well, things were put on hold when, you know, when Xavier died."

"Yeah, for sure."

They both remained quiet for several seconds.

"Fancy," Hezekiah said, breaking the silence. "I hope you believe me when I say I'm sorry. I'm not trying to get back with you or anything like that. I'm just trying to right some wrongs, starting with you."

"Well, well, well, don't y'all look cute," the woman interrupted, causing Hezekiah and Fancy to look up from their plates.

Hezekiah's eyes widened, and Fancy's face twisted into an instant scowl.

"What the heck are you doing here?" Fancy snapped, laying her napkin aside and eyeing Rianna like she was ready to pounce.

"Humph, humph, humph. Aren't you a sight for sore eyes, if I must say so myself, ex-husband," Rianna said, ignoring Fancy and standing next to Hezekiah, rubbing his balding head, a big smile covering her face.

Hezekiah bit down on his bottom lip while he forcefully removed her hand.

"Rianna?" he snarled.

"That's me. Live and in living color, baby."

She twisted her body so that her backside faced Fancy, further intimidating her. Next, she seductively lowered her head, and before Hezekiah could protest, she planted a kiss right smack dab on his lips and then broke into laughter.

"What the hell is wrong with you?" he snapped. He pushed himself away from the table and stood up. Walking past

Rianna and over to Fancy, he reached for her hand, guiding her to stand. "You done?"

Fancy nodded.

The couple walked off and stopped at the counter so Hezekiah could settle the tab.

Rianna, laughing, approached the counter next to where Hezekiah and Fancy stood. "I have a to-go order for Rianna *McCoy*. That's M-c-C-o-y... McCoy." She said her last name extra loud so Hezekiah and Fancy would hear.

Watching them walk off, Rianna laughed louder than ever. "I'll see you soon, Pastor McCoy."

"Can you believe her?" Fancy said as they exited the restaurant.

"Actually, I can," Hezekiah remarked as he walked her to her car.

†

Rianna cussed while getting into her car and storming off the lot. "I can't believe him. He gets out, and the first person he runs to is that heffa." She was furious. After seeing on the news almost two weeks ago that he had been released, she wondered when their paths would cross. Today was that day, but it was not the reunion she expected.

She gasped loudly when she entered the restaurant and saw Hezekiah and Fancy. Fancy was seated across from Hezekiah, looking all fake as they come. She wanted to belt her right in the face but focused on Hezekiah instead. Freedom looked good on him. He had lost some weight since the last time she'd seen him, but it only enhanced his good looks.

During times like this, she missed her friend, Tiny. She had no one to talk to. She called Tiny's number, but she already knew it was going to the automated message. Either that or she couldn't get through because Tiny had most likely BLOCKED her. It had been at least four months since the best friends last talked. While driving, she reached over, grabbed half her sandwich, and started eating.

"You will see me again, Hezekiah," she said between chewing.

25

BUT THE FLESH IS WEAK

"One of the best results of temptation is that it shows us what is in our hearts." A. B. Simpson

Hezekiah had been home for a month and was still living with Stiles. He was becoming increasingly frustrated about his living arrangements, having been unable to find something that matched his taste and pockets.

The two brothers sat across from each other in the mancave. "You preached another good one today," he complimented Stiles.

"Thanks, bruh. Just trying to follow in your footsteps."

"You don't have to follow in my footsteps; God is using you at New Holy Rock. He's the one ordering your steps. Not me."

"Yeah, but it's your pulpit. Not mine. It's time for you to reclaim your position."

"Not until I feel like God is directing me to do so. I told you,

I still have some things to handle before I feel worthy enough to preach in that pulpit. And don't pretend you haven't noticed the sanctuary has fallen off since my return. I think it was packed the first Sunday I came back, but that's probably because folks just wanted to come and see if any drama was going to go down. When you carried on service as usual, I guess people realized we weren't some reality TV church show. And now only the loyal ones remain."

"I don't care what things look like, I still rely on God. He's in charge. He'll provide increase when he chooses, but suit yourself." Stiles rose from the chair and stretched. "I'm about to leave. Mya and I are going to dinner."

"You like her, don't you?"

Stiles stopped, turned, and looked at his brother, and nodded. With a half smirk on his face, he said, "Yeah, I do."

"Good for you. She seems like a good woman."

"She is."

"How serious are you? If you don't mind me asking."

Stiles shrugged. "I don't know. I mean, I like her. If you're referring to intimacy, we're celibate. That makes things easier —at least it does for us. There's no pressure. We're getting to know each other and enjoying being with each other. The physical part will come at the right time."

"That's possible, as long as you don't place yourself in a position where you can be caught off guard and have that moment of weakness that can tear down all that talk about celibacy."

"I know. I know. But yeah, Mya is a good girl. I like her a whole lot."

"Would you say you love her?"

Stiles appeared lost in thought, his brows furrowed slightly. "Uh, well, I can't say that I don't. That's all I can say. What about you?"

"Me?" Hezekiah laughed. "You can't be serious."

"Yeah, you. I should say, you and Fancy."

Hezekiah threw up a hand and shook his head. "Man, she's made it clear that I've hurt her too many times. She doesn't trust me. Can you blame her?"

"She's hurting, and she's still grieving. It hasn't been that long since Xavier died, man. It's going to take time, lots of it, before she begins to act what we call normal again."

"Tell me about it," Hezekiah said, his expression sad. It was as if fresh wrinkles suddenly appeared on his face. "I still can't believe he's gone."

"Have you talked to Khalil yet?"

"Nope. That's one of the things I've yet to do, but it's coming."

Stiles looked at his watch. "Gotta go."

"Enjoy yourself," Hezekiah said.

After Stiles left, Hezekiah kicked back in the mancave and tuned to ESPN. He got up again when a commercial came on, went into the butler's pantry, and poured himself a double shot of Scotch. This would be the second time since his release that he had whiskey. He hadn't done any form of drugs while in prison, and he didn't plan on picking up that terrible habit again. Since being home, he enjoyed having a beer or two with Stiles. That was it.

As he savored the taste of the warm liquor, his mind and body started to relax. When he was finished, he poured another double shot and swallowed it quickly. The effects of the alcohol mellowed him.

Next, he retrieved his phone from his pocket and started looking for more potential places to live when he received a text notification. He was surprised to see it was from Fancy.

Fancy: Are you still looking to rent? If so, take a look at the link. It contains images of my casita.

Clicking on the link, he eagerly explored the images. It was as if it had been tailor-made for his taste. A soothing palette of light grays on the walls created an illusion of spaciousness and comfort. After scrutinizing all 32 images, Hezekiah couldn't deny that this was the exact kind of space he had been searching for.

Hezekiah: Uh, looks amazing.

Fancy: You interested?

Why am I concerned about his living arrangements? she said to Victoria days before when they were, once again, talking about Hezekiah.

Since seeing him and talking to him, Fancy had come to accept that she and Hezekiah did the best they could as parents. Both of them could have been better. She had been just as condemning at times as Hezekiah when it came to their sons and the decisions they sometimes made in life. It was time to let go and forgive him and herself. So, in the past weeks, she entertained the idea of them being cordial, maybe even becoming friends. Xavier would like that, and she told herself it would also be good for the grandkids.

She poured herself into decorating for two clients she had taken on. It kept her busy, and she could handle her grief better when she was doing something.

"*Girl,*" Victoria had said, "*you said you were ready to rent this place. The man is still looking for a place. He's someone you know. He won't destroy the place and will pay the rent on time. Right?*"

"*I guess. Anyway, I'll think about it.*"

"I'm just saying. It's worth the thought. And if it doesn't work ..."

> **Hezekiah:** I told you my budget. Is this in my price range?

The phone dinged, bringing Fancy back to the present.

> **Fancy:** I wouldn't have extended the offer if it wasn't. If you want to see it in person—

Buzzzzzzz

The doorbell startled him. He quickly turned up the remainder of his scotch and headed for the door.

"Who the heck is this? Bruh must have left his key."

Buzzzzzzz

"Dang, hol' up, man," he yelled, somewhat staggering up the hallway, feeling lightheaded from the liquor.

He opened the door while looking down and reading Fancy's text, getting ready to reply.

"How did you forget your key?" he said, looking up. He awkwardly stepped back when he saw the person at the door.

"Wha—what the heck are you doing here?" He stepped up and poked his head out the door, scanning the outside perimeter of the front yard as if expecting to see someone, perhaps even Stiles, for whatever reason. When he didn't see anyone but her, he was confused.

He noticed the car parked on the quiet street in front of Stiles's place and then returned to focus on the intruder.

"I said, what... are... you... doing here?"

The woman, clothed in a short tan all-weather jacket and sneakers, wore her hair in shoulder-length locs.

Crocodile tears poured down her cheeks as she hugged herself. "I'm sorry. I know I shouldn't have just shown up like this. But you're the only one who would understand. I need to talk to you."

"Rianna, look, I don't have time for your games. You pop up here like a crazy woman. You know this is not my crib. You don't just pop up at somebody's crib like this. Now get away from here," he shouted, pointing toward the door.

"Please, listen. Hezekiah. You remember my friend Tiny, don't you?"

"What about her?"

"Hezekiah, I just found out her baby daddy killed her," she boohooed.

"What? Man, I'm sorry to hear that, but it has nothing to do with you showing up at my brother's crib. You need to go."

"Please," she tugged at his shirt after realizing the bold-faced lie she'd made about Tiny wouldn't work. "Okay, okay, that was a lie. But I think you'll want to hear what I really came to say."

Hezekiah shook his head in amusement. "You are a piece of work. You come here, and you lie about your best friend being murdered. You're a sicko, Rianna. Get away from here before I call the cops and have you arrested for trespassing and stalking," he demanded.

"You can't be serious?" Rianna smirked. Her tears quickly disappeared. Her quivering lips tightened into a frown as her voice, once soft and gentle, now dripped with the undertone of a veiled threat.

"Oh, you heard what I *sh*aid," he said with a slur, effects of the scotch.

"So, nothing I have to say interests you, huh? Not even if it's about your trusty POA, ol' Trevor Price? Okay, suit yourself. I'll leave. But I always knew he was a crook. He didn't fool me." She turned around abruptly and took one step away from the door.

"Hol' up." Hezekiah reached out and grabbed her arm, turning her around. He yanked her up against him, closing any space between them.

"What do you know about Price? And don't play with me, Rianna?" he seethed, gripping her arm so tightly that she could not move away. You wouldn't like me when I'm mad." The smell of alcohol was strong on his breath.

Jerking and twisting, "Lemme go, you're hurting me, Hezekiah." She used her free hand to hit him in his chest.

He still held on. "Not until you tell me what you're talking about."

"Okay, okay, let me come in, and I'll tell you."

"You betta not be joshing me," he said, reluctantly leading her into the house.

"Where's Stiles?" she asked as he slightly released his hold.

"Don't worry about him."

"Please, call him to the door. I want to apologize for showing up like this." She knew Stiles was not there. She had been staked outside his townhouse for at least an hour before she saw him leave. He drove right past her. Times like this, she missed her sidekick the most. What she wouldn't do to have Tiny sitting in the seat next to her.

"I *said*, forget about Stiles. What's this about Trevor Price?"

"Dang, can't I at least sit down or something? I feel light-headed." Her limp from the accident was hardly noticeable, and she no longer used a cane.

"Stop with the foolishness. Do you know something about Trevor Price or not?"

She swooned, grabbing her head and reaching for the wall. Hezekiah stopped her fall.

"Come on," he said, forcefully leading her into the family room outside the kitchen.

He went to the kitchen and returned with a glass of water.

"What just happened? What's wrong with you?"

Her hands shook as she brought the water to her mouth and took a big gulp. "I have hypoglycemia."

"When did you develop diabetes?" he asked.

"I don't have diabetes. I have hypoglycemia. Do you have anything sweet? Like a piece of candy or a cookie? That should help."

Hezekiah returned to the kitchen and got a box of cookies from the pantry. Seeing Rianna tonight stirred up a gamut of emotions. First, she looked good when he saw her at the restaurant a few days ago. Real good. Tonight was no different. He couldn't tell what she had on underneath her jacket, but her hair was laid, she smelled divine, and yeah, she was still just as sexy as ever. Hezekiah hated to admit it, but her ability to go from sweet to downright nasty was what used to turn him on.

He poured himself another shot of Scotch, swiftly downed it, and again, without hesitation, followed up with another one before returning to the family room. He was feeling quite relaxed.

"Here," he said, passing her a pack of cookies.

"Thank you. I see you can still be the sweet Hezekiah I used to know. The one I fell in love with," she said softly, laying the cookies to the side.

"What do you know about Price?" he said, trying to ignore her fragrant aroma and the cleavage peeking out through her jacket. He sat in the chair across from her as the liquor relaxed him even more.

"Have you talked to his best friend?"

Hezekiah sat upright. "Best friend? No. Who's his best friend?"

"His name is D. J., C. J., or something like that. I don't know his last name. But they were supposed to be good friends; I know that much. Oh, and he's a lawyer, too. I think."

"How do you know this?"

"I have my sources. I don't have to tell you anything more than that." She giggled.

"What about the cookies?" Hezekiah said, eyeing them on the table where she had placed them.

"I feel fine now. The lightheadedness is gone."

"What else you know?"

"Uh, I'm not going to tell you everything I know unless I get something in return," she said, rising slowly and walking over to where he sat in the oversized chair.

"What are you doing?"

She smiled seductively while slowly and methodically releasing the buttons on her jacket until it fully opened, revealing her plump mounds encased in a see-through black laced bra. A matching thong barely covered her personal parts.

It had been over three years since he'd been this close to a woman in a setting like this. It was no surprise that he immediately became physically aroused.

Rianna took notice and smiled. She could already tell she had him exactly where and how she wanted him. He had never been much of a drinker, but she smelled the liquor on his breath and heard him slur some of his words. The fact he had been drinking gave her leverage, and she was going to take full advantage of it.

He nudged her aside, but not hard enough to make her stop. Her fragrance, mixed with the effects of the alcohol and the allure of her curvy body, made him lose all sense of self-control.

She used her Delilah-like skills to seduce him further. With her intimate knowledge of his desires, she knew what he liked and how he wanted it and was ready and willing to give it to him. When she heard a deep grunt escape his lips, she laughed to herself and grabbed his face with both hands, covering his mouth with hers without further protest from him.

Hezekiah became like an unleashed wild animal. His needs and desires came forth with furor, and he hungrily devoured her mouth and tongue while his hands traveled the contours of her body. In the throes of passion, his phone fell to the hardwood floor.

Fancy: Hezekiah, are you still there?

26

WEAK IN THE KNEES

"It's never too late for a new beginning in your life." Joyce Meyers

"I had a good time. I like it when the university holds things like this for those who teach virtually. I like meeting other professors and staff. It's great networking," Mya said as she and Stiles walked hand in hand to her front door.

"I think so too," Stiles said, tightening his squeeze. "They really go all out for the one they host for Christmas."

"Yeah, I heard they cater the food, have a live band, and have a dance floor."

"Yeah, they do."

"I wasn't there. I think I had something going on with my son around that time. Oh, speaking of my son, he's staying at his dad's all next week rather than coming home Sunday night."

"Oh, is that right?"

"Yep. He does that sometimes, you know."

"Yeah, that's good. A young man needs his father or a strong male figure in his life."

"Yeah, they do. And though our relationship crumbled, I can never deny that he's a great dad. I thank God for that."

"And I think you're a great mother," Stiles said, leaning in and kissing her lightly. "And....a great woman." He kissed her again. "And....I'm crazy about you." He kissed her again, but this kiss was long and full of desire.

When he pulled back, Mya exhaled, closing and opening her eyes slowly. "You make it hard for me to resist, you know that?" she said softly, breathing heavily.

"Um, is that right?" he said hungrily, devouring her polished lips again.

"Tell me, since your son is going to be with his dad, does this mean I get to spend more time with my favorite lady?" Stiles continued flirting as they stood by the front door.

"Duh, of course." Mya giggled.

Stiles, keeping a grip on her hand, leaned down and kissed her again, more deeply and longer. This time, he held the base of her neck and kissed her hard. When he felt himself becoming physically excited, he used every ounce of grit he could muster to restrain himself.

"I'm sorry," he whispered hungrily, his lips still touching hers as he spoke. "I better go before I can't stop myself."

He smiled into her eyes, kissed her quickly, and watched as she removed her house keys and opened the door. When she went inside, he turned and walked to his car.

Exhaling when he got in the driver's seat, he said a quick prayer. "Lord, help, I don't know how long I can remain a celibate vessel for you."

On the drive home, he reflected on the past year spent with Mya Dugard. It wasn't until this moment that he admitted to

himself that he might be in love. Those words were still difficult to utter, evoking memories of long ago when Rena had
occupied a special place in his heart. Of course, there had been
other relationships, including his tumultuous marriage to
Detria, a chapter he'd rather forget. The ties in Houston and
the one with Victoria had come and gone, each leaving its
mark, but this sensation with Mya was unique.

Mya possessed qualities that set her apart. She was sweet,
sensitive, and remarkably understanding, seemingly compre-
hending his demanding schedule effortlessly. With his responsibilities as a pastor and teacher, dedicating time to a
relationship had always been challenging. Yet, Mya seemed to
be unruffled. Stiles suspected it was due to her own busy life
and raising her teenage son. Whatever the reason, it worked
perfectly for them.

Most Sundays, Mya joined him at New Holy Rock. She
occasionally participated in mid-week Bible study sessions,
showcasing her commitment to her faith and his ministry.

Their connection deepened as their relationship grew more
official. Mya even contributed to his ministry by typing his
sermon notes, ensuring that every scripture was addressed in
his meticulously crafted messages, a loving gesture he
appreciated.

As he continued driving, Stiles contemplated the path
ahead, which seemed to lead toward a more profound connection with Mya. Meeting her had been entirely unexpected, for
he hadn't been actively seeking a romantic connection with
anyone when they met. His focus had been firmly fixed on the
demanding task of maintaining New Holy Rock in Hezekiah's
absence. Yet, destiny had other plans when he met her at the
university.

Mya possessed a sort of agelessness that seemed more
befitting a college student. Their first date ignited an attraction

that had grown stronger with each passing day. Yet, questions lingered in his mind. Was this love he was feeling? Was he genuinely ready for the commitment of marriage? Or was he allowing his physical desire to rule his heart?

Turning left onto his street, he was surprised, to say the least, to see Rianna walking down his driveway. *What in the world is going on? Man, I know you ain't have that foolish woman up in my house.*

He parked in front of his neighbor's house and watched her get into a car parked on the street.

"Nah, nah, nah. Come on, bruh. I know you're not doing this," he said aloud as he watched her drive off.

He pulled into his driveway and hurried inside. He was eager to hear Hezekiah's explanation for Rianna's unexpected presence.

"Hezekiah! Bruh," he called, almost shouting as he entered.

There was no answer. He went through the house, peeking inside the family room and the mancave.

"Hey, bruh," he called again and went to the guest bedroom. He saw Hezekiah sprawled across the bed naked from the waist down. He turned away and went into his bedroom.

Later that evening, Hezekiah strolled into the kitchen with the worst headache ever. He made himself a specialty cocktail that was supposed to help with headaches naturally. His memory was fuzzy but not so vague that he didn't recall what went down between him and Rianna. What had he been thinking? Oh, that's right; he wasn't thinking. The excessive alcohol, combined with the wiles of a woman like Rianna and the fact he hadn't made love in over three years, made for the perfect storm.

He turned to leave the kitchen and almost bumped chests with Stiles.

"What's up with you, man? I saw Rianna leaving when I was coming home. Of all the females out there, you go and get her? You know she's trouble with a capital tee, man. Why would you even tell her where I live?"

Hezekiah rubbed his head, took a gulp of his concoction, and shook his head. "I know. Believe me, it wasn't planned. And I didn't tell her where you lived. She just showed up. At your door."

Hezekiah told Stiles how it all went down with Rianna.

"You let her pull one on you, man. Do you really think she knows what she's talking about?"

"Who knows? Rianna is a true-to-life Delilah, cunning as heck. She got me at a moment of weakness for sure, but never again. Hol 'up." He ducked past Stiles and went into the family room, where he and Rianna started their make-out session before moving into the bedroom. He started looking between the edges of the sofa and on the floor around the bottom rim.

"What are you looking for?"

"Here it is," Hezekiah said, reaching down and coming back up with his phone. He immediately started reading Fancy's last text. "Dang," he scolded himself.

He hurriedly replied, although hours had passed.

> Hezekiah: Sorry, I had one too many shots of Scotch. I passed out. I hadn't had alcohol in three years, you know. 😄 Let's talk tomorrow.

He hit SEND and then returned his attention to Stiles. "What were you saying?"

"I was saying I don't want her coming here. She means you or me no good." Stiles walked past his brother.

"Don't I know? I heard from Fancy," he said. She asked me if I wanted to rent her casita."

Stiles stopped and looked at Hezekiah. "Really?"

"Yep. I got a text from her right before Rianna popped up. She made the offer out of the blue." Hezekiah smiled.

"Look, just don't hurt her, man. You've done more than enough of that."

"I know. Believe me that is not my intention. But I do need a place of my own. Living in Lion's Gate again would give me the privacy I want. What Fancy says she's charging will fit my budget, and I wouldn't have to worry about the likes of Rianna popping up. That's for sure."

"You got a point. But—"

"But what?"

"We're talking about Fancy being your landlord. You may have privacy to a certain extent, but you're still basically living with your ex. I don't know, man. Maybe you should reconsider it more before accepting her offer."

"After what happened tonight, my answer is loud and clear. Man," he said, frustrated, "I can't believe I folded like a wimp. Whew. Definitely can't let that happen again." He paused and smiled slightly. "But on the other hand, a brother got some relief."

Stiles smiled and shook his head as if amused. "Yeah, I know exactly what you mean. I also know if you're serious about moving there, this is probably a good time to talk to Khalil. You'll run into him sooner or later, living in the back of her house."

"I thought about that. When it happens, it happens. It's not like I'm shying away from talking to him."

"I'm just saying you already know not to expect him to come to you first, but at this point, he shouldn't have to. Khalil is still a boy in many ways. You know he's a man. He knows he's a man, but you still see him as your boy when you stand face to face. You've got to be the one to go to him."

"You're not telling me anything I don't know. So much has been going on, and well, I'm going to talk to him."

"Good. If you need something for that headache, there's some acetaminophen in the bathroom cabinet."

"Thanks. I'm feeling better."

27
ON MY OWN - ONCE AGAIN

"Forgiveness says you are given another chance to make a new beginning." Desmond Tutu

"Better to rent it to someone I know will pay me my money on time than having a stranger living there. Anyway, I don't think he'll be there for very long," Fancy told Khalil. "He's going to do a six-month lease for now. We'll play it by ear after that."

"I still don't like it. I know this is your crib, but having him live on this property after all he's done? Nah, Mama. I don't care how you try to make it make sense. And think about it. He's been out of prison all this time, but not once has he attempted to talk to me."

"You haven't attempted to talk to him either, Khalil. It works both ways, you know. Both of you are stubborn and set in your ways, but it's not good for either of you. That's why I had to release y'all. Give you to the good Lord. With Xavier's death and with you and your father at odds, it was weighing me down. I had to let something go. I chose to move aside when it comes to you and your father's relationship."

"Are you serious? You sound like you're on his side. Oh, I get it. You slept with him again, didn't you? All he had to do was show up, and you gave it up," he accused.

Fancy walked up to him and slapped him across his mouth. "Don't you ever in your life talk to me like that again! I don't care how old you are. You will respect me, Khalil McCoy! I'm not your little trophy wife nor that tramp you're messing with. Don't get it twisted!"

Rubbing his hand across his face, he said, "I don't get you, Mama. How could you forgive him after all he's done to you, to our family?"

"You really have to ask me that, Khalil? You're sitting there, a man of God, preaching the word two or three times a week, and you have to ask me how I can forgive him. You think I wanted to? No, Khalil, I had no choice. If I want to be forgiven for all the crappy mess I've done, I have to forgive. You know that. Life is too short, baby. Too short," she said, wiping the island countertop while Khalil resumed eating the sandwich and chips she had made him.

"Well, I'm not on board with it. And if I see him, I'm telling you now, I don't have nothing to say to him. My brother's dead!"

"You said it yourself—that's not his fault, Khalil."

"I didn't say that it was!" Khalil's anger was unleashed. After everything his father had done, how could his mother give him a place to lay his lousy head?

Fancy listened to her son's side, and she understood his frustration, but at the end of the day, she was going to let

Hezekiah move in. She thought about Xavier. Those first weeks after his death, she felt anger toward Hezekiah, too, but God had delivered her from that. Those days when she visited Xavier's gravesite, she felt his spirit and heard his tender voice telling her to keep going, that there was nothing anyone could have done. Her grief was enough to bear without holding anger and resentment. Xavier was his own enemy. She'd come to terms with that. It didn't lessen her grief, but it did lessen her anger toward others, including herself, Khalil, and Hezekiah. It was not their fault. What Xavier chose was nobody's fault.

†

Hezekiah looked around the space as he carried two armfuls of groceries into the kitchen. After placing the bags on the counter, he lifted his hands in praise.

"Thank you, Jesus! Man, it feels good to have my own spot. Thank you, Lord," he celebrated again.

He couldn't have been happier, having settled into the casita two weeks before. The layout and size were perfect, affording him abundant space to live comfortably. Adding to the appeal was a covered designated parking spot beside the garage.

Since moving in, he hadn't seen Fancy. The only indicator that she was home was at night when the glow of her bedroom light was visible from his living room. The casita's design allowed him the option to walk the covered paved trail leading to the main house. Of course, this was something he wouldn't just do. Why would he? Their relationship was strictly a straightforward landlord-tenant arrangement, and he was committed to preserving that boundary.

He started prepping his food. Tonight, he was going to grill steak and veggies on Fancy's backyard grill. Like a good tenant, he texted her and told her his plans.

> Hezekiah: Do you have anything you want to put on the grill?

Minutes later, she responded,

> Fancy: The grandkids are coming over later this afternoon. Spending the night. I'm taking them to church with me tomorrow,

> Hezekiah: Oh, okay. "Have fun."

He would love to see his grandkids but would not infringe on Fancy's time with them. He had seen the boys last week, but he'd only seen Khaliyah once in the seven weeks he'd been home. That was when Eliana was at Pepper's house on one of the occasions when he was visiting. He couldn't blame Khalil for him not seeing his granddaughter as often as he did the boys. It was because of his hesitancy to reach out to Khalil so they could talk man-to-man.

> Fancy: I'm going to make hotdogs and curly fries. We're going to watch the new Paw Patrol movie. You're welcome to join us.

Hezekiah responded right away.

> Hezekiah: I'd love to. What time?

> Fancy: Around five 😊

> Hezekiah: See you at five. I can put the hotdogs on the grill, too, if you'd like?

Fancy: Sounds good. I have everything else
covered. See you later.

The evening was one of the most fun evenings he'd had in
years. He and Fancy grilled steaks for themselves and hotdogs
for the grandkids. He couldn't recall the last time he'd watched
an animated movie. Seeing their grandkids bouncing about
and having a grand time was a memory he would always
cherish.

"When are you going to talk to Khalil?" Fancy asked while
the kids watched the movie between playing and tussling.

"Soon," was all he could muster up to say. He didn't want
to lie. He had no definitive date of when he would reach out to
Khalil, but time was passing, and he needed to move toward
some reconciliation.

Although he hadn't contacted Khalil, he had seen Jude a
few days before the boy's ninth birthday. Mariah didn't exactly
like the idea of Hezekiah coming around. Her ex-husband's
murder was something she was still dealing with. There were
no clues as to who brutally stabbed him in his prison cell.

When Hezekiah was released, Mariah acted like a certified
gatekeeper when it came to seeing their son. She didn't like
him talking about being more active in the boy's life, but that's
exactly what he intended to do. The conversation he and
Mariah had that day could only be likened to an ebb and flow.

"What I'm saying is Jude has always looked at Vernon as his
father. I mean, he knows you're his bio dad, but you had another
family, and me, well, I was married to Vernon. He raised him along-
side our other kids while you merely sent a check every month and
saw him here and there. Jude needs time to grieve. It was terrible
what happened to Vernon. And I don't think they care about finding
who killed him," Mariah cried. "It's just one less convict to them."

"I'm sorry, Mariah."

"Sorry? It's me you're talking to. I know you're far from sorry, Hezekiah. How can you be when Vernon tried to kill you twice? I'm no fool; honestly, I wouldn't blame you if you tried to do the same to him. Only somebody beat you to it."

Hezekiah listened, taking in everything his former lover said.

The court had granted him visitation rights long before he went to prison. That order still stood, and Hezekiah was going to take full advantage of it. He was determined to be a better father to Jude than he had been to Xavier and Khalil.

During the movie, he and Fancy had brief moments of talking. It felt like they were one big happy family, making him realize the life he had wasted and the woman sitting next to him who he had hurt. He shrugged off the feelings and continued to enjoy the moment.

By the end of the movie, the grandkids were sprawled on the floor, fast asleep. Sebastian was curled on her cat bed in front of the fireplace. Hezekiah rose from the sofa and scooped Davion and Zavion in his arms. Fancy picked up Khaliyah. They took the kids to the guest room, which Fancy had made into what she called the *kid cave*. It had some of their favorite toys, storybooks, stuffed animals, and more.

They put the children in their beds and went back to the kitchen, where Hezekiah assisted Fancy in storing leftovers and tidying up.

"Thanks for inviting me over," he said as he dried dishes.

"No problem. I'm glad the grandkids got a chance to spend time with both of their grandparents at the same time. I know I had a good time."

"So did I," Hezekiah agreed.

An hour later, they plopped down in the family room after making the house look like an HGTV spread and not like a home recently invaded by three rambunctious toddlers.

Hezekiah relaxed in the corner chair while Fancy rested on the cozy sofa.

"Would you like a glass of wine?"

"Uh, I don't think so. Not tonight," he said, not sure why he so eagerly turned her down.

She looked a little bothered, so Hezekiah spoke up again. "I don't want to keep you up too late. You probably have to get up extra early to get the three of them ready and on time for service in the morning."

Fancy nodded. "Yep, I do. We're going to Holy Rock, so I do have a choice of what service I'm going to attend. More than likely, it'll be the second. That way, I can take my time getting them dressed and fed. You know what?"

"What's that?"

"I'll get them dressed, and we'll have breakfast at church."

"So Holy Rock still offers breakfast on Sunday mornings, huh?" Hezekiah said, smiling.

"Yeah, they do. And lunch and dinner on Wednesdays." She smiled. "So, do you want that glass of wine?"

"Nah," he showed a hand. "I'm going to call it an evening. Let you get your rest." He stood, stretched, and then headed toward the back door.

Fancy followed.

"Goodnight." He glanced into her baby-brown eyes but immediately averted his gaze as a fiery feeling started to build up inside. He didn't want to risk ruining their relationship by making advances on her, no matter how much he desired her.

"Goodnight, Hezekiah."

She stood by the door, watching as he made his way down the winding path to the casita. Just as he glanced back over his shoulder, she quietly shut the door, her heart heavy with that familiar feeling she could never seem to deny. It was her own vulnerability, a persistent weakness she couldn't seem to shake when it came to Hezekiah. Despite the countless times he had inflicted pain, humiliation, and betrayal upon her, her heart continued to race in his presence, much like a schoolgirl smitten with her first crush. She leaned against the door, laid her hand across her heart, and sighed. *God, why did I let that man move in my backyard?*

28
FEELINGS

"Life has many chapters. One bad chapter doesn't mean it's the end of the book." Unknown

As soon as he stepped inside the casita, Hezekiah took a cold shower. Being around Fancy had aroused him, and all he could do was think about how much he wanted to lie next to her.

He thought about Rianna showing up at his brother's house a few weeks ago. She seduced him good with her sexual ruses until he succumbed and allowed his physical desires to overtake him. He vowed not to let that happen again, not with her.

His phone rang just as he finished drying off. Still clothed in his birthday suit, he retrieved the phone.

"Hey, Black. What's going on? Good news, I hope."

"I wish. The investigation of Price's friend comes up empty. His background is squeaky clean. He's a successful tax lawyer with some high-profile clients in the midsouth. He's well respected in his area of expertise. I've turned over every stone I could and still came up with nothing. I even got some of my colleagues to look into this guy. There's no proof this M. J. fellow knows any more than what we know, and that is, Trevor and his new bride were killed in the earthquake. I think it's safe to say, even though I hate to come to this conclusion, that the whereabouts of your money may have died along with him."

Hezekiah angrily slammed his palm on the nightstand, scowling deeply and unleashing a string of expletives directed at Trevor Price. "That no good for nothing, son-of-a—" Hezekiah carried on with his tirade as he strode back and forth on the polished hardwoods. "Are you sure he has no ties to Price whatsoever?"

"Other than being long-time friends, there's no evidence of them having business connections of any kind."

Hezekiah felt his chest tightening. Covering it, he stumbled slightly before collapsing onto the plush living room sectional.

"Hey, you alright over there?" Christian inquired, hearing Hezekiah's evident distress.

Hezekiah sucked in a series of deep breaths, gradually regaining his composure as his racing heart began to slow.

"What kind of question is that?" he retorted. "Heck nah, no way! I'm far from being alright. That punk took off with my life's savings, Black, and I don't have a clue where my money is. And now he's six feet under? I don't know, man. He might be out there, still alive, living it up. He could have faked this whole death crap. I can't wrap my head around it. Damn!" He yelled again, followed by a forceful slap to his forehead.

"Take it easy. Getting angry isn't going to do you any good."

"The only thing that can make me take it easy is finding my money!"

"Look, I just wanted to bring you up on the latest. Calm down. There's nothing more to do right now."

"I can't believe this," he said again. "Look, thanks, Black. I'll talk to you later. I need time to process this." Hezekiah ended the call and lay out on the sofa, his mind going in a thousand and one directions. *Almost a half million dollars. Gone? Like that? Without a trace?*

He got up from the sofa, put on a pair of boxer briefs, went into the kitchen, and made coffee. Standing by the window, his gaze fixed on Fancy's bedroom window. Her room was aglow from the soft light of a lamp, and her plantation blinds were slightly open. He caught a fleeting glimpse of her silhouette gracefully moving about the room. Not wanting to seem like a voyeur, he discreetly observed her for a few more seconds before turning away from the window.

†

After the conversation with Hezekiah, Christian went into the family room and started reviewing the adoption papers from their attorney again.

"Christian," Luna called from upstairs. "Christian," she called a second time, sounding distressed.

"I'm coming," he answered, placing the file folder back on the table before dashing upstairs.

"*Ahhh,*" he heard her scream and started taking two steps at a time while calling her name.

"Luna. Luna, baby. Are you okay?"

He appeared at the bedroom doorway.

Luna was bent over, holding on to the dresser with one hand and clinching her massive belly with the other. She was

29 weeks, and she felt like she was about to burst. The pregnancy had added 35 pounds to her already thick, petite frame.

Christian dashed toward her and grabbed her. "What is it? Sweetheart, are you okay?"

Tears flowed. "I don't know. I was getting out of bed to go to the bathroom when I got this sharp pain," she explained, still holding her belly and looking down at it. "I think I'm having contractions, Christian."

Another pain hit her, and she screamed louder.

"Come on; let's get you to the hospital!"

Luna didn't make a big fuss but did cry as Christian helped her put on her shoes and jacket.

The weather was quickly changing as fall made its arrival. Christian sped to the hospital.

Luna was monitored for several hours before she was discharged, having determined the contractions were Braxton Hicks. She was sent home and told to get some rest.

He lay beside her, observing her as she slept. She looked so peaceful, so beautiful. The thin nightshirt she wore barely covered her bulging belly; its buttons strained under the pressure of her pregnancy. His attention shifted to the gentle, rhythmic movements beneath her nightshirt—the unmistakable stirrings of the child she carried. Luna had always delighted in these moments, her squeals of delight filling their nights whenever the baby kicked. She made countless attempts to coax him into feeling those tiny movements, but he consistently found excuses to avoid it. Deep down, he wrestled with his insecurities, unable to cope with the fact that this child wasn't biologically his. Far different from adopting a kid, this kid was conceived through violent, unnatural means by a cruel individual who did what Christian could never do to Luna—impregnate her.

Christian silently reprimanded himself, realizing that if he couldn't even touch Luna's belly now, how would he handle it when she gave birth to a real, living, breathing baby? Would he genuinely connect with the child? The doubts gnawed at him until he rose from the bed and quietly went downstairs to his office. He stood at the picture window, staring at the darkness and the star-lined sky.

"God, help me to be the father this child will need. Guide me and Luna not only with this child but with the new child or children coming into our lives through adoption...."

His phone rang, waking him up. He stretched and sat up from being sprawled on his swanky, popping red leather sofa, not realizing he had fallen asleep. He saw the phone lying on his chest. NEW YORK OFFICES, the screen read. He eyed the time; it was after midnight in Virginia. Why the heck was she calling him at this time of the night? Or any time, for that matter? What would it take for him to get it through Lorie's head that she was not welcome in their lives? Luna's sister or not, he couldn't have her come to Memphis and possibly ruin his life.

He pressed IGNORE. Seconds later, she called again. He pushed IGNORE again. True to Lorie's abrasive attitude, she called again. And for the third time, he pushed IGNORE.

When she called a fourth time, he answered. "Look, I'm not playing these games with you, Lorie. I'm telling you, do not call me again."

"Christian—"

He ended the call and immediately put his phone on DO NOT DISTURB.

"I don't need this tonight," he muttered, his hand nervously massaging his temples.

In recent months, Luna's pregnancy had turned into a thrilling yet challenging rollercoaster for her and Christian, sending their emotions soaring and plummeting. The last thing he needed was Lorie popping up again with her mess.

Luna was going through enough without Lorie ushering in a fresh set of problems. She was still dealing with haunting memories of the assault, which cast a shadow over their once-happy marriage. There were days when her frustrations erupted into heated arguments over the most trivial things, and hurtful words flew like sparks. Her emotions were all over the place. She would shed tears of happiness because she was carrying a child. Then she would go from happy to sad, thinking about him and how difficult this had been for him. There were nights she was plagued by night terrors linked to the trauma. Although it had been seven months since the traumatizing incident, and while the terrors had lessened, their impact still lingered. Then, there were times when she pushed him away as if resenting his presence. These were the times Christian's love faced its most daunting test.

Deciding to return to work had helped Luna cope, mainly because it kept her busy mentally and physically. But three weeks ago, Christian convinced her to take an early leave, mainly because of the approaching adoption. Their recent call about the possibility of adding a child to their family had ignited great excitement in them.

Luna followed his suggestion and reveled in her time at home, pouring her heart and soul into preparing the nursery for their upcoming baby and transforming another room for the toddler they hoped would soon occupy their home. Fancy came over on several occasions to lend her design expertise.

Sometimes, Luna tried to avoid acting overly excited about the baby growing inside, but this was something she had always dreamed of, something she always desired—carrying and giving birth to a child. It had happened, but totally in an unexpected and unwelcome way. Christian could not produce kids, yet an evil man had impregnated her. Some things were just beyond comprehension. This was one of those things.

Knowing he hid many of his emotions, Luna tried to understand and empathize with Christian and how her pregnancy
probably made him feel. She wanted so much to enjoy this
pregnancy fully, but knowing how the child was conceived and
seeing the hurt it caused in her husband, it was difficult for her
to do so. Those times when she felt the baby kicking and
keeping up a fuss, she wanted Christian to enjoy those
precious moments along with her, but he always managed to
come up with an excuse for not doing so.

When they received the call about a child that was up for
adoption and were told they were at the top of the list as
parents, she felt like a prayer was being answered. She hoped
having another child in the home would help Christian accept
the child she was carrying.

29
THAT'S WHAT FRIENDS ARE FOR

*"Friendship isn't about who you've known the longest; it's about
who walked into your life, said 'I'm here for you,' and PROVED it."*
Anonymous

Today, Luna joined Eliana and Pepper for lunch at a
charming mom-and-pop deli a few miles from her
home. A couple of months prior, Eliana had extended
an invitation to Luna. Luna was grateful for Eliana's
thoughtful gesture, especially since she hadn't built many
connections in Memphis yet. She wanted friends she could
trust enough to talk to and share things she didn't want to
share with her husband. She still talked to Tiffany, the execu-
tive she met at work, and she and Fancy had struck up a friendship, but neither lady offered her the kind of friendship she
desired. She found that in Eliana and Pepper, perhaps because
the three of them were closer in age.

Luna pushed aside the weight of her worries when she

thought about what Pepper was going through as a grieving widow raising two toddlers.

"How have you been feeling?" Eliana asked Luna.

"Christian had to take me to the ER a few nights ago."

"OMG," said Pepper. "Why?"

"I thought I was in labor. I was hurting so bad," she said, placing a forkful of food into her mouth.

"Braxton Hicks, I bet," said Pepper. "I had them something awful starting the end of my second trimester."

"That's exactly what they said it was. They monitored me for a few hours and then sent me home. Other than that, I'm okay. I wish—" she paused.

"What?" urged Eliana.

Luna threw aside her hand. "Never mind."

"You know you can talk to us."

"Eliana's right. We're not judgmental, and what we discuss is kept among us."

"Well, I just wish things were different."

"Different, how?" asked Pepper.

"You know how I got pregnant. I thought I would never carry a child of my own. But God knows I didn't think it would be like this."

"How does Christian feel?" asked Eliana.

"He's been a champ through this whole ordeal. I don't know how I would make it without him. But whether he shows it or not, I know he has to be feeling some way, knowing I'm carrying a rapist's child. I don't understand how God operates sometimes. I really don't." Luna looked down and grabbed her belly. "Ooops," she yelped. "He just moved."

The ladies giggled.

"So, it's a boy?" said Pepper.

"Oh, I don't know. I feel like it's a boy, but we don't know. We decided to wait until I give birth."

"Oh, cool," said Pepper, smiling.

"Yeah, I think that's a great idea. So, what's going on with the adoption? You're going to have your hands full when it goes through."

"She's right," Pepper eagerly agreed.

"Well, we've had the pre-placement visit. Next, we have to sign the Placement Agreement. We do that this Friday. Once that's done, we have to wait for the release from DCS. That can take another week or so. After that, our attorney will file an adoption petition, and a hearing will be held before a judge. The judge will finalize the adoption, and we will pick up our precious little boy."

"Sounds like you and Attorney Black could have your child within a few weeks."

"Yes, that would be good. I would like to have some time to bond with him before the baby comes."

"Have you finished the nursery?"

"Yes, it's done. Now I'm working on our adopted son's room."

"Have you decided on a name for him, or are you going to stay with his birth name?"

"Can you believe they never named him, not officially anyway? The foster parents called him Bobby, but that's not what we're going to name him.

"Christian Junior?"

"No, there won't be a Christian Junior. I was on board with him being Junior or the Second. But Christian wanted Dax, so then I chose Everett. So we're going with Dax Everett Black."

"I love that."

"Thank you."

"Have you thought of names for that one?" She pointed at Luna's belly.

"A few. If it's a boy, we're thinking of Reed."

"Okay," Eliana nodded. "I like it. And if it's a girl."

"It's not going to be a girl," Luna playfully insisted, "but if it *is* a girl, Laiyah Rose."

"I love that too."

Luna smiled. "Here, let me show you some pictures of what I've done with Dax's room so far." She pulled out her phone and began scrolling through pictures, showing off her decorative skills. "I decorated it in all the things little boys love. Fancy helped a lot. She gave me lots of ideas. She's good!"

"Yeah, she is. She can decorate her behind off," Eliana said.

"She sure can," added Pepper.

"I'm so excited but also a little nervous," Luna admitted.

"I know you are," Eliana said. "Two kids under two? Girl, you are certainly going to have your hands full. I can barely keep up with Khaliyah, so I can only imagine having a newborn and a toddler underfoot."

"If I can do it, you can do it," Pepper assured. "You'll have help from Christian. When Xavier," she hesitated, sucked in a breath, and proceeded, "when Xavier was alive, he helped so much with the boys. You may not know this, but I had postpartum psychosis. For the first year of their lives, I could not care for myself, let alone two newborns. The third baby, a little girl, died at birth. It was hard. Xavier was my hero." Her words trailed off.

"I am so sorry," Luna said. "No, I didn't know," shaking her head.

"Anyway, what about you and Khalil, Eliana? How are the two of you?" asked Pepper.

Eliana shrugged. "Um, we're okay. I mean, he takes care of home, he adores his daughter, and Holy Rock loves him," she said almost casually.

"And?"

"And what?" Eliana focused on Luna, who had directed the question.

"Is that it?"

"What else is there to say?"

"There's a lot to say," said Pepper. "You didn't say a thing about your needs. What's he doing for you?"

"Khalil has a full plate. And before you say anything, what I mean is overseeing a megachurch like Holy Rock isn't easy. He's always on the go. He's either here, going there, speaking somewhere, or attending this or that function. I can't say too much because, being First Lady and the mother of a toddler, my schedule is busy, too. It's expected for the first lady to go wherever the pastor goes. I don't attend all of his engagements, but I accompany him about eighty-five percent of the time."

"Do you take your little girl with you?" asked Luna.

"I do most of the time. Other times, Sista Mavis—Khalil's office assistant, will watch her. Of course, Fancy helps. And thank goodness for the senior couple who live next door. They love Khaliyah. That's who's watching her for me today."

"That's good. That's one of the things I worry about—getting someone trustworthy to watch my kids when or if I decide to return to work."

"You're going back to work? I didn't know that," said Eliana, drinking some of her soda.

"I think so. I haven't fully made up my mind. I might want to stay home until the kids are school-age, I don't know."

"What about your husband? What does he say?"

"Christian likes the idea of me staying home with the kids. It's just deciding if I want to give up my career to become a stay-at-home mom."

"Not trying to be nosy, but can you afford to stay home and not be bothered financially?" asked Pepper.

Luna nodded. "Yes. We're in a very good place from that aspect. Thank God."

"Then what's the problem? I don't get it. You say money is not an issue. Every day, there are women who wish they could afford to stay home and raise their kids."

"Look, I say pray about it," Eliana spoke up.

Pepper nodded and turned up her lips. "Okay, okay, she's right. Just listen to what your spirit says. All I'm saying is you'll never have this moment in time again. They grow up so fast. I still can't believe Zavion and Davion are going on four!"

"What are you going to do now that they're pre-school age?"

"I'm going to keep doing things the way I'm accustomed. Xavier left me in a good financial position, so it's not like I have to rush out and get a job. Thank God for that. I plan to stay home with the boys as long as possible and homeschool them. There's too much craziness in the world for me to trust my kids to just anybody, including teachers and people in authority."

"That's why I've been working to reopen Holy Rock's pre-k through six academy. It was open for almost two years, and then the pandemic hit. We have a grant writer to help locate and secure funding," Eliana said.

"That is so good. We haven't gotten to that point yet. I'm sure it'll be some time before they think about starting a school or daycare," said Luna.

"Has Hezekiah returned to the pulpit?" Eliana asked Luna.

"No, and I'm not sure when he plans to. He sits up there every Sunday. Sometimes, he presents the scripture and prayer, but he hasn't delivered a message yet. I mean, people are slowly trickling back, but attendance is still nowhere near what it used to be."

"Is that what's keeping him from preaching? The people, or lack thereof?"

"I don't know," Luna replied.

Pepper turned her head away as her voice trailed off into a whisper. "I haven't been back to church since Xavier died."

"You'll go back in your own time. Don't let anybody make you feel guilty about it either," said Luna.

"I know that's right," Eliana emphasized, looking at Luna and Pepper. "Don't get me wrong, I know they want you back at New Holy Rock, but at the end of the day, we have to remember that we carry the church in our hearts."

"Thanks for that."

"Anyway, getting back to the question. Who knows when my daddy-in-law will start preaching again. And why would he when he's already back on the church payroll? All I'm saying is Hezekiah McCoy is one of a kind. There's no telling what he could have up his sleeve," Eliana mouthed her disapproval.

"We still have to respect his decision. We have to accept him as he is," said Pepper, picking up on Eliana's attitude.

"I know that. That's why I would never say anything negative about him around Khaliyah. I'm just saying to you and Luna the man is slick as oil. You know that, Pepper. And Khalil has ways just like him. That's why they can't get along. The man's been out of prison, I know, for at least three months. Do you think he's tried to contact his son?"

The ladies looked at Eliana but remained quiet.

Eliana shook her head and pursed her lips. "Nope, not a word. You would think after what happened..." She quieted down and looked at Pepper sadly. "I'm sorry, Pepper. I didn't mean to bring—"

"No, I understand. You would think after Xavier's suicide that he would try to make amends or talk to Khalil."

"Exactly," said Eliana, gesturing.

"I haven't spoken to him in length, so I don't know what kind of fellow he is. But from what I know of his past, he used to be a take-charge kind of man. I've only spoken to him a couple of times at church. So what's the deal with him?" Luna's eyebrows furrowed, and she glanced around the room, searching for some clue or sign that might provide an answer.

"Let's just say you'll see the real Hezekiah McCoy in due time. And when you do, *babeee*, all I can say is you better have your seatbelt on good and tight because he'll take you for a wild, crazy ride you'll never forget. He can deliver prolific messages in the pulpit, but behind closed doors, he's known to get what he wants. Then again, who am I to judge? God can change the worst person there is into his mouthpiece," Eliana spoke.

"Yeah, we'll see," Pepper said with a smirk. "Are we ready to get out of here? Fancy has the kids with her, but she has something to do later this afternoon. I want to pick them up so she can regain her life." Pepper laughed.

"Well, thanks, ladies, for the invite. I've had so much fun and learned a lot about the McCoys." Luna laughed and pushed back from the chair. With Eliana's help, she stood up, clutching her belly. "Please include my husband and me in your prayers—especially my husband. I pray he can open his heart to love and accept this child. Don't get me wrong, I've told you he's been supportive, but I know he's hiding a lot. I know it." She placed a hand over her belly.

"We will," Eliana assured. "And like I said, nothing goes beyond this table. We're here for each other. So you can talk to me about anything."

Pepper raised a finger in the air. "That goes for me, too," she said, patting Luna's hand.

30
N-TICED

"There is no pain more acute than loving someone who can never be yours with their whole heart." Unknown

Sista Mavis observed with keen interest as Detria Graham confidently waltzed into Holy Rock in a pink thigh-length tweed skirt and cropped jacket that gracefully hugged her perfect waistline. She switched past the front office, disregarding the staff, like she owned the church.

In an instant, Sista Mavis sprang from her chair like a lioness rushing to shield her cubs. "Hold on," she shouted, running into the hallway, her voice echoing through the corridor. "Where do you think you're going?"

Detria halted in her tracks, turned around, and fixed Sista Mavis with a look that could have turned Medusa to stone. She needed more patience for Sista Mavis. The older woman had worked at Holy Rock for years. Detria and her had a history from when Detria was first lady. Sista Mavis seemed to think she ran things around Holy Rock, including Khalil. She acted like Khalil was her son or something. *Nosy heffa.*

"What is it, *Mavis?*" she said disrespectfully.

"I shouldn't have to repeat myself, but I forgot I'm dealing with the likes of you. Let me remind you that you are no longer the first lady of this church. You lost that title years ago, thank God! So let me repeat myself—where do you think you're going?" Sista Mavis crossed her arms and stepped back, standing firmly on her chunky legs.

"Look, ol' lady, if you were as good as you think you are, you would know I have a counseling session with Khalil. Oops," she covered her mouth and giggled, "I mean Pastor McCoy."

"I don't think so," Sista Mavis rebutted.

At that moment, Khalil appeared from around the corner, surprising them. "Everything okay?" he asked, eyeing both women, knowing they disliked one another.

"*Humph*, she says she has an appointment with you, but I don't have it on my calendar, and you've said nothing about it." Sista Mavis rolled her eyes at Detria, claiming victory.

"Oh, I'm sorry, Sista Mavis. Sista Graham is right. We do have an appointment. I was coming up here to tell you. She and I spoke earlier. Come on back, Sista Graham." He reached out toward Detria.

Detria followed him. "Thank you, Pastor McCoy." She looked over her shoulder, rolled her eyes, and gave Sista Mavis a cold stare followed by a haunting smile as she sashayed behind the pastor, disappearing into his office.

Once inside Khalil's office, Detria ran up to him. Using her good arm, she lifted her small frame off the ground and wrapped her legs around him. Planting her lips on his, she kissed him like she hadn't seen him in forever.

He abruptly pulled her arm from around his neck and

guided her back to the floor. "What is so important that you couldn't just call or text? You always have to make a scene, don't you?"

"Don't be mad. And I *did* call," she cooed, rubbing her body against him.

"Yeah, when you were in the parking lot. Okay, so you're here now. What is it that couldn't wait, Detria?"

"I wanted to let you know I'm going out of town," suddenly sounding serious and sad.

"Okay, so why is that important? You and Brooke go to Nashville and Atlanta all the time. How long will you be gone this time, not that it matters?" he said and sat in his chair.

"I'm serious, Khalil."

Clasping his hands and resting his elbows on the oak desktop, he said, "And what makes you think I'm not? Where are you going? You following your baby daddy to Nashville? Or is it Chattanooga?" Khalil laughed lightly.

Detria's baby daddy had relocated to Nashville, where he had opened more Subway franchises. When he told Detria his intent to relocate with their son, she wished him well, and that was the end of that.

Detria sat in the chair in front of his desk. "I'm going to New Mexico. Priscilla hasn't been in the best of health since the pandemic."

"Yeah, I know," said Khalil. "So are you saying you're leaving because of Priscilla? I don't get it."

"Yes. She's moving to New Mexico. She has a sister there."

"I recall you saying she had a sister and that she was considering moving closer to her."

"Well, she made up her mind to do it. And she asked me to come with her."

"Cool," Khalil said nonchalantly.

"She's been good to me over the years. She was a lifesaver after my car accident. I can't see myself telling her no in her time of need. I'm going to help her get settled and see if I can find some programs and services she might benefit from. Her sister is a widow. She has a three-bedroom house the two of them are going to share. While I'm there, I'm going to look for a condo or bungalow to lease or buy as a second home. That way, when I go back and forth to see about her, I'll have my own place. You know, for you and me," she teased. "I assume I'll be gone for two or three months."

"Well, well, well, aren't you special?" he said sarcastically, fidgeting with an ink pen and half twirling in his chair. His attention to her was barely noticeable. "Who knew you had a sympathetic streak?" Khalil mocked. "Well, I still don't see why you had to rush over here with that news. When are you leaving?"

"Tomorrow morning."

Khalil stopped fidgeting and looked at her like she was a stranger. "Tomorrow, huh? What's the rush? For you, that is?"

"No rush. Priscilla finished moving a few days ago. As for me, it's not like I have a job or anything to go to or kids under my feet to deal with. And as for you and me," she eased up to him, "it will be perfect. You can always fly to New Mexico, and we can have our private little getaway."

She stood up from the chair, walked over to him, leaned in, and began kissing and nibbling on his bottom lip.

"I don't think so," Khalil said, dismissing her suggestion and easing her off him. Either way, this should be good for you." He rose from his chair and walked from behind his desk.

"What do you mean? Why will it be good for me?"

"Look, I've been telling you for a while now that you need to move on. I'm a married man with a kid. I've never given you false hopes. You know the deal—I don't love you. I know that may sound harsh, but it's the truth. Then again, I've always been straight up with you. Anyway, I wish you well, baby girl."

Detria looked at him. Tears formed in her eyes and trickled down her reddening cheeks. "You can be so heartless sometimes, Khalil."

"Heartless?" Khalil chuckled while he rose from his chair. "Women always talk about how they want a man to tell them the truth. But when we tell you what's up, you say we're doing y'all wrong. But, I've been straight with you since we started kicking it, Dee. You know that, and I know that. I won't change my stripes to make you feel better. Now, am I going to miss that sweet...yum yum," he said, walking up to her and guiding her until her back was pinned against the office wall. He continued to whisper into her ear while his hands went where they pleased, and his lips hungrily devoured her neck, forehead, and mounds but swiped over her mouth. Khalil told himself this was the last act of betrayal he would commit against his wife and against God. But for now, he would enjoy his last feast of Detria Graham to the fullest.

At first, she resisted his advances, but her weak protests faded, and she gave in. Despite the one-sided nature of their relationship, Detria convinced herself that deep down, Khalil loved her. She couldn't see herself anywhere but in his arms. She hoped he would ask her not to go. Instead, he made it clear he could care less if she left.

Maybe he was right. She needed to leave for a few months to clear her mind and maybe even move forward. She was getting tired of being his sidepiece. She wanted and needed more. It would be hard to move on, but New Mexico might be the portal to her new beginning.

31
THE DAY NOR THE HOUR

"Pain doesn't always show itself on the outside; sometimes it hides behind a beautiful smile that only you can see through." Unknown

Eliana phoned her neighbor on her way home from the restaurant. The relaxing girl time with Luna and Pepper was much needed.

"Hi, honey. Take your time," the seventy-nine-year-old silver fox told her. I fed her a good lunch. She was watching Cocomelon until Cocomelon started watching her." She erupted in laughter. "She's sound asleep."

Eliana laughed. "Okay, perfect. I can run some errands before I come home if that's okay with you."

"That's fine, sweetie."

"Thanks. I'll be there in an hour or so."

"Take your time, baby."

She drove through the city rather than using the interstate.

She stopped at the dry cleaners to pick up Khalil's suit and shirts. Next, she went into Kroger's and picked up a few items.

When she was done with her errands, she hadn't planned it, but as if the car had a mind of its own, she went in the direction of Holy Rock. She glanced at the dash. Khalil should be done with his Tuesday staff meeting. She would stop by and surprise him. When she worked in the office, she and Khalil would have an occasional make-out session in his office or hers. That hadn't happened for quite some time. It especially stopped when she discovered that he was still seeing that slut, Detria. For the life of her, Eliana couldn't seem to grasp the reason he kept messing around with that woman. She had prayed for God to let her husband be faithful. So far, God hadn't answered that particular prayer.

Focusing on their child helped Eliana cope with his infidelity. The little girl adored her father. Sometimes, she thought about leaving him and starting life anew with just her and Khaliyah. But she loved Khalil, and she wanted their marriage to work. Thus, the reason for her surprise today. She wanted to show him she could be spontaneous. That everything didn't have to be black and white. Khalil craved excitement. She was going to take advantage of Khaliyah being with the neighbor and spend an hour seducing her man.

On the drive, she stopped and picked up some cinnamon rolls from the bakery near the church. Khalil loved cinnamon rolls, especially the ones from this particular bakery.

She soon arrived and turned into the vast church lot. She saw a car parked in her assigned spot.

"Who is this in my spot?" she mouthed as she drove up and parked next to the car. She got out and proceeded to go inside.

Sista Mavis watched First Lady Eliana approach the front entrance. Part of her was happy that a scene was about to unfold that would hopefully put Detria Graham in her place.

That woman had been causing trouble ever since Sista Mavis could remember. She cheated on Pastor Stiles when they were married. She had slept with Hezekiah McCoy and now she was sleeping with his son. The woman had no morals.

Sista Mavis didn't particularly want Pastor K to get caught in the arms of another woman, but today, he might find himself in deep trouble because there was nothing she could do but watch.

First Lady Eliana smiled and raised a quick hand. "Hi, Sista Mavis," she said, zooming past the front office. "Is he in his office?"

Sista Mavis didn't have a second to respond. She eagerly got up from her desk, raced to the door, and watched Eliana parade up the corridor toward Khalil's office.

Eliana lightly tapped on his door and reached out to turn the knob. Just as she reached for the door to open it, it flung open, and out pranced a flushed-looking Detria Graham.

"Oh, well, uh, excuse me...First Lady."

"What the heck are you doing here?" Eliana snapped.

Khalil appeared behind her, his eyes blazing like he'd seen a ghost.

"Khalil, what is this...this *thing* doing here?" It was bad enough she was screwing Khalil behind her back, but now this heffa dared to be up in Holy Rock doing only God knows what with her husband.

"Uh, I *am* a member here," she said coyly to Eliana. "A good paying, committed member," she emphasized. "I had an appointment with my pastor."

Sista Mavis remained at a distance, her head sticking out of the office where she could get a pretty good view of the scene unfolding.

"Pastor K and I were just finishing up a personal counseling session," she cooed, smiling and rolling her eyes as she dashed past Eliana while smoothing out and pulling on her short skirt. Her cheeks were bright red.

"Uh, what are you doing here, sweetheart?" he asked, looking guilty as the sin he'd just committed. He eyed the white box she held, displaying the bakery's logo.

"Oh, I just thought I would surprise my husband with his favorite dessert, but it looks like I'm a little late for that." She rolled her eyes as Detria whisked past.

Looking back, Detria paused. "Thanks again, Pastor K. A girl wouldn't know what to do without you." She giggled as she passed by Sista Mavis and exited the building.

"How are you embarrassing me like this? Having that wanch up in here. Everybody knows what the two of you are doing, Khalil," Eliana retorted as he persuaded her to come into his office.

He closed the door. "Look, nothing was going on. Like she said, she had an appointment. She wanted to ask for prayer for her housekeeper. The woman is ill. She has to relocate to live close to her family. Sista Graham was telling me that she was going to go with her, help her out, and hopefully see the woman get healed."

Eliana stared. There was nothing she could say short of exploding and cussing him out. But she had to respect her position as First Lady. She was not going to clown up in the church.

"Uh, is that for me? Is that what I think it is?" he asked, pointing at the familiar blue and white square box. He reached for it, peeped inside, and smiled.

She remained quiet, folding her arms and giving him a fixed stare.

"Thanks, babe. My favorite." He took a bite out of one. "Um, it's good and fresh." He leaned in to kiss her, but she quickly turned, and his lips landed instead on her cheek. She snatched the box back.

Scanning the office, she saw a few papers scattered on his desk and a folder on the floor. Studying him closer, she noticed his tie was loose, as were the first three buttons on his white starched shirt. His belt was half fastened. She was nobody's fool. She knew clearly what had gone on.

"I've had enough," she said.

"What are you talking about? Had enough of what?"

"Are you serious right now, Khalil? Your whore just left your office, and you're standing here, half-ass dressed, looking at me like I'm boo-boo the fool. Look at you. Do you have *any* morals?" She looked at him in disbelief, shaking her head. "It's obvious you don't!"

"Look, don't start, Eliana. Come on," he said, pleading, "I told you nothing was going on. The woman had an appointment. I talked to her about the move and told her it might be good for her and certainly for her assistant."

"And just how do you know what would be good for her and her assistant, Khalil? I wish you would stop playing me for a naïve little fool. I'm far from that!" she continued screaming.

"Look, stop it, already. We're in the house of the Lord. Don't be up in here hollering and acting all ghetto, for chrissakes!"

"Ghetto? How dare you! You low-life scum of the earth. You just finished screwing your mistress—right here! In God's house," she snapped, looking around. "You're just like your no-good, trifling, cheating pappy!"

"And you're delusional!"

"I'll show you delusional!" Eliana removed the remaining cinnamon rolls from the box and threw them. One landed on his face, and the other hit his shirt. A glob of white glaze oozed down the center of his face.

"Are you crazy?" he said, wiping his face while dashing toward her and grabbing her arm.

"Let go of me!" she demanded, twisting out of his grip. She drew back, slapped him with all her might, and stormed out of the office, past Sista Mavis and another office worker who had suddenly appeared.

Khalil stood in his doorway, furious but choosing not to go after her.

Eliana got in her car, sped off the lot, and headed home.

†

Arriving home, Eliana hurriedly packed some things for her and Khaliyah. She'd had enough of Khalil. Catching him with Detria was the last straw. She had to get away, or else she couldn't be responsible for what she might do to him or her. She was just that mad. So before she let him push her to the brink of no return, she thought it best for her to get as far away from him as possible until she could sort her life out. What better place than with her parents, who recently sold their home in Murfreesboro and purchased their dream home in Tempe, Arizona, after her father's retirement?

Before going next door to pick up Khaliyah, she called Jocelyne and briefly told her what had transpired. Jocelyne had always been in Khalil's corner until recently. She always tried to make Eliana see the good in him.

"I can't believe him," Jocelyne said, dumbfounded. "This is too much. You know I want you to be happy and enjoy married life like I do, but he's gone too far this time," Jocelyne sighed.

"I know, right."

"I'll be there in about fifteen minutes. I was already headed to that side of town to pick up my daughter's dance uniform. I'm glad you caught me."

"Me too. Thanks, Jocelyne. I'll be ready."

Her next phone call was to her mother. When she didn't answer, Eliana left a detailed message.

"Mama," she cried, "I need to get away for a few days. I wanted you and Daddy to know I'm coming there. I hope you don't mind. I'm catching the next flight. It leaves Memphis at three-forty, so I've got to hurry. Khaliyah and I should arrive tonight around nine. I'll tell you about everything when I get there. Make sure you let Daddy know. Oh, and don't try calling me back because I'll probably be going through TSA or already on the plane, and my phone will be off. And, Ma, tell Daddy to please not call Khalil. Anyway, I'll let you know when I land. Buh-bye. Love you."

For a split second, she thought she should go where Ian was instead. But that would be the first place Khalil would look, and she didn't want her brother involved in her drama. When it came to her parents, Khalil didn't know exactly where they lived in Arizona, only that they had moved there not long ago. He might call them to see if they could tell him where she was, but he wouldn't think she and Khaliyah would run to them. That was quite unlikely. He knew how Eliana felt about what she called her mother's *outdated* beliefs. Her mother did not believe husbands and wives should sleep apart, let alone move out of the home and run home to their parents under any circumstances, no matter how angry they got at each other.

She looked at Khaliyah sitting calmly on the sofa, nursing her binky.

"It's time to let Miss Binky go to binky heaven, Khaliyah."

Khaliyah cast a puzzled glance at her mother, gently shaking her head from side to side while tightly gripping the pacifier in her tiny hands.

Eliana shrugged, then shifted her thoughts to what had happened. Khalil had stooped to another low, and it caused her major embarrassment. She had gotten out of her first lady character by yelling at Detria and going off on him. It's not like she should have been surprised to see Detria parading half-naked out of Khalil's office. *That outfit she wore left little to the imagination. Skirt heisted up so high it almost showed her flat behind. And that top was so low her breasts looked like they could fall out. He was probably in there drooling all over her. That wanch has a lot of nerve. Prancing around, flaunting her affair with my husband in front of those folks at Holy Rock. Yeah, enough is enough, Khalil. I'm not taking another minute of your mess!*

She needed to escape the craziness of her life. Maybe spending time with her parents could be the perfect way to clear her mind and gain clarity on the next steps for her marriage. She may disagree with her mother, but she also knew her parents would provide a supportive environment for Khaliyah during this valley-low period in her life.

†

"You know you messed up, mi amigo," Omar told his buddy the following morning while they were working out at the gym. "I told you before you got married to make sure you knew what you were getting yourself into. No more messing with the ladies. No more single life," he warned with a thick Spanish accent.

"I know, I know you did, man. The crazy thing is I had just told God this would be it for me, and I wasn't going to cheat on Eliana again. I wasn't going to betray Him either. I would be the man of God He called me to be. Then look what I go and do." Khalil hit the punching bag with his full might. "Who would have thought of all the days and times that Eliana, of all people, would pop up? She even brought me my favorite dessert, man, only to see Detria coming out of my office." Khalil wiped sweat from his brow.

"From what you said went down in your office, you better be glad that's all Eliana walked up on. So what are you going to do to fix this?"

"I don't know, Omar. When I got home, she was gone. She sent a text telling me she was giving me some space to figure out what I wanted. She wouldn't say where she went. But I have a suspicion she went to Atlanta, you know, where her twin brother lives. She left her car here, which means she didn't drive there. She probably caught a plane." He walked away from the punching bag and headed toward the weight area.

"She and her brother are close, right?" Omar asked, lying back on a weight bench and reaching for an overhead barbell.

"Yeah, they are." Khalil positioned himself on the bench next to Omar. The friends continued working out. "I just hope he doesn't try to talk her into leaving me. He doesn't care for me, and the feeling is mutual."

"All I can say is," Omar strained to lift the weight, "if you have not started already, now is the time to seriously start petitioning God. He's the only one who can save your marriage."

32
THE CALL

"Adoption is the most intentional process on Earth." Unknown

The call Christian and Luna had been anticipating came Thursday morning. The process had moved faster than expected, and they were heading to pick up their little boy after two weeks. The forecast for the day couldn't have been more perfect.

"Do we have everything?" Luna asked, nervously going back and forth through the house, picking over one thing after another.

"Baby, slow down. We have everything. If we don't, it's no problem. Remember, our little fellow is coming home with us. Whatever we don't have, we can get."

"I know, I know," she said, holding her giant belly and approaching Christian's outstretched hand.

Walking up to him, he wrapped his arm around her, kissed the top of her head, and they left.

At the adoption agency, they met Dax for the first time. He had a head full of curly sandy brown hair, fair skin, sunken eyes with circles underneath, and hollow cheeks that caused Luna's heart to ache for the little boy. He looked frightened, lost, and sad, unable to understand the unfair plight he had already experienced in his young life. The picture they were shown of him initially was nothing compared to seeing him face to face. He wasn't walking yet, and they were told he barely tried to crawl. As for talking, he grunted.

She could feel her heart expanding to accommodate all the love he would need. She reached for him, but he pulled away, clinging to the social worker's shirt.

Christian stood beside her, silent but visibly overwhelmed by emotion. This frightened little boy was about to be placed in the care of him and Luna. For the first time, Christian felt an indescribable longing to give him every ounce of love he had to offer. He wondered if he would feel the same depth of love for the baby Luna carried.

When the child refused Luna's arms, Christian stepped up.

"Come on, fella. It's okay. Daddy's got ya."

The little boy looked at Christian. His expression of fear and uncertainty remained, but Christian kept his arms extended. "Come on, I've got you. I'm going to watch out for you. We're going to do fun things together," he spoke softly.

The little boy leaned forward and slowly reached for Christian. Christian's face was filled with a smile as he embraced him in his arms, hugging him against his chest as he walked with him around the room.

Luna's eyes rushed with tears, and she covered her mouth with her hands.

Christian and Luna were embarking on a new journey. Many twists and turns were likely, but Christian told himself he was ready for the challenges.

†

Hezekiah sat in his office at New Holy Rock, scrolling through one site after another, hoping to find information about his missing money. He was still not one hundred percent on board with them saying Trevor was dead. The memorial service the family held for him and his wife was not enough to convince him. Especially since there was no physical body, only pictures of the couple, giving him more reason to believe Price could be alive and hiding across the ocean. When he found himself losing it, he pushed back from the computer, got up, and went to his brother's office to see if he wanted to grab a bite for lunch.

"Hey, I just got a text from Black."

"Oh, yeah?" Hezekiah responded as he walked into the office. "What'd he say? Everything okay?"

"Yes, their adoption is being finalized today. He asked if I would attend as a support person and as their pastor. I told him I would. That's where I'm heading in," he said, "about an hour, " eyeing his phone.

"Good for him. Black's a good guy. I wish him and his wife the best. I was coming to see if you wanted to grab something to eat, but you already have plans."

"Yeah, it's going to be a full day. After I leave court, Mya and I are going to a stage play the university's Theatre Department is putting on this evening. It's already going on one. I need to get out of here in about ten minutes or so."

"Black is going to have his hands full with a newborn and another kid under two." Hezekiah laughed.

"He sure is," Stiles agreed. "How is it going living with Fancy?" he asked jokingly.

"I do *not* live with her," Hezekiah corrected. "I'm her tenant. It's strictly professional. But to answer your question, it's all good. It's peaceful living in the casita. I have no complaints. I get a chance to see my grandkids more often, too."

"That's right. Fancy gets them, mostly on Saturday evenings, so that she can bring them to church," Stiles added.

"The last couple of times the grandkids came over, she invited me to the house. I'm telling you, I felt like my world was perfect. I imagined this is how it would have been for Fancy and me, living our best lives, enjoying our grandkids, traveling whenever and wherever we want." Hezekiah paused, "But I messed that up."

"Stop looking back. Press forward. Enjoy each moment God is giving you now. We've all made mistakes. We'll do so as long as we live. But I'm not telling you anything you don't already know."

Hezekiah nodded. "I just don't want to mess up again. That's all I'm saying. I know Fancy and I are over. Then again, I haven't tried to get back with her. As much as I'd like to, I can't do it. I don't want to hurt her again, Stiles."

"Then don't. Be grateful for a decent place to lay your head, and who knows, maybe another lady will come into your life. You never know what God is up to. Know what I mean?"

"Yeah, like you finding Mya. I'm happy for you. Real happy. She seems to keep you smiling. You still ain't hit that?"

Stiles laughed and shook his head. "Nah, man. I told you, I'm living a celibate lifestyle. I'm going to be led by my heart and spirit this time. Not by my flesh. I want to do it God's way. Satisfying my flesh is one of the things that contributed to my fall in my other relationships, mixing physical with spiritual. I've learned it won't work like that. It has to be God's way if I expect anything lasting."

"You're a better man than me. I know I have some changes to make, but I'm not going to lie; I don't think I want to go through that again. I was forced to go without while I was in prison. But hey, I'm a free man now," Hezekiah said.

"Yeah, but be careful out there, man. Pray about everything. You're too old to be out there just chasing tail. Find you a good woman and get somewhere and sit down."

Hezekiah laughed. "You said a mouth full.

†

Christian, Luna, and Stiles anxiously occupied their seats in the near-empty downtown courtroom. Their attorney delivered a persuasive argument, highlighting the couple's strong qualifications to be nurturing and caring parents.

Following the attorney's presentation, Christian and Luna stepped forward. They pledged to provide a permanent, safe, and loving home for the little boy they longed to call their own. Twelve tense yet hope-filled minutes later, the judge signed the Decree of Adoption, sealing a new chapter of love and family for Christian, Luna, and their son.

33
UNCONDITIONAL CONDITIONS

"You don't have to look like someone else to love them." Leigh Anne
Tuohy

D ax had a rough start adjusting to his new
environment. For the first week, he cried and
whined daily. It was also a big adjustment for Luna
and Christian. With a toddler in the house, their time with Dax
consisted of adjusting, rearranging schedules, and learning a
seventeen-month-old's needs and wants.

Christian had taken time off from his practice to bond with
his son. It was a hectic learning curve, but they did not
complain. They found their new roles as parents rewarding
and entertaining but also challenging. It was preparing them
for the next addition to their family.

By the end of the second week, Dax began to allow Luna to
cradle and hold him close. Yet, it became clear that he had a
special bond with his father. Whenever Christian was around,

Dax's little face would light up, and he would reach for him. Christian had even managed to coax a faint smile from the boy.

When they introduced him to his room, brimming with toys that any child his age would typically adore, Dax clung to Christian as if uncertain about what to do.

Daily, Christian patiently talked to him and showed him *how to play*, and Dax began interacting with his toys and stuffed animals. He was still used to being given a bottle, but from what they had learned, the bottle often contained water mixed with a small amount of apple juice or sugary soda. He had ten or twelve teeth. He had a hearty appetite and grabbed for any food Luna and Christian fed him to the point they had to feed him slowly so he wouldn't make himself sick from eating too much too fast.

In the middle of the third week, it became less stressful as Dax began to warm up to them, and they began to get accustomed to having a child around 24/7.

It was enjoyable to see Dax finally adapting to his new home. Soon, he started crawling, pulling up, and walking around furniture.

Their lives together, though haunted by the memory of Luna's abduction, was otherwise perfect. They had a precious little boy who was all theirs to love, care for, and cherish. Christian was already deeply attached to his son.

Luna was okay with that. She hoped his relationship with Dax would make it easier for him to accept the child she was carrying.

During her appointment earlier this week, the doctor informed her that the baby could come any day but no later than the next week. He would arrange for her to be induced if she went past seven days.

Trying to take care of Dax, address his needs, and tend to herself was proving harder each day but rewarding. It was becoming more difficult for her to move around because her belly seemed to have grown substantially. She was often out of breath, had to pee every few minutes, moved around like a turtle, and had to take mini breaks throughout the day.

Christian was a lifesaver, assuming many of the roles, including caring for Dax.

This morning, while Christian showered, Luna hummed a tune and made funny faces at Dax while making him a breakfast fruit bowl.

Dax was sitting in his high chair, not impressed with his mother's singing skills. He tried to reach for the fruit bowl while still holding the pacifier in his mouth, taking it in and out playfully.

Unexpectedly, Luna let out a chilling shriek, and poor Dax, obviously frightened, burst into a loud cry.

"Ahhh," Luna yelped, grabbing her belly and dropping the fruit bowl she was trying to put on Dax's high chair.

Christian appeared at the door. Seeing her in distress, he ran to her and guided her to the bar stool at the kitchen island.

Still holding the bottom of her stomach, she bent over, her other hand resting on the island counter.

"I might be going into labor."

"Do you think you are?" Christian asked, going to the high-chair and picking up the bowl and fruit from the floor. "The doctor said it could be any day."

He prepared another bowl of chopped fruit and placed it before his son.

As they had grown accustomed, Dax quickly picked up pieces of the fruit, devouring it.

"Slow down, son." Christian guided the food and assured his son wouldn't choke. He looked back at his wife.

"Give me a second. I'll help you to the bedroom. Maybe you'll feel better if you lay down for a while."

"Yeah, that's a good idea. I do feel tired and a little nauseated, too."

He removed Dax from his high chair and walked over to Luna, using his free hand to hold on to her and lead her to the downstairs primary bedroom.

With his son clinging to him, he guided Luna to the chair in the bedroom.

Just as she was sitting, another hard contraction hit her.

"I'm in labor! Uhh. I know it," she cried, causing Dax to cry too.

"I'll start timing the contractions," Christian said, doing what the doctor had instructed him for when this time came.

Luna cringed, rested her head against the chair, and breathed deeply. When the contraction subsided, she exhaled, wiped the sweat off her forehead, and closed her eyes momentarily.

"I felt that one in my back, all the way around my stomach. It's nothing like when I had Braxton Hicks. These are way worse." She reached for her son. "Oh, Dax, sweetheart, please don't cry," she said. "Everything's fine."

Dax pulled away from her, clinging to his father.

"I don't think you should try holding him, honey. At least not right now. Your contractions are strong, and you don't know when the next one will come."

"Okay, you're right. Get his pacifier. Better yet, give him some juice in his sippy cup."

Christian rushed from the room and returned moments later with a calm Dax. He sat the boy on their bed with his sippy cup.

"Good, that should keep him satisfied for a while," she said. "I think you should call Sista Fancy. I think we're going to need her. I don't think this is a false alarm this time."

†

Fancy had committed to being there for the couple when the time came for Luna to deliver, especially since Luna's parents wouldn't be coming to town until after the baby was born.

"I'm on my way," Fancy assured when Christian called. She got her purse, phone, and sweater jacket. The wind had picked up, making the fall day much cooler than predicted.

She hurried to her car. When the garage door opened, she began backing out but stopped when she saw Hezekiah pulling into his parking spot.

She released the window. "Christian's wife is in labor. I'm on my way to their house to watch their son."

"Okay, tell him they're in my prayers. Do you need me to come with you?" he offered.

"No, I'll be fine. I've turned on the timer for the lights. I'm not sure what time I'll be back or if I'll even be back tonight."

"If you don't mind, will you keep me posted about how she's doing and when you're on your way home? That way, I can be on the lookout for you."

Fancy smiled. "I'm a big girl. You don't have to wait up for me," she giggled. "But yeah, I'll let you know when the baby arrives. Talk to you later. I gotta go."

She backed out of the driveway and disappeared up the street.

Hezekiah stood at the side of his car. What he wouldn't give to have another chance with Fancy McCoy.

Ding.

He opened the text message. He laughed, frowned, and shook his head as he read the X-rated text before deleting it. As much as his body reacted to the text, he wasn't going to fall into her trap again.

†

After twenty-one and a half grueling hours, Luna gave birth to a baby girl weighing six pounds, nine ounces, and nineteen inches long.

Luna was worried about her baby's health during her pregnancy since she didn't know who the father was or if he had any diseases or deformities that could be passed on to the child. However, her baby girl was born healthy, which was a great relief.

Christian was present in the delivery room when the baby was born. He had not shared his curiosity with anyone except Stiles, but he was eager to see what the newborn looked like.

The newborn bore a caramel skin tone, an oval-shaped head, noticeably monolid eyes, and a few barely visible strands of straight reddish or dark brown hair.

After cleaning up the baby, the nurse unexpectedly handed her to Christian. As he held her in his arms, his heartbeat quickened. He felt nervous and awkward, but to his surprise, he experienced emotions similar to the ones he felt when he first saw Dax.

"Isn't she beautiful?" Luna said, crying and reaching for her baby girl.

Christian nodded with a smile. The tiny human looked so innocent and pure. Christian became overwhelmed with feelings but couldn't pinpoint exactly what those feelings were. He watched as the baby continued to squirm, but she didn't cry. Next, he gingerly placed the child into Luna's arms.

Luna tenderly kissed the cradle of her little girl's head and caressed her face, feeling an inexplicable connection with this tiny human who entered her life under unconventional circumstances.

34
THOSE TIES THAT BIND

"You don't choose your family. They are God's gift to you, as you are to them." Desmond Tutu

Caring for two little ones was far more complex than they expected. Immediately, their days became filled with sleepless nights, feeding Laiyah Rose around the clock every three hours and diaper changes for not one but two because Dax wasn't even close to being potty trained.

They were still bonding with Dax. He had started exploring independently, which was challenging and exciting for them to see. But, he was also prone to tantrums when he didn't get what he wanted when he wanted it. He seemed curious and a little jealous of the baby. Luna maintained a sharp eye on him when he was around his sister.

The good news was Luna's parents were arriving the following week.

"I can't wait until Mom and Dad get here," Luna said after

breastfeeding and burping Laiyah Rose. "Or should I start getting used to saying YaYa and PopPop, as they want to be called now that they're grandparents?" Luna laughed.

"They'll give us some relief, that's for sure," said Christian, sitting on the floor with Dax playing with building blocks.

"Yes, I know. As much as I enjoy being a mom, it's not easy. But I wouldn't trade it for anything," she said, kissing a now sleeping Laiyah on the forehead and then getting up and placing her in one of the cribs they had set up in the family room. "I thank God we have people who offer to help. I appreciate all the warmth and love we've received since moving to Memphis, and even more so now that we have two little ones. What happened to me, to us, I should say, was horrific. I didn't think I would make it through that, but because of God's help, I'm here with you, Christian. I'm safe and sound. We've been blessed with not one but two beautiful, precious babies."

Christian got up and walked to his wife, sitting down beside her. Wrapping his arms around her, he held her close.

Luna began to cry softly. "All I'm saying is I'm grateful for Dax and our sweet Laiyah Rose." She looked over at the baby peacefully asleep and then at Christian. "I'm especially grateful for you. I love you so much, Christian."

Dax crawled over and began pulling at Christian's pant leg and whining, wanting his daddy to pick him up. Christian obliged and picked up the little boy, who immediately quieted down.

Christian was still trying to adjust and accept the baby girl who was now part of their forever family. He had recently talked to Stiles about being uncomfortable around the baby.

Stiles suggested looking at Laiyah Rose the same way he did Dax—like she was adopted. He told him, "Dax is adopted, and he's not your biological child, but Laiyah Rose was born with your name. She is Luna's biological child, with Luna's

DNA. Knowing that you are recognized as the father without adoption but because of your relationship with Luna? That's powerful. It's a sermon in there," Stiles said over the phone one day.

Christian listened to his friend, pastor, and confidante. He respected Stiles and his advice. Sometimes, Stiles didn't offer advice but instead allowed Christian to vent.

Christian felt a different bond with Dax than with Laiyah Rose. Perhaps it was because she was still such a tiny little thing. He was nervous whenever he held her. He had told Stiles that Luna's baby felt like a stranger in his arms. He didn't feel like that when he first held her, but since bringing the little girl home, he felt different and didn't know why. He didn't say a word to Luna about his feelings. He just prayed that God would change his mindset and heart.

"I wonder what the surprise is?" Luna said, returning to the chair and curling her legs underneath her bottom.

"Don't spend too much time trying to figure it out. You know your parents; they're probably bringing us money or maybe tickets for you and me to go on a romantic parents' getaway," Christian joked. "Some of the fellows at the office said once grandbabies arrive, your parents look right past you. It's all about the grandkids." He laughed.

"I admit, a parents' getaway would be nice, but we couldn't leave the kids, at least not right now. They're too young, and Dax hasn't gotten fully accustomed to you and me, not to mention Laiyah Rose. I caught him trying to take her pacifier again. He would have scratched her if I hadn't pulled him back," Luna shared, her voice ringing out her frustration.

He patted Dax on the head and got up from the floor. Going over to where Luna was, he got in behind her, pulled her into his arms, and planted light kisses along her neck. "I was just fantasizing," he clarified.

Luna relaxed in his arms, laying her head against his chest. "I know. But let's enjoy being parents."

"Anything you want," he replied.

Her phone started ringing. "Dang, I left my phone in the kitchen." She began to get up.

"Wait, I'll get it."

Christian retrieved the phone and brought it to her.

"Hi, Eliana," Luna said.

Hi, Luna," Pepper said.

"Oh, hey, Pepper. I didn't realize you were on the line too." Luna chuckled, happy to hear from her friends.

"We were checking on you," Eliana said. "I know your hands are full."

"Yeah, let me know what day is good to come over and give you and your husband some relief. At least for a few hours," Pepper offered.

"That is so nice of you two. But so far, we're good. I told Christian earlier about how grateful I am to have people like you, Eliana, and Sista Fancy. You all mean so much to me and Christian."

"Awe, you are so welcome. We know how it can be. Motherhood is no joke." Eliana giggled.

"But the good news is my parents will be here next week. They plan on staying all month. I can't wait. It will be so exciting seeing the babies interacting with their grandparents, you know, bonding with them."

"Yes, I know," Eliana and Pepper said.

"Enough about me. Eliana, how are you? Are you back in the city?"

"No, I'm still out of town."

"You still don't know when you're coming back?" Pepper asked.

"Nope. Khalil has been calling and texting nonstop. He was

begging me to come home. He still thinks I'm in Atlanta. I hate to have my parents lie, but he's called them asking if they know how to reach Ian or when they last heard from me."

"What did they tell him?" asked Luna.

"They just say they don't get between people's marriages, no matter if it is their daughter, unless physical or verbal abuse is involved. In other words, they didn't tell him a thing."

"Oh, my," said Pepper. "I'm so sorry for all of this, Eliana."

"Me too," Luna added. "How is Khaliyah?"

"She's good. They're spoiling her rotten. "You know how that goes."

"I sure do. My mom and Fancy are always giving in to the boys." Pepper laughed. "Do you know what you're going to do? I mean, about your marriage?" Pepper's voice lowered.

"No, I just know I need more time. Time away from him, from Memphis, from everything. I'm not going to go into full detail about my marital woes, but let's say I will no longer change who I am for someone who doesn't treat me the way I deserve. I used to tell myself that because I wasn't upfront with Khalil at the start of our marriage, I had no right to complain or fuss over how he was treating me. No more. Whatever that means for our relationship and this marriage, I will accept. Even if that means divorce."

"Oh, no. I hope it doesn't come to that. Just keep praying about it. I'm going to pray for you and your husband as well. Maybe this will be the wake-up call he needs to save his marriage and keep his family together."

"I agree with Luna," said Pepper. "But I also see where you're coming from. I mean, please do not stay in a marriage where you aren't respected and where you aren't put first. I disregarded Xavier and what I knew to be true. He was not in love with me. I knew that from the start, but I tried to force it. Look where it got me."

"Ladies, we will not do this today, not over the phone anyway. Luna, I know you have your hands full. Pepper, you said you were going to take the boys to see their grandmother, and me, well, I'm going to get freshened up and meet some friends for dinner," Eliana chirped.

"Friends? Dang girl, you've only been there a week," chimed Pepper. "Good for you."

"Uh, no. I've been here nine days, to be exact. I have two friends who moved here after graduating from college that I keep up with, mostly online. We're going to get together and do some catching up."

"You don't owe us an explanation. Do what you need to do to protect your mental health," Pepper said.

"She's right," said Luna.

"Anyway, I told them I was visiting my parents in Tempe. They drove over the other day to see me."

"Do they live close to your parents?"

"Sort of. They live about twelve miles from Tempe, in Phoenix. They're picking me up in about an hour, so I need to get ready. I know one thing: I am so excited to be getting out— no baby to worry about, no husband to cry over. For the first time in forever, my mind feels free."

"Good for you," said Pepper. "You deserve it."

Luna sounded more apprehensive. "Just be careful. Make wise decisions, and please don't think you can do what he does —you can't. Remember, you're still a woman of God. You never know who's watching, including your friends."

"I know that," said Eliana, sounding irritated. Luna was beginning to rub her the wrong way. She was a grown, married woman with a kid and a cheating husband who called himself a man of God. Yes, she knew exactly who she was and who she represented. That's why she hadn't put her husband on blast for the congregation and the whole city, for that matter, to learn he was an undercover adulterer. No, she didn't need Luna or anybody telling her how to act.

"Thanks for the word of caution, Luna, but all I'm doing is enjoying the company of old friends. We're going to grab some food and have some good, clean fun. Well, I have to go. I'll talk to you ladies tomorrow." She ended the call and sucked in her breath. She would not let Luna or anyone mess up her good mood.

Ding.

She picked up the phone while looking for something suitable to wear. The only thing she had packed that would work was a pair of straight-leg designer jeans and a crisp white long-sleeved cotton shirt. She highlighted it with a wide designer belt. It was fall in Memphis. The weather was unpredictable. But in Tempe, the temperature was a perfect seventy-three degrees. If asked to go out again after tonight, she would have to go to the nearest TJ Maxx and grab a few things. But for now, jeans and a cotton shirt would do.

She looked at the screen while stepping into the jeans.

"Please answer. We need to talk, Eliana."

She chose to ignore it and continued to get dressed.

35
EVERY MAN NEEDS A DAD

"Forgiveness doesn't forgive their actions. Forgiveness stops their actions from destroying your heart." Unknown

Khalil, Omar, and Stiles stopped at the sports bar inside the FedEx Forum before tonight's game.

"You need to get your mind right, nephew. You're not a kid anymore. You're a grown man. You have a successful ministry, a beautiful, committed wife, and a precious little girl. You're blessed. I hope you don't allow the enemy to come in and tear apart everything God has given you."

Khalil nodded, sipped his soda, and toyed around with his bean and cheese nachos bowl.

"Nothing I haven't been telling you since day one," Omar reminded him.

"I know, and both of you are right. I've got to get it

together. I hope it's not too late," he lamented. "She's stopped answering my calls and texts."

"Have you tried calling Ian? Maybe he can convince her to talk to you."

"I did, but the number I had for him is no longer his. I called her parents, too. Her father said they were not going to be in the middle of marital problems, but that she's okay, and she'll be in touch when she gets ready, and to take this time to decide what it is I want."

"Think about it, bro. Can you blame her old man for feeling the way he does? You've been cheating on his daughter. How do you expect him to feel? As for Ian, that's her twin. You know he's not going to tell you a thing."

"Stiles is right," Omar agreed. I think the only thing you can do now is give her space and time. Let things cool down, try calling again in a few days."

"Has Detria left town yet?" Stiles bit into his footlong chili cheese hotdog.

"Yep, she left the day after Eliana caught her coming out of my office."

"And she hasn't been blowing your phone up?" Stiles asked.

Omar laughed.

"Actually, she hasn't. I told her, for the umpteenth time, that it was over. Maybe she got the message this time. I sure hope so."

"Man, haven't you heard of BLOCKING people? That's what you need to do when it comes to her. She's never taken no for an answer," Omar said. "I don't see her starting now."

"That's probably because he says one thing, but his actions say another. You keep telling her it's over, but you still communicate with her and run to her whenever you don't get what you want at home."

"I say you should change your number, amigo. That or BLOCK her."

"You know, Omar, that's not a bad idea," said Stiles.

"I just might do that. Thanks, bro," Khalil said.

After the game, Khalil dropped Omar off and headed to take Stiles home.

"I appreciate your advice, Unc. It means a lot. You know it's not like I can talk to my dad."

"You two still haven't talked, huh?"

"You know we haven't." Khalil's jaw twitched, a sign of his mounting frustration. He didn't understand his father, but then again, folks kept telling him he was just like Hezekiah, a bonafide chip off the block. He sure as heck hoped he wasn't. He didn't want to be anything like his father.

"Give him time. He's got a lot going on."

"Stop making excuses for him! I'm sick of you trying to give him a pass. Admit it, he ain't worth—"

"Quit it, Khalil. Okay, so your father isn't perfect, but he's still your father. Stop letting bitterness overrule you, man. Admit you've done things that hurt him too, but it's time you let the past remain in the past."

"All I know is that I'm not going to him."

Stiles wrapped a comforting arm around his nephew. "Fair enough, but give him a little more time. God is going to work this thing out with the two of you. He's going to heal your relationship. You have to be open to receiving. Okay?"

Khalil nodded. "Yeah, I hear you, Unc. I hear you."

36
SURPRISE!

"Not everything that is faced can be changed, but nothing can be changed until it is faced." James Baldwin

"You're sure they said not to pick them up?"

"That's what they said. Daddy said they were going to get a LYFT, I didn't argue."

Christian shrugged, "Okay, if that's how they want it, but you know I don't have a problem playing UBER, LYFT, OR whatever."

"I know that, and so do they. They just said they were going to catch a LYFT this time. I think they're just trying to be considerate of our time with these two precious little ones." She looked at her kids and smiled.

"Honey, it's them," Luna exclaimed, stepping outside onto the front porch, carrying Dax high on her hip while leaving Laiyah Rose inside the house asleep in her crib.

Christian appeared behind her. The couple stood and waited until Luna's parents exited the car.

Christian rocked, suddenly becoming unsteady on his feet. *This was the surprise? What on earth are you up to, Lorie?* He shot her a glance, rolling his eyes, while a mischievous smile crept across her face.

Next, he saw his wife's weirded-out facial expression. She looked just as surprised, if not more so, than him.

"Mama! Daddy!" Luna cried, temporarily dismissing the guest with them.

"Honey," her mother said with outstretched arms as she walked towards her.

"Hi there, cutie." She tried to rub Dax's little hand, but he pulled back.

"He's still adapting," Luna said while side-eyeing her sister.

"Before we leave, he's going to love his YaYa and PopPop. Isn't that right, honey?" Luna's mother looked at her husband as he walked up.

"That's right," he said.

"Christian, will you help your father-in-law with our bags?"

As if suddenly brought back to earth, he shook his head slightly with a faint smile and replied, "Uh, sure."

Luna's words got stuck, "Lor...Lorie? Is it ... is it really you?" Luna was stunned. "Talking about a surprise! OMG, I don't know what to say." She didn't know if she should be happy or angry. It had been years since she'd seen her sister.

Lorie didn't give Luna much time to decide how she should react or feel. Instead, she eased past their mother, ran up to Luna, and pulled her and Dax into her arms.

"Yes, it's me, sis," Lorie exclaimed.

Luna recoiled as Lorie embraced her, and a sudden rush of

unpleasant memories flooded her mind. When Lorie was seventeen, she suffered a mental breakdown, and she attempted to stab Luna. That incident sent Lorie to a youth detention center for eighteen months. After she was released, Lorie left home, and Luna had seen her only a handful of times since then. Any type of sisterly bond was nonexistent.

Luna couldn't erase the memory, but she had managed to suppress it to maintain her mental strength. Now that Luna had children – her sister's presence made her even more nervous. Why had she returned without any prior notice? And why hadn't their parents said anything? An array of unanswered questions swirled in her mind, but she pushed them back and put on a brave smile.

"Christian, this is my sister, Lorie."

"Uh, hello, Lorie," Christian said awkwardly, extending his hand. "Nice to finally meet you."

"You too." Luna casually accepted his handshake.

"Luna, I know this is all a shock. You weren't expecting this, but I'm just thankful God is bringing our family back together," her mother exclaimed.

"Yes, shock is an understatement," added Luna, unnecessarily bouncing Dax up and down on her hip.

"We'll all sit down and talk later at dinner," their father said.

Christian side-eyed Lorie. She looked away swiftly and followed everyone inside.

"Luna, uh, I have to go to the office," Christian said after placing his in-laws' luggage in the downstairs bedroom.

"To the office?"

"Yes, I just got a text. I need to locate a file for Jim. He's managing a case for me while I'm away. It shouldn't take too long. I'll call you on my way back to check if you want me to pick up dinner." He leaned in and kissed Luna's cheek just as Lorie approached.

"All right, that sounds like a plan," Luna replied.

"You leaving, brotha-in-law?" Lorie said, sneering.

"Yes, something came up at the office. I'll be back as soon as I can." He hurried out the side door and into the garage before Lorie could reply.

Inside his car, he slammed his palm against the steering wheel in disbelief. Lorie's audacity in showing up at his home left him stunned. The situation was beyond messed up. His mind raced with questions as he navigated out of the neighborhood, making his way toward the town square. Finding a parking spot on one of the lots, he sat in his car, pondering his next move.

His phone rang.

"What the heck kind of game are you playing?" he yelled.

"Chill out, lover boy." Lorie laughed into the phone. "You're so uptight. I've repeatedly tried telling you that I needed to see my sister."

"And I told you to stay away from us! My wife has gone through unbelievable pain and trauma this past year. Now, she has not one baby but two. The last thing she needs is more stress. I'm telling you, Lorie, you need to leave, and you need to leave right away," Christian demanded.

"Sorry, not gonna happen. Oh, and so you know, I'd like pepperoni pizza with extra cheese and jalapeños. That's if you stop and bring dinner," she mocked and ended the call.

Christian was even more furious after her call. Lorie was trouble with a capital *T*. He had to get her to leave as quickly as possible.

He exited the car, entered a diner in the square, sat at the bar, and ordered a vodka on the rocks. He rarely drank, but when he did, vodka was his liquor of choice. Sipping on the booze, he began to relax. An hour later, he returned to his car and called home before leaving the parking lot.

"Honey," Luna said, "Lorie wants pizza. Mama and Daddy said pizza is fine with them, too. I'll call in the order, and you can pick it up. Tell me what kind you want."

Christian told her what kind of pizza he wanted and then asked about Dax.

"He's asleep. Can you believe he let Daddy hold him? It was just for a few minutes, but that was huge," Luna said, elated.

"Yeah, that's my boy," Christian said proudly as he drove off the town square parking lot.

"Oh, and Christian," Luna whispered. "Wait a sec. Let me go to our bedroom. I want to tell you something."

"You mean, now?"

"Yes, it won't take long. Lorie and I talked. She came to me and told me she was sorry for the terrible sister she was to me. She asked me if I would give our relationship another chance, that she wanted to be the sister she should have been when we were growing up. She said she wants to be an aunt to the kids and be more present in our lives. I didn't know what to say, Christian. If she means what she says, I think having her in their lives would be a blessing for the kids."

He could hear Luna starting to cry. "Look, you're getting yourself all worked up. We'll talk tonight."

"Okay, it's just that this is an answered prayer, Christian. God is restoring my family. He's blessed us with two beautiful children. I have a wonderful husband. Now my sister wants to be part of our lives. I'm so grateful, Christian."

"I know, I know. Look, go ahead and call the order in. I'll be there soon, okay?"

"Okay."

"And Luna."

"Yes?"

"I love you. I really, really love you. You know that, don't you?"

"Yes, I know that, but it's always good to hear. I love you too."

Lorie stood outside Luna's half-opened bedroom door, eavesdropping. When she heard the call end, she knocked.

"Come in," Luna invited.

"I just wanted to tell you again how much I appreciate you welcoming me into your home. I realize this whole scenario could have played out differently, especially with me swearing Mama and Daddy to secrecy. I know it wasn't the best way to do things. I should have called and talked to you first. But I thought you wouldn't want to talk to me. I mean, your last memories of me aren't the best. I was messed up back then, Luna. I'm so sorry for the way I treated you."

"No, it's okay. Everything worked out like it should."

"I sure hope so. What about your husband?"

"What about him?"

"How do you think he feels about me just showing up? Does he even know about our relationship and the trouble I caused?"

"Lorie, there's nothing Christian and I can't talk about. He's a good man. And if you think he's going to hold something against you for what happened with you and me years ago, then you're wrong. Christian is a loving, forgiving person. He really is. That's why I love him so much."

Lorie walked into the room and embraced Luna. "I'm so happy for you, sis."

"Thank you, Lorie. So, tell me about you. What's been going on in your life?"

The sisters sat on Luna's bed and talked, filling in all the missing gaps from their estrangement over the years. They only stopped an hour later when Christian arrived with piping hot pizzas, a huge salad, cheese bread sticks, and two-gallon containers of sweet tea.

†

Later that night, lying in bed with Dax between them, the couple talked low enough to keep from waking him. The baby monitor on the night table gave them a clear view of Laiyah Rose asleep in her nursery. If only they could get Dax to sleep in his room and bed, something he was not willing to do just yet.

"So what's your verdict?"

"My verdict? Are you talking about my long-lost sister?" Luna eased up and rested her back against the headboard.

Christian nodded.

"I mean, it was shocking seeing her after all these years. But I have to admit, once we talked, I felt better. I'm glad she's back. She looks good. From what she told me, she's quite successful. Talking about changing your life around, she's done it. She lives in Virginia and owns her own real estate brokerage firm. One of the reasons she came with Mama and Daddy is because she's going to leave here to attend some big real estate convention in Nashville. Oh, and she's divorced, has no kids, and right now, she isn't in a relationship, but she wants to eventually get married again, she said."

"Good for her. It sounds like she has definitely changed from the person you described when you and I first met."

"She has. God is good."

"It sounds like you're excited she's here."

"I am. I'm glad we can move forward. You know, forget the past. All of us have messed up. I know I have. Maybe not the same as my sister, but yeah, I've done some things I'm ashamed of. But the key is to forgive. That's what Christ expects of us."

Christian leaned over and affectionately kissed her forehead. "That's why I love you. You have the ability to look past a person's faults. Some people would have turned her around at the door."

"She's my sister. Now, the kids will know their aunt, and she can be part of their lives. I'm so happy how this day has turned out, Christian."

"I'm happy for you. Goodnight, my love."

Within minutes, Luna was asleep. Dax lightly snored, with one of Luna's arms draped across him like a seatbelt. The little boy could barely move.

Christian smiled, seeing the display of love.

Later, over in the night, he climbed out of bed and went downstairs when his stomach growled. Leftover pizza sounded perfect. He warmed up three slices, poured a glass of tea, and stood at the island, chowing down.

"That's what I was coming to do," Lorie said, startling him. She walked past him and opened one of the pizza boxes. "Do you mind?"

"Go for it," he said calmly. "Have a good night." He popped the last of his slice into his mouth and started to walk off.

"Christian, wait."

He paused and looked at her. "What is it?" his tone dry.

"Look, I just want to tell you I'm not here to cause trouble. Really, I'm not. I tried to tell you that I wanted to make amends with my sister. I couldn't let you interfere with that."

"I told you not to come here. To leave Luna alone," he said between clenched teeth.

"Luna is my sister. I love her. I messed up in the past with her, but I've changed, Christian. Okay, so you and I were involved at one time. But, like you said, that was before we discovered you were married to her. I've moved on from that, and so have you. Sure, I gave you a hard time, calling you and putting you on edge. I'm sorry about that, too. But I've come to realize how important family is—I want to be around mine. My parents are not getting younger. I want them to see me all cleaned up and living a good life. Like Luna and you."

"That's what you're saying, but I have a hard time believing you. You've been calling for months, basically threatening to tell Luna about us. Now you pop up here, and you think I'm supposed to believe you're here on a goodwill mission or something?"

He moved in front of her, and Lorie took hold of his arm. "Please, Christian. You have to believe me. I would never do anything purposely to hurt my sister or you."

"What's going on?" Luna appeared, looking surprised.

Christian looked like a deer caught in headlights. "Uh, I got hungry. I came downstairs to warm up some of this pizza."

"Me too. When I got in here, he was devouring that pizza like it would be his last meal." Lorie laughed.

"What are you doing up?" Christian asked.

"Dax woke up wanting a bottle. I gave him his binky. That should hold him until I get back up there with his bottle.

"I'll make him one and bring it up there," Christian told his wife. He then headed to the sink, rinsed Dax's bottle, and filled it with warm almond milk.

"Well, goodnight," Lorie said, swallowing her last bite of pizza. "That should hold me for the rest of the night."

She walked past the couple and disappeared upstairs.

"What was that about?" Luna asked when Lorie was gone.

"What do you mean?"

"I thought I heard the two of you arguing. It sounded like you were having a serious discussion about something or other. You said something about her being on a goodwill mission. What is that supposed to mean?"

"It was nothing, honey. And we weren't arguing. I just met the woman, what would there be to argue about? She was telling me that she wants to make things right with her family. I told her it wasn't a goodwill mission, and from the look of things, her family had already forgiven her and accepted her back. That was it. Come on, let's get back upstairs. I don't like Dax being left in the bed by himself. It only takes a quick second, and he could land on those hardwoods."

"You're such a good Poppa," Luna whispered, smiling as they headed upstairs to their room.

Lorie stood out of view underneath the staircase, again eavesdropping. She was relieved when Luna didn't press Christian about their discussion. The last thing Lorie wanted was to hurt her family again. But also, she couldn't help but feel a bit envious seeing her sister's life—a good husband, two beautiful kids, a successful career, and plenty of money. As Lorie thought about it on the way to her bedroom, she told herself it might be worth ruffling the feathers in her sister's so-called idyllic marriage—just to see how strong it really was.

†

Christian felt a fresh burst of relief when the day came for Lorie to leave for Nashville. After the convention, she was going home to Virginia. During her week-and-a-half stay, she and Luna reconciled, and Lorie was a perfect aunt who helped Luna with the kids. That was the positive thing Christian gleaned from her visit. But it didn't make him feel any better about her. He didn't trust her as far as he could throw her. Hopefully, her promise to leave their past behind was true.

37
EASY LIKE SUNDAY MORNING

"The sweetest of all sounds is praise." Xenophon

S unday morning, the Black household was up hustling and bustling. YaYa helped get the babies ready for church while Luna made breakfast and filled baby bottles with pumped breast milk. Christian and his father-in-law sat back and allowed the ladies to do as they pleased. Usually, his father-in-law was the resident chef, but with Luna and her mother practically taking over, it was like being on vacation because he wasn't required to do anything but stay out of their way.

"Here, you can put Dax's shoes on. He seems to like you," Luna's mother said, placing the little boy on her husband's lap.

"Come on, tiger." PopPop beamed and eagerly reached for his grandson.

The family filled half a pew when they arrived at New Holy Rock. Dax sat on his father's lap. He did not adapt well to strangers or new environments, so they kept him in service with them rather than taking him to the nursery. He would get accustomed to things in his own time. Laiyah Rose was asleep in her mother's arms.

Hezekiah presented the scripture and said the congregational prayer before turning the pulpit over to Stiles. The sanctuary was half full, but attendance had improved.

"I want to talk to you today about the art of deceit taken from the passage of scripture Pastor McCoy just read." Stiles looked over his shoulder and nodded at Hezekiah.

"Amen," some people in the congregation responded.

"Let me repeat what the good book says in Jeremiah seventeen, specifically verse nine. It says, and I'm reading from the NIV, the heart is deceitful above *all* things and beyond cure. Did you hear that? It's deceitful above *all* things and *beyond* cure!" he heavily emphasized.

"You know, I am reminded of a story I heard a while ago. It's a story about this upstanding pillar of the community, a church-going guy. I'll call him Donny. Donny had it going on. He was what one would call a master of deceit. He went about manipulating others by playing what he called innocent, clever games and carrying out elaborate schemes. He cared little, if anything, about how his endless lies and tricks affected others."

"Preach, Pastor," someone from the choir stand yelled.

Stiles looked out over the congregation. "For a while—in fact, for more than a while—for twenty-something years, Donny was a successful business owner and entrepreneur. His money afforded him and his wife a mansion, luxurious cars, island vacations, and passes into exclusive VIP clubs and resorts.

"Yes, Donny had it made until his tangled web of lies and deceit came back to bite him—like a boomerang. He lost his business and all of his wealth during a real estate crash combined with the pandemic. Soon after, his wife left him.

"Listen, people," Stiles preached, "dishonesty and deceit are not in alignment with the path of righteousness and integrity. It will lead you down a treacherous road..."

Stiles stepped to the side at the end of his sermon, and Hezekiah came up.

"Let us stand and celebrate God's greatness. Raise your hands, people of God," Hezekiah said with hands upraised. Next, he burst into a song by Marvin Sapp. "*I thank you for it all...the good, bad...*" he sang.

Stiles and his deacons lined in front of the sanctuary with stretched-out hands, inviting people to come to the altar for prayer or to join New Holy Rock.

The church was on fire, and the congregation shouted praises to God. YaYa removed Dax from Luna's arms, and Luna jumped up from the pew, waving her arms and singing along.

†

In the meantime, across town at Holy Rock, Fancy was on her feet, standing next to Sista Mavis and some other ministry wives. Khalil did his usual at the end of service—performed. He broke out in song. Unlike his father, Khalil was a showstopper. Today, he chose a hip and upbeat song called "Amazing" by gospel artist Pastor Mike Jr.

"*My God is amazing. Simply amazing,*" Khalil crooned, with several choir members joining him at the front of the sanctuary. Their steps looked like a choreographed performance.

Missing from the pew, however, was the first lady. Days prior, she had flown back to Memphis but did not attend today's services because no one knew she was back in town. Temporarily, she and Khaliyah were housed in a hotel downtown. She planned on remaining at the hotel until she saw where things were headed with Khalil. So far, she was not impressed with his weak apology and pleas. All this time, he still thought she was in the ATL. That proved that he didn't care too much about her whereabouts to find out exactly where she was. He proved more each day that he was selfish, arrogant, and stuck on himself.

Fancy went to Khalil's office after service to tell him how much she enjoyed his message about relationships.

"Thanks, Mama," he told her as they stood in his office.

"You still haven't talked to Eliana?"

"Nope, not in a few days. If she wants to stay gone, that's on her now. Enough is enough, but I want to see my daughter, Mama. She has no right to keep Khaliyah away from me."

"I know, sweetheart. You're right, but give her time. I told you, while they're away, you need to get yourself together. You've allowed a slut like Detria Graham to tear your marriage and family apart. Come on, Khalil. How ridiculous is that? I know we're at church, so Lord forgive me, but I can't help but say it. Is she that good between the sheets you would throw away everything you've built?"

"It's not that, Mama. I told you before that Dee is convenient. Eliana is so closed-minded about a lot of things, especially in the bedroom."

"And I told you to get over it, Khalil. And if that's the case, talk about it. Don't be demanding and pushy. Women will do just about anything to please a man when they're in love. If Eliana isn't, then you must not be making her feel secure. That's easy to see. A blind man can see that you don't put your wife first."

"That's not true."

"Oh, but it is, son. I'm the last one to lie to you. If you want your family back, if you want to be whole again, you better do some praying. Ask the good Lord to give you a change of heart and to control your wandering eyes. It's going to lead to nothing but destruction. Don't you see that? Look around. Your family is gone. You can't say where they are because you don't know where they are. You say she's at Ian's, but what proof do you have of that? If you love my precious little grandbaby like you say you do, which I know you do, then you need to do better. Get your family back."

"I am, Mama. I am."

"I hope so." Fancy walked up to her son and hugged him. His tall stature dwarfed her petite frame as he returned the hug.

When they pulled apart, she smiled. "Oh, can you come by the house tomorrow?"

"Sure, what's up?"

"I want to rearrange some of my design supplies. I have a ton of boxes filled with sample tiles, fabric, upholstery materials, just a whole lot of stuff. I want to move it from the bonus room to the garage storage. Get some much-needed organizing done."

"What time?"

"Whatever time is convenient for you. I'm going to be home all day for the next few days until I can get it all put away. If I'm going to start designing more, I need to get myself together. Anyway, don't come too early."

"Oh, yeah, you like to sleep in late."

"I don't consider sleeping until nine as late. I could sleep later than that, but I make myself get up and move around." Fancy laughed.

"I hear you, Mama. By the way, how are you doing?"

She knew what he meant when he had that look on his face and that tone.

"I'm okay. I don't cry every day anymore. Maybe every

other day," she giggled again, "but I'm taking it one day at a time. The grandkids keep me busy. I miss my little sweet cheeks, though," Fancy said. "But just keep the faith. Work on you, and they'll be back home before you know it." She gave him a pat on the cheek. "I love you. Now, let me get out of here. My stomach is growling. I'm starving."

"I love you, too, Mama, but you're telling me you've been here for all three services and haven't eaten? Why didn't you get breakfast this morning when you first arrived? You could have brought it to my office if you didn't want to eat in the fellowship hall with everyone else. And what about the fruits and snacks we serve in between services? I'm saying there's no excuse for you to be walking around hungry, Mama."

"Stop fussing. I wasn't hungry when I first got here, and I hadn't planned on staying for all three services, but after the boys didn't spend the night, I knew I could stay, so I did. I'm going to get something when I leave here."

"I hope so. Where are you headed?"

"I don't know. I want something good and filling. After I do that, I'm heading home. What about you?"

"I was going to do the same, except I was thinking about going to that Thai restaurant close to the house. You got a taste for Thai?"

"Yeah, you know I love Thai."

"You want to join me? You can leave your car here. I'll drop you back off after we're done," Khalil suggested.

"As long as you're paying, you've got yourself a date." Fancy laughed, looping her arm inside his.

38
LOVE CHILD

"The worst feeling in the world is when you can't love anyone else because your heart still belongs to the one who broke it." Unknown

"Can you come back tomorrow? It shouldn't take as long as it did today," she asked as Khalil exited the guest bathroom.

"Yes, but remember, tomorrow is Tuesday. My weekly staff meeting."

"That's right. Tomorrow *is* Tuesday; I wasn't thinking. So what time do you think you can get here?"

"Umm, around twelve, twelve-thirty at the latest. We put a big dent in getting the boxes packed and moved. What you have left shouldn't take too long to knock out."

"I think so too. Either way, I'll have lunch ready."

"Sounds good. That sandwich you made today was chef-worthy," he complimented. "I thought I was eating in an

Italian restaurant. It tasted just like an original Italian muffuletta."

"Thank you, baby."

"Well, let me get out of here, Mama. I'm meeting Omar at the gym." Khalil hugged his mother and left.

Shortly after, sitting in the family room reading, Fancy heard a car pull up. She figured it was Hezekiah. She went to the window and peeped through the oak plantation blinds, ensuring she was out of view. Yep, it was him. She watched as he got out of the car. When she saw the passenger door open, she moved closer to get a good look at whoever it was with him.

A little boy who looked about nine, maybe ten years old, stepped out.

"Who is that?" Then she quickly shook her head while talking to herself, "You know exactly who that is. That's Jude. The child he had outside of your marriage, silly. Who else could it be?"

At first, she felt angry, but she soon calmed down by reminding herself that Hezekiah was her tenant. As a renter, he had the right to bring his son to his home; nothing unusual or disrespectful about it. She shook her head and continued to watch.

Hezekiah held the boy's hand as they laughed and talked, looking around the yard. Seeing this fatherly gesture, Fancy's thoughts drifted towards Xavier. She imagined it was Xavier's hand he was holding instead of little Jude's. Tears formed, but she quickly wiped them away. She remained at the window, watching until they disappeared around the corner of the garage.

She retreated to her bedroom and peeped out the bedroom window. A light was on in the front room of the casita. She could make out Hezekiah's shadow but didn't see Jude.

"Stop being nosy, Fancy," she chastised herself. When her phone rang, she was relieved, especially when she saw Victoria on video chat.

"Hey, bestie, what's going on?"

"I was calling to ask you the same thing. We haven't talked in a few days. Is everything okay?" Victoria asked.

"Yes, everything's good. Khalil came over and helped me organize some of those supplies."

"I told you I would help you with that."

"I know. You're the one who talked me into organizing all that stuff instead of having it strewn all over that guest room. You helped me separate it and label the boxes. I couldn't have gotten this far without your help."

"Still, I told you I would help until you finished."

"Girl, please. I do not have a nine-to-five like you. Thank God I can work at my leisure, or I can work from home. I'm blessed that Holy Rock pays me well as a consultant. And before you say anything crazy, I'm not saying I'm in a better position than you are. I'm just saying that you have to go to the office every day. Sometimes you're tired when you get home, and on weekends, you're trying to spend time with the grand-kids and do your own thing. I get it. Plus, as heavy as those boxes were, neither of us could have moved them to those high shelves. Khalil was a godsend."

"I'm glad you got it done. Now we can decorate that room and make it a real office."

Fancy laughed. "One thing at a time, plus I'm not quite done. Khalil is coming back over tomorrow to finish."

"So what else is going on? Have you or Khalil heard from Eliana?"

"He showed me a video and some pictures she sent. I'll show them to you when I see you. Khalil thinks she might be coming home soon. I sure pray she does. They need to settle things. Being separated like this and not talking will only put more strain on their marriage. I already don't know if it can be salvaged. I have no idea what Eliana thinks."

"So she hasn't texted or called you?"

"She'll text if I text and ask about Khaliyah, which I have done several times. I ask if she and Khaliyah are okay, to which she'll send back a quick reply, a word or two. She isn't answering my calls."

"But you haven't done anything to her for her to cut you off, especially from Khaliyah."

"I know that, but I'm Khalil's mother at the end of the day. I think she thinks I'm automatically on Khalil's side. At least that's how I feel. I don't fault her for that, although I wish she understood that I do not condone his actions. I only want what's best for my granddaughter and for my son to be happy, as well as Eliana."

"Yeah, but she doesn't need to put you in their mess. But I also understand she needs time away to think. It's hell dealing with an unfaithful spouse. I've lived through it. I wouldn't want that heartache on anyone."

"You forget, I've gone through it too, so I told Khalil I would not uphold him in his mess. I prayed for him not to be a whore-monger like his father. But that's between him and the good Lord," she sighed into the phone.

"Do you want to go out to eat this weekend?" Victoria asked, swiftly changing the subject. "I have a taste for spicy tacos from that place that serves those supersized tacos and burritos."

"Yeah, I'd love to."

"Okay, cool. Now, let's get to the juicy stuff. Tell me, what's going on with the uhh man living in the back of your house who also happens to be your ex? How's that going? Have you invited him to the house yet? And I'm not talking about when the grandkids come over either." Victoria snickered. "Catch me up."

"Girl, you know you're crazy," Fancy laughed and then told Victoria about her seeing Hezekiah with the boy.

"One thing you're right about; he's a tenant, and he's allowed guests, especially his kid. I know seeing the boy reminds you of Hezekiah's infidelity, but as you said, the kid's innocent."

"Right. What kind of pisses me off, though, is that he can have a relationship with this little boy, but he's yet to make amends with Khalil. I don't understand."

"I can't answer that, Fancy. But hopefully, he'll reach out to him soon."

"Soon? Vicky, he's been out of prison for months. What's he waiting on?"

"Your guess is as good as mine." Victoria hunched her shoulders.

"Anyway, that's enough about my mixed-up, chaotic life. Tell me about this guy you met. I'm dying to hear all about your date."

They talked and laughed over video chat for half an hour or more. At the end of the chat, they had planned a weekend outing at the taco joint.

Fancy showered and changed into PJs. Just as she was about to get in bed, she heard voices coming from the back-yard. She took a peek through the window. Hezekiah and Jude were going up the walkway toward the front of the house.

"Where are they going at this time of night?" she spoke to herself.

"We've got to get you home, buddy...school," she barely heard Hezekiah say.

"Oh, yeah, school. That's right. Hezekiah, you know you should have taken him home earlier. That child should already be at home and in bed." She raised her hand dismissively and shook her head as she turned from the window.

Kneeling beside the bed, she bowed her head in silent prayer. Afterward, she settled into the comfort of her bed. Retrieving the novel from the nearby table, she resumed reading from where she had left off the night before.

39
SECOND CHANCE PLEA

"What a painful thing to taste forever in the eyes of someone who doesn't see the same." Perry Poetry

K halil texted Fancy, notifying her that he was en route.

Fancy: Ok, see you shortly.

Khalil: 👍

He got into his car. His text notifier dinged again as he was about to drive off.

Detria: I miss you.

A string of racy, intimate pictures of Detria followed the text.

Khalil looked at them briefly, shook his head, and then proceeded to do something he wouldn't have thought of doing not very long ago—he deleted the thread and BLOCKED her number.

When he arrived at Fancy's house, he sat in the driveway and Facetimed Eliana.

"Hey, I'm surprised you answered."

"Hi." Her reply was dry and emotionless, and the scowl on her face let him know he was still on bad terms.

"Uh, how are you and Khaliyah?"

"Khaliyah's good. She's right here if you want to talk to her."

"Yeah, I do."

"Hi, Daddy," Khaliyah said, looking all cute.

"Hi, Precious. What you doing?"

"I went on the slide," she giggled and bounced, her profile going in and out of the screen's view.

"Oh, you're a big girl if you're on the slide. Are you doing okay?"

"Uh-huh."

"Are you being good for Mommy?"

"Uh, huh."

"I miss you, and I love you so much."

"Ok, Daddy, bye." She gave the phone back to Eliana and ran off.

"Ok, is that it?" Eliana said calmly.

"Uh, when are you coming home?" he pleaded. "We can't resolve anything with you in Atlanta and me in Memphis. Baby, we need to work this out face to face."

"Now you want to work things out? What's going to be different this time, Khalil? Tell me. I want to hear this. Are you going to trade Detria Graham in for a newer model?"

"Come on, Eliana. I told you that's over. I know I've done

you wrong on so many levels, but I also know I want my family back."

Eliana saw the look on his face. His expression matched his words. He looked broken, sad, and hurt. After how deeply he hurt her, it should have been hard to feel sorry for him, but she loved him. Hearing him pleading and seeing tears form in his eyes softened her—just a bit.

"I don't trust you, Khalil. You're a cheater. And it's not like this is anything new. You've never been faithful to me. The thing is, I knew who you were before I walked down that aisle. So, I blame myself. Blinded by love, and look what it got me." Her expression suddenly hardened and grew more serious as her voice got louder.

"What about Khaliyah? We have a beautiful daughter together, Eliana."

"She's the one good thing that's come out of this." Eliana began to cry. "She makes it worth it."

"Eliana, please...just come home. No, I tell you what. Send me Ian's address, and I'll be there."

"No, I don't want you coming here," she said quickly. "I'll be home in a few days."

Khalil sighed. "Thank you, Eliana. I promise you won't regret it."

"We'll see. Anyway, I gotta go," she said, wiping her tears away and ending the video chat.

Khalil remained in the car, thinking about the call. Not once during the chat did he tell Eliana he loved her. He told his little girl he loved her but didn't think to say those words to his wife, the woman he said he wanted back. Maybe she would be home now if he had told her those words more often. But the truth was he had never quite felt like he was *in love* with Eliana. He cared deeply for her. She'd given him a beautiful daughter and stuck by him through thick and thin. When she was his assistant, she looked out for him. She was loyal. That's the main reason he married her. If anyone deserved to wear the title of First Lady, it was Eliana.

"Khalil. Why are you just sitting in your car?" Fancy asked, appearing on the front porch.

He looked up when he heard his mother's voice. "I was on the phone with Eliana," he said, stepping out and walking around the front of the car toward her.

He kissed her cheek and side-hugged her before following her inside. "Ummm, smells good in here."

Sebastian appeared and followed them through the house. Khalil leaned down and gave the cat a couple of rubs.

"I made fried potatoes, broccoli and cheese casserole, baked chicken wings, and garlic toast. And before you say anything, I know I told you not to expect me to cook a big meal, but I wanted to ensure you had something to fill you up —not that fast food."

"Mama, you're the best. Remember when you used to cook like this just about every day for me and ..." his words trailed off.

As if knowing what he was about to say, she said, "It's okay, sweetheart. I can talk about him now."

"Mama, it seems so unfair."

"I know," she sighed. "But enough of that. We're not going to do that today. Come on," she grabbed his hand, "I know you're hungry."

"Yep, sure am. I didn't eat at church since you said you were making lunch." He hugged and kissed her again.

"I made enough for you to have some to take home, too."

"I love you." He washed his hands at the kitchen sink before grabbing a plate on the counter and going to the containers of food.

"Yep, that's right; take care of your appetite before I put you to work." Fancy laughed.

Fancy made herself a plate and joined Khalil in the dining room. "I'm not trying to get all in your business, but is everything okay? Is my grandbaby all right?"

"Yeah, Mama," Khalil put a forkful of food into his mouth. "Ummm, this is *so* good."

"Thanks, sweetie."

"Yeah, Eliana said she's coming home in a few days. She didn't give me the exact day, but at least I know she's returning with my daughter."

"Is Khaliyah the only reason you want Eliana back? What about your wife? Are you ready to be the husband she deserves?"

"Of course, I want my little girl home with me. I'm her father. That little girl is my heart. You know that, Mama."

"You didn't answer my question, but I guess you did."

"What?"

"I asked if you're ready to commit to your wife and marriage. Stop all of this running around. Get that other woman out of your life. I can't understand why you can't see that Detria is nothing but a certified demon. You and your father fell to whatever she does that has y'all jeopardizing your families. I'm sure your Uncle Stiles also told you how nasty and lowdown that woman is." She shook her head. "It's a darn shame. But I'm going to say this, and then I'm going to leave it alone. You say you want your daughter back?"

"You know I do."

"Well, if you want her back, you better get serious about your life, Khalil. You better get yourself right with your wife *and* with the Lord."

"I'm trying, Mama." He picked up a chicken wing, popped it into his mouth, sucked on it, and pulled back a bare bone.

"As for Detria, I'm done with her. And I mean that. Anyway, she left town for a few months."

"Thank you, Lord, for answered prayers. Maybe she'll stay gone forever," Fancy said, getting up from the table and entering the kitchen. "You ready for some dessert? I made a butter pound cake."

"Fa sho!" Khalil applauded and rubbed his hands together in excitement.

"So, you got my daddy shacking up in the backyard, huh," Khalil shook his head, laughed, and put a forkful of the delicious cake into his mouth.

"How many times do I have to tell y'all the man is a paying tenant? Nothing else."

Khalil chuckled. "So you're saying he hasn't made not even one trip," Khalil raised a finger, "up to this house?"

"He's been here a few times when the grandkids were here. That's only because I invited him. It was nothing else. Just two people enjoying their grandkids."

"Uh, huh? You know, Mama, I don't get that guy. He'll entertain my daughter, but he and I are worlds apart."

"That's because both of you are stubborn and selfish. I held a lot of anger toward him in my heart at one time, too, baby, especially after Xavier's death. Then, my mindset changed. I can't say what my wake-up call moment was. All I know is I took a good, long look at myself. I realized I was flawed and messed up, too. I was ashamed of who your brother was. I wanted him to live the life I wanted him to live. I pushed Pepper and him to get together. I don't know if you know that, but I did."

"Maybe you did, but still, Xavier chose to marry her. He didn't have to do something because you wanted him to."

"I know, but he still based his life on pleasing others. He knew his family didn't support his lifestyle."

"Okay, so we didn't support him being gay. I won't and don't apologize for that. Could I have just supported him as a brother? I admit I was lacking in that area. But, Mama, talking about the past, bringing up painful memories, what good is that doing us? I will not carry any more guilt over whether I was a good brother or not. There's nothing I can do about that now. There's nothing we can do but be good to his sons. Try to guide them in a positive direction."

"True," Fancy replied.

"Lunch was delicious, but I need to get up from this table before I decide to take a nap."

"You can take a nap. Go get in one of those beds and sleep as long as you want to," Fancy said as they tidied up the kitchen.

"I wish I could, but if I take a nap now, I won't be good for the rest of the day." He laughed.

"Just remember, get your carryout plates on the counter when you leave."

"Oh, believe me, I'm not going to forget those. Come on, show me the rest of what you want me to put away."

Khalil arranged and moved boxes around for the next two hours.

"If you don't need me to do anything else, I'm going to leave. I need to run back by Holy Rock before I go home."

"Okay, baby, and thank you so much. I love you."

"No problem. I love you too."

Fancy walked with him to the door and kissed his cheek. "Call me later."

"I will. See ya."

She closed the door and went to her bedroom.

†

Khalil walked toward his car but paused when he saw the Mercedes pull into the side drive. He started walking toward his car as the figure exited.

Their eyes met, and a heavy silence hung in the air until Hezekiah spoke up.

"Hello, son." Hezekiah closed the car door and walked ahead, his voice sounding uncertain.

"What's up," Khalil replied, his voice slightly nervous. He stood in front of Khalil. "So... uhh, it's been a while."

"If that's what you wanna call it," Khalil said, looking off.

Though they were outside in an open space, Hezekiah felt like he was back in a cramped six-by-eight cell with the walls closing in on him.

"So, uh, you were visiting your mother?"

Khalil nodded. "I helped her move some things around."

"Oh, I wish she had told me; I could have helped."

"And why would you do that? You think you can get a month of free rent out of her or something," Khalil chided.

"Look, I know things have been on a bad note for a while between us."

"Hah, you think?" Khalil replied bitterly.

"Look, come with me to my spot. I think it's time we talked. That is if you have time. I just left New Holy Rock, stopped, and grabbed a couple of sandwiches and fries." He held up a white bag. "There's enough for two."

"Nah, I'm good. Mama made me lunch, and I have these containers of leftovers." He held up his own plastic bag of goodies.

"Okay, but what do you say? You have a minute?" Hezekiah tilted his head, beckoning for Khalil to follow.

Fancy walked to the front of the house, talking to Victoria, when she saw through the living room window Khalil's car was still in the driveway, and now Hezekiah's car was in its designated spot.

"Vicky, girl, you won't believe it."

"What?" Victoria asked excited.

"I don't see him, but Hezekiah's car is here. He and Khalil must be at the casita."

"Why do you say that? You said Khalil had left."

"I thought he had. Hezekiah must have driven up when he was getting ready to leave. Wait, let me go to the back."

She went to her bedroom and looked out the window. "His blinds are closed. But I know they're in there. Where else could they be?"

"You're probably right. It's about time they talked."

"Yeah, I know."

"God has a way of doing things."

"Yep, he does."

"Well, I gotta go. I'm having dinner with my Tinder guy."

"Again?"

"Yep."

"Guess that means you like him." Fancy chuckled.

Victoria giggled. "Yeah, I like him. He's good company. Anyway, I gotta go. I'll call when I get home so you can tell me what happened with Hezekiah and Khalil."

"Okay, sounds good. Oh, yeah, text me where you're going. Safety first, you know."

"Yes, ma'am, will do, although I've already told Pepper."

"Okay, as long as someone knows."

Seconds later, Fancy's text dinged with the information from Victoria.

Fancy smiled, shook her head, and walked to the front of the house. Khalil's car was still outside. She shrugged, turned around, went to the bonus room slash office, and began making the design plans for a new client's glam closet.

40
IT'S GONE BE ALRIGHT

"Courage is what it takes to stand up and speak; courage is also what it takes to sit down and listen." Winston Churchill

Hezekiah stood at the kitchen counter, doctoring his sandwich and warming his fries. Khalil watched from the family room.

"You sure you don't want any of this?"

"Nah, I told you I'm straight."

Hezekiah had aged since Khalil last saw him. Wrinkles on his dad's face now told the story of those missed years.

Hezekiah entered the family room with his tray of food and sat across from his son, but the stiffness between them was so thick it could be cut with a knife.

Hezekiah sucked in a breath as if he didn't know how to begin. Words had never failed him in the past. But this time, he felt like someone whose tongue had been ripped out of his mouth.

"I... I think it's time we talked. Air some things out, you know."

"Hol' up right there, bruh. Don't start out lying. The only reason I'm sitting here in my mother's casita with you," he emphasized, "is because I just happened to be leaving when you were coming. You've been out of prison for months. Not once have you tried to reach out to me. You've only seen my daughter because of my mother and Eliana. So quit with the lies. I'm not up for it. I'm not." Khalil held his head in his hands and sighed in frustration.

"Okay. You're right. I could have reached out earlier. I should have, but we were all going through so much. Xavier's death, me trying to find my way again after being released, my lawyer running off with my life's savings."

"Wait. What?"

"What lawyer? What are you talking about? Attorney Black ripped you off?" Khalil knew it was not like his father to sit back and do nothing when someone crossed him. He used to have George and another dude to help him carry out his revenge acts when he felt he had been wronged. But George had died, and Khalil had no idea what had happened to the other fellow.

"No, not Black; I'm talking about Trevor Price."

"Price? Wasn't he killed in that earthquake in Morocco?"

"That's what they say. I didn't find out until after I got released that Price had scammed me, stole my life's savings, and fled the country. I've tried tracing his steps, looking into things he did before his death, but I found nothing that can tell me what he did with almost a half million dollars of mine. It's hard to feel sorry about his death, not after what he stole." Hezekiah fumed, just thinking about it. "If he *is* dead, it may be bad to say, but I hope he's rotting away in hell," he spewed.

"What? A half mil? Are you serious? How did that happen?"

"I don't want to talk about Price now. I'll get myself pissed off all over again. Right now, I want to focus on us, on getting things right with you," Hezekiah said.

"Why now? You're the one who walked out on your family. You walked out on me *and* Xavier. You went and got a kid on the outside while married to Mama. Not to mention, you accused me of stealing from you."

"And you're saying that you didn't?" Hezekiah said, sticking some fries into his mouth.

"What if I did? Would it be any worse than what you stole from Mama? You practically put us out on the streets. You set my mother up with some wanna-be Casanova dude who tricked her into falling in love with him and broke her heart. What kind of sick, crazy crap is that! And you want to talk about me stealing money from you? Where did *you* get the money you say I stole in the first place? Was it money you stole first—uh, like from Holy Rock?" Khalil accused.

"It's none of your business where I get my money or how I make it. You're sitting up here talking about Holy Rock when it was you who tried to send me to prison. You and Xavier are the ones who tried to set me up. But, you know what, Khalil, you're my firstborn son. I've already lost Xavier. I don't want to lose you too." Hezekiah's voice cracked. "So, let me start over by saying I regret the terrible things I did, but I can't undo any of that now. I would do anything if I *could* go back and have a chance to do things differently."

"What brought on the sudden change of heart?" Khalil inquired, his tone laced with skepticism.

"Life's short. I've missed out on a lot. I'm not talking about the three years in prison—that's a given. I'm talking about all I missed in your and Xavier's lives. I'm sorry."

"Sorry is easy to say," Khalil said, his tone softening, "but it can't erase the damage you caused."

"Look, I'm not asking you to forget about all the pain I brought on y'all, especially your mother. I'm not even asking you to forgive me. I'm just asking for a chance to be a part of your life again. I want to be around my beautiful little grand-daughter. I don't want us to be awkward and warring against each other anymore. I want us to come together again as father and son."

Khalil rose from his chair. "We'll see, Dad. We'll see. Look, I've got to bounce."

Hezekiah slowly rose, too. "Understood. We'll talk again soon—I hope."

"Yeah, soon."

Walking up the walkway and heading toward his car, Khalil felt a mixture of nervousness and resentment. The reasons for their estrangement were deep-rooted, and neither had let go of the hate that had driven a wedge between them. This evening was the breakthrough they needed so that healing could take place.

Hezekiah stood at the door and watched until Khalil disappeared from view. He mumbled a prayer, thanking God for the unlikely meeting. He understood they had a long way to go, but today was a start.

A soft rain had begun to fall. He closed the door, his shoulders tense. He looked away, his gaze fixed on the rain-streaked window. The wounds from the past were still fresh, and forgiveness seemed like a distant dream. He asked God to show him how to rebuild the crumbled and broken pieces of his life and the relationship with his son.

The longstanding flame of bitterness between them was still present, but perhaps the flame had dimmed a bit after tonight's talk. Father and son had come together, whether for closure, redemption, or for some reason unbeknownst to either of them.

Hezekiah's mind fell on Pastor. Pastor was someone else he needed to make amends with. Unlike the desire to reconnect with Khalil, he didn't have that same urge toward his father. Stiles had told him more than once that he should see Pastor. His dementia had worsened, according to Stiles, another excuse Hezekiah used. Why see him when it was highly likely that Pastor wouldn't know who he was? *Call*, he heard the voice in his head say—*just a quick call.*

He listened to the still, small voice and scrolled through his CONTACTS until he came upon Pastor's number. He dialed the number, not thinking about what he would say and not knowing the reason he was calling in the first place. He'd never had a relationship with Pastor. Why start something now?

"Hello," Josie answered.

"Uh, hello, Sista Josie?"

"Yes, who is this."

"Sista Josie, this is Hezekiah...Pastor Hezekiah McCoy. How are you?"

"Oh my, Lord. Hezekiah? I'm blessed, honey. Blessed and highly favored. I can't believe this is you on the phone."

"Yes, it's me. Uh, may I talk to Pastor? Just for a minute."

"Baby, I wish you could, but he's already asleep. I have to give him a sedative every evening. If I don't, he'll be up all night rambling around the house, mumbling, getting into some of everything."

"I understand. Well, look, I'm not going to hold you. I'll give you a call later this week or next week. I want to come by and see him, and you too, of course."

"Okay, that sounds nice. I look forward to seeing you. Is everything okay? How are you making it since you've been home?"

"Oh, I'm good. I'm just trying to get back to living life."

"Well, you take care of yourself. I'll tell Pastor you called.

He may or may not know who I'm talking about. His memory is fading fast." Her tone softened.

He detected sadness in her voice. "Josie, you hang in there. God's got you."

"I know, baby. I know. Well, thanks for calling. We hope to see you soon."

41
HOME SWEET HOME

"If you change nothing, nothing will change." Unknown

Khalil mentally replayed the encounter with his father. He wished he could believe he had genuinely changed and meant it when he said he was sorry, but doubt lingered. Hezekiah had always been highly articulate and had what was often referred to by older folks as the *gift of gab*, which he used to manipulate others when he deemed it to be for his benefit.

Turning onto his street, his phone rang. "Hey, Uncle Stiles. What's up?"

"Nothing much, just checking on you. It's been a minute since we talked. You straight?"

"I'm good. I would be even better if Eliana would bring my baby home."

"Have you talked to her?"

"Yes, I talked to her today."

"Did she give any indication as to when she was coming back?"

"She said soon. That was it. I told her I wanted to make this work between us."

"Do you?"

"What kind of question is that? Of course I do. The last thing I want is for Eliana and me to go our separate ways, and I look up and another man is raising my daughter. That's not gonna happen."

"You know what I have to say. It's the same thing I've said before. You need to leave my ex-wife alone. Detria is nothing but trouble. Can't you see that, man?"

"Yeah, I know, and I've ended things between us. But you were married to her, so you should know how hard it is to get Detria to back off. The good thing is she's left town. She's supposed to be gone for at least a couple of months, hopefully more. But, honestly, I wouldn't care if she never came back," Khalil said, shaking his head and chuckling into the phone.

"The thing about Eliana is that whenever she comes home, things can't be the same, man. It's going to take time before she trusts you again. I hope you realize that," Stiles said.

"I do." Khalil sighed.

"It's not like she's going to run into your arms and forget how you hurt her. Then again, maybe she will. She loves you, at least; that's the impression I get. I believe she wants her marriage to work."

"If that's true, then why did she leave?"

"Come on, Khalil. You're not slow. There's only so much a person can take. Especially from a guy like you."

"Hey, a guy like me? What's that supposed to mean?"

"Figure it out. Look, we'll talk later. Mya is calling."

"Okay, later," said Khalil.

Arriving home and pulling into his driveway, he pressed

the remote inside his car and slowly drove toward the garage door as it opened. When he saw Eliana's car in her spot, he hurried to get out of the car and rushed into the house.

"Eliana! Eliana!"

"I'm upstairs," he heard her reply.

He dashed up the stairs, two at a time. Rushing into their bedroom, he stopped and looked around but didn't see her. He went into their bathroom, but she wasn't there. On to the next room, Khaliyah's bedroom on the other side of the house. He stopped in the doorway. His heart swelled with happiness seeing his little girl and his wife.

"Hi, Daddy," Khaliyah said with a big smile on her precious little face.

Khalil rushed toward her and scooped her into his arms. He planted butterfly kisses all over her, embracing her tightly as they swung around and around. "I missed you so much, my sweet baby girl."

Eliana folded her arms and watched the loving scene of father and daughter. She knew Khalil had missed his daughter, but what about her? Did he miss her? Or was Khaliyah the only reason he wanted her to come back home? She'd asked herself this question over and over.

She loved Khalil, but his cheating ways had all but killed their relationship, and she felt like her love for him was beginning to wane. Nevertheless, she had come back to him. Her mother told her that all marriages have problems and men are likely to cheat—as long as he took care of home and wasn't abusive.

Still holding Khaliyah, he approached Eliana and pulled her into his arms. Embracing both of them, he kissed Eliana long and hard as if he did miss her.

Eliana melted in the safety of his arms, succumbing to his

demanding kisses. As if something had pinched her, she pulled away.

"Oh, my God. You don't know how glad I am you're home," he whispered. "Home where you and my baby belong."

Later that evening, after putting Khaliyah to bed, Khalil made his desire for his wife known. He wanted her but was still determining whether she would welcome his advances. To his disappointment, she did not respond when his kisses and touch became more eager, revealing his desire.

"I hope you didn't think I came home to run into your waiting arms. This is not a movie. The only reason I came back was because of Khaliyah. She kept asking about you. As for running into your arms and getting in our bed, it's not going to be like that, Khalil. I can't do it. But don't worry, I won't embarrass you in public. On the outside, everyone will think we have the perfect marriage and family. I'll continue my role as First Lady until we decide," she pointed at herself and him, "if this can survive. Oh, and I'll be sleeping in the guest room. Goodnight."

An awkward and uncertain tension hung in the air as she turned and left their bedroom. This moment served as a reminder of the emotional abyss that had grown between them, leaving him worried that his marriage could very well be over.

†

Eliana sat in the center of the bed and checked the baby monitor. Khaliyah was sleeping peacefully. She grabbed her phone and texted Pepper.

> Eliana: I'm home.

Pepper: Good. Was he there when u got there?

Eliana: No, He got here not long ago.

Pepper: How'd it go?

Eliana: You already know he wanted some. Girl, please. Lol

Pepper: LOL. You give him some?

Eliana: R u serious? No way. He has to earn this. I still don't trust him. No telling who he was screwing while I was gone.

Pepper: You said the slut was out of town.

Eliana: So? Doesn't mean he didn't hook up with another one.

Pepper: I hope not. That's nasty. SMH.

Eliana: It sure is.

Pepper: I'm glad you're back. Maybe you and Khaliyah can come over tomorrow.

Eliana: Maybe. Depends on the weather. supposed to be freezing rain.

Pepper: Aww. We'll see how it goes.

Eliana: Okay. TTYL.

42
JUSTICE BEST SERVED WARM

"Someday, you'll look back on this and see it as a blessing. Just not today." Anonymous

Fancy spent most of her afternoon meeting with the ministry leaders at Holy Rock. The church's various ministries gave her something to do as a ministry consultant, but it was not a full-time position. It was more or less a made-up position assigned to her by Khalil to keep her on the church payroll. But Fancy took her role seriously.

Being a ministry consultant and taking on clients for her interior design business was beginning to keep her quite busy. She welcomed the busyness because it helped her cope with her ongoing grief.

"I'm leaving," she waved and said to Sista Mavis as she passed the front office.

"Goodnight. Be safe out there," Sista Mavis replied.

"I will, and you too."

As soon as she settled into her seat, her phone rang. She closed the car door and then looked at the screen. "Umm, Hezekiah? What could he want?"

"Hello."

"Fancy."

"What is it, Hezekiah? Is everything all right?"

"Yes, everything's fine. Look, I'm about to leave New Holy Rock. I'm going to stop by Brady's Barbeque Joint. I know how much you like their food or used to like them," he auto-corrected himself.

"Yes, I still love them. They have the best barbeque spaghetti. Um...mmm," she said. "I just haven't been over their way in a while."

"Do you want me to bring you something? That's the reason I was calling."

She thought about it for a second before replying. "Uh, sure," and proceeded to give him her order.

"Okay, I'll see you in about forty-five minutes."

"Okay." Her lips curled into a smile as she replied, "Thanks," before ending the call.

No sooner had the call ended than her phone rang again. This time, it was Stiles calling on video chat.

"Hey, there."

"Hey, how's it going? I haven't talked to you in a few days."

"I know, but whose fault is that? Mya is the one keeping you on a tight leash."

Stiles laughed. "I won't lie. The girl has my head spinning."

"I'm happy for you. Mya seems like a good woman."

"You don't have to tell me. Believe me, I know. That's one of the reasons I was calling. Her birthday is coming up in a few weeks, the day before Thanksgiving. I want to do something special. I need some suggestions."

"The day before Thanksgiving, huh? Maybe on Thanksgiving this year, we can have a side celebration, like a birthday cake in her favorite flavor. And if you find her favorite color, maybe I can incorporate it into decorating."

"That would work."

"Okay, good. Well, I'm headed to the house. We can talk some more when I get there."

"Okay, cool. So is, uh, everything okay with you?"

"Oh, yes. I'm leaving Holy Rock and heading home. Oh, and guess what? I don't know if you heard, but he saw Khalil. It was not planned, but nothing is accidental with God. I believe it was a divine setup."

"Yeah, Hezekiah told me."

"Did he say how Khalil reacted?"

"Not really, only that Khalil seemed receptive. He didn't shut him out. I say it was a big move for Khalil to even sit down with his dad, let alone have a sit-down conversation. I believe this could be the start of healing between them."

"I sure hope so, Stiles."

"Oh, what surprised me, too, was Hezekiah calling Pastor. He told Josie he would come by and visit them soon. That was another step in the right direction for him. He said he had amends to make before he felt worthy of preaching again."

"We'll see what redemption looks like for him," said Fancy, frowning. "I just hope he's changed."

"Give him a chance, Fancy."

"You're easier on him, I guess, because he's your brother, but if he got out of prison only to hurt my son again, I would never forgive him, Stiles. Never."

"If I believed he was on that path again, I would do everything I could to stop him. You have my word on that."

"Thank you."

"No need to thank me. I'm just telling the truth. You are too important to me. You're more than a sister-in-law. You're my road dawg." Stiles laughed, and so did Fancy. "How is the land-lord-tenant situation?"

"I have no complaints. I rarely see him. If the grandkids come to the house, I might call him up sometimes and invite him over. He brought his other kid to the house the other day. But there's nothing I can say about that."

"To the house? You mean he brought him to the casita, right? Not to your actual house?"

"Yes, the casita."

Stiles saw her expression and said, "Right, but as tough as it might be for you to see him with Jude, that *is* his son. It's only right that he wants to spend time with him."

"I know that, but it still hurts to know that he had a child during our marriage. It's just another something that keeps me from being able to trust him. I say I'm not angry at him, but then again, how can I not be, Stiles, when he's caused so much pain?"

"I wish there was a blueprint to healing, but it doesn't work that way. You can only move past it with God's help."

"Yeah, you're right," she reluctantly agreed. "Ok, enough about that. Has he heard anything about his missing money?"

Stiles shook his head. "You mean, *if* there's any money left. But nah, nothing's turned up. And since Price and his wife have officially been declared dead, there's not much, if anything, that can be done. Hezekiah is sick about it, of course. He wants to hurt Trevor Price. The thing is, the dude is already dead."

"I'm glad he has Black to help him. He and his wife are good people."

"Yeah, they are. But as for his money, I don't see what Black can do about that. The secret to where that money is, if there's any left, is buried with Price."

"Surely, that man did not rob him of all his money. You think?"

"I think he did, Fancy. There's not a single trace of where it could be. And it looks like there's nothing Hezekiah can do. The man was his POA. He had the right and the means to control his accounts and assets."

"That's a shame. I want to feel bad for him, and in a way, I do. But I also know what the Bible says. You reap what you sow."

"Right," Stiles agreed.

"Well, let me get off this call and head home. I'm still sitting in the parking lot. We'll talk more later about Mya's birthday."

"Okay, later."

†

Hezekiah stood at Pastor and Josie's door, hesitating before knocking.

"Come on in here," she said, opening the side door and gesturing for him to enter.

He hugged her tightly. "It's good to see you, Josie."

"It's good to see you too. You look good," Josie said, chuckling.

She led him through the kitchen and into the family room. Dark furniture and hardwoods made the space appear dreary and lacking in light.

Pastor was seated in a well-worn brown fabric recliner, his legs slightly tilted. He was fixated on the television.

"Pastor, look who's here."

Hezekiah walked up to Pastor. Pastor didn't move, didn't look up, or say a word.

"Hi, Pastor, how are you?" Hezekiah kneeled in front of the frail man. He took hold of his hand. Pastor pulled back slightly, and Hezekiah released his grip.

"I came to check on you and Josie. I know it's been a while since I've seen you. But life has its own agenda, you know."

"Sit right there," said Josie, pointing to the matching recliner next to Pastor.

"But that's your chair, isn't it, Josie?"

"Don't mind that. Sit there. I'm going back here and roll my hair while you visit with him."

"Sure, go right ahead."

Josie left the room, and Hezekiah focused on his father. "I don't know how much you can understand, but here goes." Hezekiah sat in the chair and turned toward Pastor. "I came here to get some things off my chest. Here I am, sitting across from a man who never acknowledged me as his son. But you raised my brother, a kid who isn't yours." Hezekiah chuckled. "I know I shouldn't hold it against you. I understand that my mother was crazy as heck, and she didn't tell you about me. I get that. Either way, I'm here."

Pastor remained stoic and quiet.

"Why am I not surprised that it would be like this? Your firstborn son, and you don't know me from those people on the screen." He pointed briefly at the screen.

Hezekiah stopped talking and looked at Pastor for some reaction.

Pastor said nothing. Hezekiah kept talking.

"I'm here because I'm trying to be a better man." He looked around and peered over his shoulder. He heard Josie in the other room talking on the phone, so he kept talking.

Pastor was still staring at the screen. An episode of Judge Mathis, one of Pastor and Josie's favorite TV shows, was playing.

Hezekiah picked up the remote and turned the volume down. "Pastor, I'm here to tell you that I forgive you. I look in the mirror sometimes and see a version of you in me. And you know what? It sickens me because I have to keep reminding myself that you didn't know about me." Hezekiah chuckled. "I spent the past three years in prison, so I had a lot of time to think. Now that I'm home, I wanted to tell you personally that I forgive you."

Slowly, Hezekiah rose from the chair. "Look." He stood in front of Pastor, blocking his view of the screen. "I'm going to head to my side of town. I'm glad I got a chance to see you and Josie." He tapped Pastor on the shoulder, moved aside, and went toward the hall. "Josie."

"Coming," he heard her say.

While waiting for Josie to return to the den, Hezekiah studied the framed certificates lining the walls and pictures of Pastor in his preaching days. He imagined himself being in a museum of history that was all about his father.

"Thanks for staying," Josie said, piercing his thoughts.

"You don't have to thank me, Josie. You said someone comes to put him to bed?"

"Yes, he has a CNA that comes in the evening. He should be here in a minute."

"I can still help put him to bed." He looked at Pastor.

Josie approached Pastor. "Okay." She looked at Pastor. "Honey, it's time for bed. Here," she placed the remote in his hand. "Turn it off," she told him. She put her hand over his and gently pressed the OFF button. "Come on."

Pastor slowly rose. Hezekiah got on the other side of Pastor and helped him stand.

With Josie's arm looped inside one of his, they walked up the hallway to Pastor's bedroom and helped him get in bed— soft gospel music filtered through the room, which seemed to soothe Pastor.

"That was easy tonight. Thank God," she said as they left the room.

"What? Is it not always like this?"

"Not always. Sometimes, he can be combative. Thank God for Sam, his CNA. He's good with Pastor. The sedative helps, too, of course."

Hezekiah waved at Pastor. He began to feel bad for Josie.

"Thanks for coming. Now that you're home, maybe you'll come by more often. I know you probably think he doesn't understand you, but believe me, he does. Watch, he's going to start rambling about it in a day or two, in bits and pieces, out of the blue." Josie laughed.

"Is that so?"

"Yeah. That's how it usually happens, and then he'll go silent again until," she shrugged, "until the next time."

Standing at the open back door, Hezekiah gently asked, "Have you considered placing him in an extended memory care facility?"

"I have, but early in our marriage, Pastor and I promised one another that we would never put the other one in a nursing home unless, of course, one of us could no longer care for the other. I think that time has come. I love Pastor, God knows I do, but honey, I'm eighty-eight years young," Josie cackled, "this body wears out quicker. I thank the good Lord for allowing me to do what I do."

"Josie, God bless you. You've got to take care of yourself too, though."

"I know, I know. And I already talked to Stiles about finding a place. It's in the works." Her eyes wandered over his shoulders, causing Hezekiah to turn around.

"Excuse me," the bronze-skinned young man said.

"Good evening, Sam," Josie said.

"Hello, Mrs. Graham."

"Sam, this is Pastor Hezekiah McCoy."

The young man, in his thirties, greeted Hezekiah with a

firm handshake and eye contact.

"Sam comes four nights a week. Pastor hardly ever puts up a fight with him. Isn't that right, Sam?"

"Yes, ma'am. He rarely gives me a hard time." Sam laughed.

"He's a godsend." Josie smiled and affectionately squeezed Sam's arm.

"I'm sorry to tell you that I'll be leaving the agency at the end of the month," Sam apologized.

"Is that so?"

"Yes, ma'am. I got a job making more money with better hours and great benefits."

"What a blessing, and no need to be sorry," Josie said, moving to the side so he could come inside. "God is promoting you. You have a wife and a new baby. I'm thankful for the time God sent you to us."

Hezekiah patted Sam on the back. "Congratulations, and God bless you, young man."

"Thank you, sir," Sam said, disappearing into the house.

"What about the days when he isn't here? Does someone else come?"

"Yes," she said, nodding. "I pay out of pocket with Stiles's help. But he still says having Pastor in the house is too much for me."

"I think I agree with my brother, and we're going to figure it out. Don't you worry. I'll call you." Hezekiah hugged her and left.

His father was in worse condition than he expected. Why in the world was the man still living at home with Josie? That woman could barely get around herself, let alone be a caretaker for a man with dementia. He called Stiles. No answer.

"Hey, call me when you get a minute. It's about Pastor." He ended the call and continued driving. More rain was in the forecast.

43

I'LL BE THERE

"Love is giving someone the power to destroy you but trusting them not to." Unknown

Entering the gate and following the paved walkway, Hezekiah heard Fancy weakly calling his name. Looking to his right, he saw her sprawled on the slick, wet concrete surface. He rushed over to her. The constant rain carried a flow of blood from her head wound along the path like a red river.

"Good Lord, Fancy! What happened?"

"I was taking out the trash and lost my footing. I didn't know it was so slippery," she winced as she looked over her shoulder at the trashcan with its contents scattered across the soggy grass.

"Come on, let's get you up. That's a nasty-looking gash over your eye. And it's bleeding pretty bad." He swooped her into his arms and rushed through the rain to his car.

"Where are you going?" she cried.

"I'm taking you to urgent care."

"No, Hezekiah, that's not necessary," she weakly protested. "I have a first aid kit in the house. I can clean it up."

"Nope. It's deep, I told you. I don't like the way it looks. And your eye is just about swollen shut."

"Okay." She laid her head against his headrest. He went inside his trunk and returned with a bag of towels with the tags still attached.

"Uh, I bought these a few weeks ago."

"You never took them inside?" she tried to laugh, but her head was splitting.

"Yeah, something like that," he said, pulling off a tag and lovingly covering her head with one of them.

Three and a half hours later, they were back home. Fancy required eight staples above her left eye. She was given an injection for pain—another shot of antibiotics, and a prescription.

She was exhausted by the time they arrived home. He assisted her to the bedroom.

"Do you need anything?" he asked as he went to her dresser, got her a fresh nightgown, and took it over to where she lay.

She put on the nightgown, not bothering to shield herself from her ex-husband. She was not in the frame of mind to hide from him. She only wanted to crawl into bed and go to sleep. The effects of the pain shot were quickly taking effect.

"I'm cold. Will you give me a blanket? It's one on the top shelf in the bathroom closet."

Hezekiah retrieved the blanket and placed it over her.

"Thanks for everything," Fancy mumbled drowsily, the shot seemingly taking over.

"You're welcome. If you're okay. I'm going to go now. I'll

lock up. Okay?"

"No, don't go. Stay. I don't want to be alone. What if I have to get up to pee? I don't want to fall again," her words slurred.

He grinned. "Okay, I'll be in the family room. On the couch."

He glanced back to find her sound asleep just that quick. He quietly shut her bedroom door before heading to the kitchen. After pouring himself a glass of wine, he went to the family room.

†

Hezekiah made a veggie omelet, buttered toast, and coffee. With a smile, he carried the food tray into Fancy's room and found her still sleeping. Despite the row of staples across her forehead and a swollen, purple bruise framing her eye—she was perfect in Hezekiah's eyes. He placed the tray on the nightstand beside her and turned to leave.

"Thank you," she whispered, inhaling the aroma waking her from her sleep.

He turned and saw her sitting in bed, rubbing her uninjured eye.

Her phone rang. "Good morning. Yes. Thank you," she said and ended the call, returning her attention to the tray of food. "Smell's good. It looks delicious, too, but you didn't have to do this."

She took several bites, humming her approval as she indulged. "Aren't you supposed to be at New Holy Rock? What time is it anyway?" she looked around, confused.

"A little after nine. And no, I'm not going to the office or anywhere else. It's Saturday."

"Oh, dang. Saturday. That's right." She felt her head. "Ewww, that hurts." She grabbed a napkin off the tray and wiped her hands and mouth before picking up the cup of coffee and taking a sip.

The doorbell rang.

"Expecting somebody?" he asked, looking at her as he stuck his head in the bedroom door.

"Oh, yes, the guard gate called. That should be Vicky."

He went to the door.

A big smile spread across Victoria's face when Hezekiah opened the door.

"Uh, why, good morning, Pastor McCoy." Stuttering, she said, "Uh, I is...uh."

"Come in, Victoria," he quipped. "Fancy's in the bedroom. Would you like some breakfast?" he offered as she followed him, in shock, inside the house.

"Breakfast? Uh, no. I don't guess. Is everything okay?"

"Victoria?" Fancy weakly called out.

"I'm coming."

"Come on in, Vicky," Fancy beckoned when her friend appeared at the doorway.

"Oh my gosh, What's going on? What happened to you?" she rushed to the side of Fancy's bed when she saw her face.

"I fell outside last night taking out the trash. I didn't realize until it was too late that the rain was beginning to freeze up. Before I knew it, my feet had slipped from under me, and I hit my head. Thank goodness Hezekiah showed up when he did. I was still on the ground when he came. He took me to urgent care." Fancy instinctively touched her bandage and the line of staples across her forehead.

"Are you sure you're okay?" Victoria sat on the side of the bed.

"Yes. I feel better than I did."

"Is she okay, Hezekiah?" she asked for reassurance.

"Other than a slight concussion and that nasty wound, yes,

the doctor says she's going to be fine. Say, are you sure you don't want anything?"

"No, I'm good, Hezekiah. Thanks, though."

"I'm going to the back while Victoria's here," he said. "I'll be back up shortly."

"Okay."

"I'm not going to be here for very long, Hezekiah. Maybe about half an hour or so."

"Okay, I'll be back before you leave, or you can call me on the baby monitor when you're leaving.'

"Baby monitor?" Victoria eyed him curiously.

He threw up a hand and disappeared.

Fancy spoke up. "He took it to his place so he could see me and make sure I'm okay. You know, just until I feel better."

"*Ohhhkay*. How thoughtful." Victoria smiled.

"Yes, I thought so, too." Fancy ate more bites of food.

"Hmmm, I see Reverend McCoy is taking good care of you." Victoria laughed and winked at a yawning Fancy.

"Don't start, Victoria." Fancy giggled, her voice trailing off when it caused pain. "*Ohhh*, my head hurts."

"Okay, well, seeing that you went and almost killed yourself, I'm going to give you a pass, but you know what I'm thinking about the two of you."

"Will you put this over there?" she asked Victoria.

Victoria picked up the food tray and took it into the kitchen instead. She returned with a glass of water and sat it beside the bed.

"Thanks." Fancy removed a pill from the prescription bottle and took one, followed by a swallow of water.

The ladies discussed the upcoming Thanksgiving gathering Fancy and Victoria planned to host.

Fancy yawned again, and her words became loopy.

Victoria rose and pressed the baby monitor. "We'll talk

some more when you feel better."

"Yeah, later this week. I'll be better by then, I'm sure."

"I'm just glad you're going to be okay. It could have been so much worse. I'll check on you later." She rose from the side of the bed and left. Before she reached the front door, Hezekiah walked in through the back door.

"Take care, Victoria," he said as he escorted her to the door.

"Thanks, you too."

"Need anything?" Hezekiah asked, appearing at Fancy's bedroom door after Victoria left.

"No, I'm good. Thanks. I'm going back to sleep. That delicious breakfast plus that pain pill have me sleepy again. What are you about to do?"

"I'm going to make sure everything is picked up in the kitchen, and then I'm going to call Stiles. I called him earlier and told him about your fall. He said he may stop by later."

She laughed. "I fell, Hezekiah. It's not that serious. I don't need to be treated like the sick and shut-in."

He chuckled. "I don't know about that."

Hezekiah was a man of many sides. He could be kind, concerned, and sympathetic, with a sensuality that could set her soul ablaze. As she lay in bed, reveling in his innate ability to be attentive and loving, her body tingled with desire, even amid her throbbing headache. She missed the touch of his lips and the warmth of his embrace. But she was also all too familiar with the side of him that awakened inner turmoil and reminded her why she had kept her distance. She knew that it would be a difficult path to tread if she ever accepted him back into her life. The reality of their tumultuous history echoed in her mind. Still, her heart couldn't lie.

Later the same day, Khalil called. "I'll be right over," he said after she told him about her fall.

"I'm okay, Khalil. Really, I am," she tried convincing him.

"I want to see for myself. I'm leaving Holy Rock now and heading your way. You need me to bring you anything?"

"No, I'm good, son." Fancy shook her head, sighing. *Thank God for people who care.*

†

"Hello, Khalil," Hezekiah said, opening the front door.

"Hi, how is she?" Khalil asked, stepping into the house.

"See for yourself," Hezekiah said and pointed toward the back of the house.

Khalil went to his mother's room and saw her reading a book in her bedroom chair. Her head was swollen, and one eye was black and blue. He frowned, seeing the staples along her forehead.

"Mama." He walked over to her. "Good grief. You definitely had a bad fall." He studied the staples and her eye.

"It looks worse than it actually feels," she reassured him.

"Mama, why were you outside at night and in the rain, taking out the trash anyway? That could have waited."

"I told her I would take it out from here on out, at least as long as I'm living out back."

Khalil nodded. "You hear that, Mama? Dad said he'll take out your trash."

"Ok, okay. I hear you. And thanks, Hezekiah."

"I'm going to the casita. Khalil, let me know when you're leaving, and I'll come back up here."

"Please, Hezekiah, you don't have to come back. I told you I'm fine. I know how to call for help if I need it. Really, please don't treat me like a baby."

"Mama, let him check on you."

"Ugh, okay, whatever, y'all."

"I'll be back," Hezekiah said again. "Take care, son."

When she heard the back door closing, she looked at Khalil and said, "Seems like you're civil. That talk you had must have done both of you some good." She smiled.

"I wouldn't say all that. I mean, I appreciate what he said, but it can never erase how he did you."

"I told you to let it go, Khalil. You see, he's trying to be a better person."

"Maybe he is, but a lot of folks don't think he is. And look at what's happening with New Holy Rock."

"What about New Holy Rock?"

"Come on, Mama, I heard people have been leaving ever since he came back. They say the church would be empty if he got up to preach. Stiles is the only reason they're holding on to the members they have."

"It's not that bad," Fancy said, throwing up a hand. "Yes, I can attest that the sanctuary is not as full as it used to be. But I think that'll change once Hezekiah addresses the church like he should. He says he's not ready, that God is still preparing him."

"Yeah, well, I can't say what's in his heart. That's between him and God. I'm trying to get my own house in order. I can't get caught up with what's going on with him. All I'm saying is don't *you* fall for him again, Mama. I don't trust him."

"I know, sweetheart. I know. But I'm just trying to let the past stay in the past and move forward. This family has been through too much as it is. I can't stand any more heartache. Not now. I want things to be better."

Khalil kneeled next to his mother and took hold of one of her hands. "Look, I told you about worrying. I want you to be happy. I don't want you walking around looking like you're carrying the world's weight on your shoulders."

Fancy leaned back and gave Khalil a weird look. "Boy, please, I hope I'm not looking that bad."

44
PREPARING TO GIVE THANKS

"When eating fruit, remember the one who planted the tree."
Vietnamese Proverb

One week after her accident, Fancy was back to feeling like her usual self, but the physical signs of her injury were still present. The staples were set to be removed the following week, but only time could heal the bruising around her eye.

Fancy and Victoria finally met for lunch, sharing a spicy taco from the Taco House.

"I think we should have a traditional Thanksgiving menu. What do you think?" Fancy asked.

"Traditional is good, but we should also have nontraditional selections and celebrate Mya's birthday. I was thinking about a big seafood platter and vegetarian options, too. You know, something for everyone!" exclaimed Victoria.

"Yeah! That's a good idea," Fancy replied, adding items to the list she was making on her phone.

"Are you sure Mya will enjoy celebrating her birthday on Thanksgiving?"

"Her birthday is the day *before* Thanksgiving, so I don't see why she would. This was Stiles's idea; it will be a surprise, nothing big. He said she doesn't have family here other than her son. I think he's around seventeen. According to Mya, he spends a lot of time with his father and his new family. So, he may or may not come."

"Well, we need to get our shopping and ordering done. Thanksgiving is only three weeks away."

"Right. Stiles said Mya's favorite cake is coconut layer. We can have that as her birthday cake. Of course, we'll have more than one flavor of cake."

"Okay, let's stop at the bakery when we leave and put in our order," Victoria said.

"I hope it's the same bakery where you got those cakes from on Easter."

"Yes, Eve's Bakery. Her cakes and pies are the best," Victoria said. "And she makes them from scratch. Yum." Victoria sat across the table, licking her lips. "I can taste one of them now."

"I know that's right. Let's use the same caterers we used last year for the Thanksgiving dinner.

"Sounds perfect," said Victoria.

"Okay, so let's recap. Thanksgiving menu will be catered." She rattled off the list of things they had discussed. "Oh, we need to order the decorations."

"That's right. We can order those today. I have some of the ideas saved in my online cart."

"Okay, we can take a look after eating."

"Good. I told Stiles that he and his crew were responsible for decorating the clubhouse."

Victoria raised an eyebrow.

"Under our supervision—on his dime," Fancy added, and both ladies started laughing.

†

Fancy finished the leftover dessert from the taco restaurant and headed to the kitchen to clean up. Suddenly, she heard a tap on the back door. She immediately knew it was Hezekiah. Since her fall, he had been stopping by every evening to check on her when he returned home. When she pulled back the curtain, she saw his handsome, rugged face.

"Hi," she said, opening the door dressed in a knee-length, plain but cute oversized nightshirt.

"You good?" he asked, remaining just outside the door.

"Yes, thanks for asking. I've had a good day. Vicky and I went to the Taco Spot for lunch. I have one left if you want it?"

"Nah, thanks. I'm good. We had a hearty lunch at church today. That's what's in here," he said, half holding up a brown paper bag. "Good ole leftovers."

Fancy smiled. "Okay. Well, thanks for stopping by."

"Is that the trash?" he asked, pointing with his eyes to the large white plastic bag at the door.

"Oh, yes, I'll take it out in the—"

Hezekiah stepped past her and picked up the trash bag. "We've had this discussion. Have a good night, Fancy." He turned to leave.

Fancy blushed. "Thanks."

She closed the door but continued peering through the kitchen window and watched him strut up the walkway, stopping only to throw the bag in the trashcan.

Checking the door to ensure she locked it, she then turned off the kitchen light and went to her bedroom. After saying her prayers, she got in bed and went to sleep with thoughts of, surprisingly, Dr. Micah Daniels, her old love. May he rest in peace. Micah was one of the good ones. She thought about how smooth their relationship was going, only to have it tragically end all too soon. In some ways, he had reminded her of the good things she saw in Hezekiah.

The sound of her text alert interrupted her stroll down memory lane.

Hezekiah: May your sleep be as sweet as you.
🤍

She smiled at Hezekiah's text. Then she turned on her side, closed her eyes, and fell asleep.

45
A DAY OF THANKSGIVING

"We can only be said to be alive in those moments when our hearts are conscious of our treasures." Thornton Wilder

Thanksgiving morning, Fancy and Victoria did a final walk-through of the clubhouse. The night before, Stiles and a small crew met them at the clubhouse to prepare it for today's event.

The space was transferred to look completely different. The decorations were beautifully done and added a festive charm to the area. The Thanksgiving theme was evident in the decor, with golden tablecloths and rustic centerpieces featuring pumpkins, gourds, and autumn leaves. The aroma of spiced candles filled the air, creating a warm and cozy ambiance combined with soft lighting.

Among the Thanksgiving decorations were subtle tributes in remembrance of Xavier. There were also more apparent salutes to Mya's 45th birthday, with teal accents, her favorite color, seamlessly blending into the overall design, including table runners, napkin rings, and a string of edible delicate teal ribbons embellishing the celebratory cake. It was a welcoming space for family and friends to celebrate.

"Everything looks perfect," said Victoria.

"Doesn't it," added Fancy.

"Girl, you decorated the mess out of this place. Then again, your designs are always fire," complimented Victoria.

Fancy responded with a grateful grin. "I couldn't have done any of this without your help," she expressed, giving her best friend an affectionate squeeze. "Oh, we have to remember to give Stiles an extra pat on the back, too. He did everything just like we wanted."

"He sure did. Well, let's get out of here. We need to get changed so we can be back in time to meet the caterers and greet the guests."

†

Stiles picked up his keys, put his wallet in his back pocket, and gazed at the gift in his hand. If Mya accepted it, their lives could change forever. He was worried that it might be too much, too fast. Yesterday was her birthday, which she celebrated with her son at a fancy restaurant. This afternoon, Stiles was taking her to his family's annual Thanksgiving celebration.

Mya was unaware that Stiles had asked Fancy to include a small birthday recognition in her honor. But her chosen attire was perfect. She was stylish in a teal blue pantsuit with a tailored embroidered jacket. Along the way, after picking up Mya, Stiles stopped and picked up Pastor and Josie.

Mya's mouth fell open when they entered the clubhouse.

Tears welled up in her eyes when she saw her favorite color, teal, woven into the space.

"You like it?" Stiles asked. "I told Fancy it was your birthday, and I wanted to do something special." He squeezed her hand as they walked further into the clubhouse.

"Like it? This place is stunning."

Fancy and Victoria appeared.

"You did this, Fancy?"

"Yes, me and Vicky," Fancy answered, grabbing Victoria's elbow and squeezing her best friend. "And, of course, none of this could have happened without your man and his crew." She laughed and walked up and embraced Stiles and then Mya.

"I don't know what to say. Is this... I see my favorite color, and there's a...a 45th birthday cake over there," she said, spotting the table ahead in the corner, adorned with a massive cake with a 45 topper. "I'm speechless. What do I say?"

"The look on your face says it all. Stiles, please take Mya to your reserved table."

"Reserved? Thank you, thank you, so much," Mya said, wiping tears, grasping Stiles's hand and looking lovingly into his eyes.

Fancy then turned and focused on her ex-father-in-law and his wife. "Pastor and Josie," I'm so glad you were able to come," she said more to Josie than Pastor, who looked like he had no idea where he was. "Stiles, thanks for picking them up."

"My pleasure," he said to Fancy.

"Everything looks so pretty," Josie said, holding Pastor's arm so he wouldn't get away from her.

Pastor looked around the clubhouse, his eyes bright as a baby's. His extremely frail frame made his suit look like it was about to swallow him whole. He gripped his walker.

"Take your time, Pastor," Stiles told him as he and Mya guided the couple to their table.

"Thanks again," Stiles said, kissing Fancy and Victoria on the cheek before walking slowly away with Pastor.

"Thank you so much," added a still overwhelmed Mya. "We'll see you a little later."

†

Khalil stood before the floor length mirror, surveying his chosen attire for this afternoon's Thanksgiving gathering. He donned black trousers tapered at the calf and a sleek black jacket tailored to enhance his broad shoulders. Beneath the coat, he wore a crisp white and black checkered shirt, the fabric immaculately pressed to perfection. The shirt's collar framed his face, drawing attention to his chiseled jawline and well-groomed appearance. He was definitely a younger version of his father.

The carefully put together outfit created a polished and sophisticated look. This man effortlessly captured attention with his commanding presence and impeccable fashion sense.

Baby Khaliyah was just as cute. When they were done getting dressed, they paraded into the kitchen to gather any last-minute items for Khaliyah. On the outside, they could pass for the ideal perfect family—if only folks knew what went on behind closed doors—or what *didn't* go on behind closed doors.

"You look beautiful," he complimented his wife.

"Thank you," she said dryly. There was a time when a compliment from him would have melted her heart, but not anymore. She didn't doubt his sincerity. She agreed with him, not in an arrogant way, but she was confident that she looked good. The seventeen pounds she'd lost, not all the way intentional, had given her an extra boost to her self-esteem. Her outfit of choice was a festive pumpkin-colored blazer with long sleeves and a knot at the waist that she paired with straight-leg pants and matching stilettos.

Khalil walked up to her. "Hmm, looking good *and* smelling good too? Girl, what you tryin' to do to me?" he said, smiling devilishly.

Eliana was too quick; she stepped back as he reached for her. Half-turning, she extended her hand toward their daughter. "Come on, Khaliyah."

Khaliyah ran up and took hold of her mother's hand.

"Ready?" she said to Khalil.

Expressionless, he nodded and turned to the door leading to the garage.

On the drive, she scrolled on her phone, Khaliyah played on her tablet, and Khalil, a bit salty after Eliana shrugged him off, paid attention to the road.

When they arrived at the clubhouse twenty minutes later, they were greeted by Fancy and Victoria. They made small talk, but Eliana carried the conversation more than Khalil.

"Excuse me, sweetheart," he finally said as she chatted.

"Yes?" she paused her conversation and looked at him.

"I see Pastor Eddins." The pastors had spoken at each other's churches on special occasions. "I'm going to go over and say hello."

"Sure," she said. "Oh, honey, Khaliyah wants to go with you. Right, baby?"

Khaliyah ran up to her daddy. Khalil grabbed his little girl's hand, and they walked off.

"I'm so glad you and Khaliyah came back home," Fancy said when Khalil left.

"Look, you two go on and talk. I'm going to check on the caterers and make sure everything is in place." Victoria excused herself and walked away.

"You look fabulous, by the way."

"Thanks," Eliana blushed.

"I just hope you're not *worrying* your weight off, though," Fancy said, concerned.

"In the beginning, maybe it was worry and stress, but these last pounds are because I intentionally changed my eating habits."

"Good for you. I don't want my son to be the cause of, well...you know what I'm saying."

"He's not, at least not anymore. I made up my mind—I'm no longer going to let him stress me out."

Fancy nodded. "I'm glad to hear that. He's my son, but no man is worth losing your peace of mind and sanity."

"You know, he swears he's not cheating anymore. I don't know if he is or not. I told him he has to prove himself because his words don't mean a thing. At this stage in our marriage, so much damage has been done that I can't say if things will work out in the long run for me and Khalil. My feelings are different, and that's a little scary. I want to do something for myself. Maybe put my degree to use."

"Have you thought about doing something outside the house? Maybe for a few hours until Khaliyah gets older."

"Yes, but I haven't decided what I want to do. But I'm going to do something," Eliana said.

"One thing I can say is going through what you're going through with him is making you strong. I see it in you. I hear it in your voice," Fancy said and embraced her daughter-in-law.

"Thanks, Fancy. That means a lot coming from you."

†

Hezekiah helped Pepper get Davion and Zavion out of the vehicle.

"You ready?" he asked.

"Yes," she said, forcing a smile. "As ready as I'm going to be. Are you sure I look okay?"

"You look perfect," Hezekiah reassured his daughter-in-law. He then looked at the boys. "Doesn't your mother look pretty?"

"Yeah, yeah," they said and broke out into laughter.

Pepper chose a tasteful knee-length, paisley print Boho dress while the boys wore jeans and colorful polo shirts.

This would be the first Thanksgiving without Xavier. Nothing would ever be the same. The heartache remained as she strived to create a sense of normalcy for her two small boys, who, in their innocence, still searched for their father's comforting presence.

Today's gathering was like a bittersweet dance. She was stuck between honoring Xavier's memory and forging ahead as a solo parent. Her loss was made even more difficult as she found herself amid a holiday meant for gratitude. Despite her overwhelming grief, she mustered the strength to attend. Needless to say, the Xanax she'd taken before leaving the house helped take the edge off some of her apprehension.

Eliana and Luna appeared almost as soon as Pepper walked into the clubhouse.

"I am so glad you came," Luna said, hugging her.

"Me too. You said yesterday that you didn't know if you would come."

"Yeah, I know, but Hezekiah convinced me to bring the boys out for at least a while. So here I am," she said, her face grim and lifeless.

"Come on, let's walk around."

"I need to find my table first."

"You're at the table with us."

"I am?"

"Yep," Eliana said. "And don't worry about the kids. The

grandparents have the table across from us. They're getting VIP treatment." She laughed.

Pepper turned and looked at Hezekiah.

"You go ahead. I've got them," he insisted. "Did you say there's a table for grandparents somewhere in here?" he laughed.

"Yes, it's over there," Luna said.

"Oh, I see. Come on, boys." Hezekiah held the chubby little hands of his grandsons as they went in the direction Luna pointed. His salt-and-pepper beard added an air of distinguished charm to his appearance. His tailored, earth-toned blazer complemented the atmosphere of the holiday by creating a warm and inviting visual appeal. Underneath the blazer, he wore a light-colored button-down shirt tucked into fitted dark jeans.

The four-hundred-dollar brown suede tassel loafers were a far cry from the seventeen-hundred-dollar Tom Fords he would have customarily donned had Trevor Price not ripped him—he stopped the thought. He refused to get himself worked up. There was nothing he could do, not tonight, not tomorrow, probably not ever, about that situation other than give himself a heart attack or another stroke. He wanted neither.

He put on his game face, striking the perfect balance between easygoing charm and bold confidence, ready to leave a lasting impression at this afternoon's celebration.

†

"I know Dax will miss his YaYa and PopPop when you have to go. We all are, but I'm just saying he's definitely a spoiled little boy with you here." Luna giggled.

"We aren't leaving until Sunday. So you better know we're

going to use every minute spoiling them even more," her father said, holding Laiyah Rose and kissing her. Dax laid his head on PopPop's thigh and curled his little body on the sofa.

"Okay, I think we have everything," Luna said, stepping into her shoes. Her chestnut hair cascaded in loose waves around her shoulders. It was easy to see that she celebrated her curves in her choice of stylish, distressed boyfriend jeans and a loose-fitting, off-the-shoulder burgundy sweater. A delicate pendant necklace, a recent gift from Christian, added a touch of femininity.

Tall and distinguished, Christian sported a navy blue designer shirt and dark, slim-fit jeans with leather loafers.

Upon arrival, Christian and Luna smiled as they entered the clubhouse and settled at their table, ready to enjoy an afternoon of good food and fellowship with friends and acquaintances.

This afternoon's gathering made it easy for Christian to avoid interacting with Laiyah Rose, as many guests stopped to admire the kids and talk to their grandparents. When a server approached holding a tray of Thanksgiving-themed cocktails, he grabbed an apple cider sangria for himself and a pumpkin spice martini for Luna.

46

ALL YOU NEED IS LOVE

"If the only prayer you said in your whole life was, 'Thank you,' that would suffice." M. Eckhart

The celebration was filled with joy. Children ran around while grandparents shared photos, and other guests danced and sang to various music played by the DJ. Food was plentiful, both traditional and non-traditional, there was something to whet everyone's appetites.

An hour or so into the festivities, Fancy returned to the podium at the front of the room.

"May I have your attention, please?"

The room grew quiet, except for the sounds coming from the little ones.

"At this time in this afternoon's Thanksgiving celebration, I wanted to come up here and openly thank God. Even though," she struggled to keep talking, "this has been one of the most difficult years I've ever experienced in my life. Most of you, if not all of you, know my son, my baby boy Xavier, took his life earlier this year," she cried. "Losing a child is a pain like no other. But God is faithful. I'm blessed beyond measure despite my loss. I have my son, Khalil," she looked at Khalil, my precious grandbabies, two beautiful daughters-in-law, and friends who love and support me." She looked at Stiles and Victoria as well as Eliana and Pepper. She paused and wiped her tears with the tissue she held. Knowing she would likely cry, she'd been smart to bring the tissue with her. "If any of you would like to share what you are most thankful for, you can do so now, starting with the table at the back."

Table by table, individual guests stood and shared what they were thankful for. When it came to Mya's table, she stood and told everyone how grateful she was for her son, Stiles and his family, and to celebrate another trip around the sun.

Stiles stood beside her, clearing his throat before addressing the room. He began to give thanks, similar to what many others had said. Then he locked eyes with Mya.

"Mya, on this special day, your birthday, uhh, well, yesterday was actually your birthday." He laughed. "Anyway, today, the day *after* your birthday," he joked, and Mya giggled. "I know what I'm about to say might come as a surprise, but I realize life is too short to keep our feelings hidden."

He took a step closer, holding her gaze. "I want to tell you in front of my family and friends how thankful I am for you. I'm grateful God connected our paths. I can't think of a day better than Thanksgiving to tell you I love you, Mya. I know I've never said those words until now, but it's the truth, and I had to tell you."

A wave of 'oohs' and 'ahhs' swept through the room. Some guests were teary-eyed.

Mya covered her mouth with one hand as emotions she couldn't describe consumed her. It was like she was living a dream, a beautiful fairytale.

"I love the person you are. You're beautiful inside and outside," Stiles continued. "I love the laughter you bring into my life. I love the way you make every moment brighter. What I'm saying is I want to be with you, to share my life with you. Today, the day *after* your birthday," he chuckled, "on Thanksgiving, I have so much to be grateful for."

He dropped to one knee while pulling a square navy blue box from his pocket.

Mya's hand flew up to her face again, covering her mouth while guests gasped.

"I'm asking if you would share the rest of your life with me. Mya Dugard, will you marry me?"

The room went quiet as everyone waited for her response.

Mya allowed him to gently move her ring hand away from her face.

She looked into his eyes and smiled, tears glistening in the corners of her eyes. "Stiles, this is so unexpected," she said, her voice trembling as were her hands, "but I've heard that sometimes life's most beautiful moments are the ones we didn't plan." She paused as if savoring the moment before continuing, "I love you too, Stiles. I love you so much. And yes," she said, "I will marry you."

Tears streamed down her face as he placed the sparkling three-carat diamond solitaire on her finger.

The room erupted in applause as Stiles and Mya shared a passionate kiss. Afterwards, happy birthday was sung.

Later in the afternoon, toward the end of the celebration, Fancy returned to the podium.

"I am grateful for all of you who came to celebrate and give thanks for another year. I thank God for each of you. We will close by allowing anyone else who wants to say what they are thankful for to come forward. After that, we'll have a closing prayer by Pastor Hezekiah McCoy."

Several more guests, including children, stood up and told the things they were thankful for. At the end, the room went quiet again as Hezekiah approached the podium.

"God is good," he said, his voice booming over the room.

"All the time," several people responded.

"Uh, ladies and gentlemen, family and friends, I stand before you with gratitude and humility on this Thanksgiving day. As we gathered here today, we shared laughter, had fun, enjoyed good food, remembered our loved ones, and celebrated new loved ones. I have been reminded of just how precious the moments are with family and the importance of forgiveness and healing.

"As some of you may know, probably most of you," he said, his eyes scanning the room, "I've emerged from a chapter of my life marked by dark shadows, a period of incarceration that tested my faith, character, and relationships. Today, I stand here a free man. My conviction was overturned. It is a vindication I humbly accept with gratitude."

Some in the room applauded and shouted, "Amen, Praise God." Others remained quiet and expressionless.

"To my firstborn, Khalil," Hezekiah continued and locked eyes with his son, "I want to publicly acknowledge the pain I've caused, the distance that grew between us, and the struggle to find common ground. Our conversations have begun, and though the path to redemption may be hard, I am committed to rebuilding our bond as father and son. I pray that time will heal the wounds that divide us."

Khalil sat at his table. Quietly, his eyes penned to his

father's. He detected what he could only describe as sincerity as he listened to his father speak.

Hezekiah continued talking to a captive audience. "You see, the loss of Xavier cast a sad shadow on our family. His memory lingers in our hearts, a reminder of the fragility of life. As we give thanks today, remember the moments we shared with him and find solace in the love that endures and will forever continue through his sons." He looked at Zavion and Davion squirming at their table.

Khalil remained quiet, holding Khaliyah on his lap as his heart opened up to his father for the first time in years. Maybe he could forgive his father now. Maybe it was time. He reached for Eliana's hand. He felt her tense up, but she didn't pull away. He had a long way to go to prove he had changed. But if his father could try to fix his life, so could he.

"To Fancy, the mother of my two sons. Fancy, I publicly ask your forgiveness. I acknowledge the pain I've caused you and the wounds that need healing. I promise you that I am a changed man. I will strive from this day forward to show you that I am a better person."

Fancy's eyes welled up with tears, prompting her to bow her head and brush them away.

"To my church family, those of you who are here and represent New Holy Rock Ministries, I ask for your forgiveness as well. I haven't always lived up to the standards of a man of God, and I am truly sorry for that. If you allow me to return to the pulpit, I am dedicated to showing you the transformation that has taken place within me during my time away. If you decide I am no longer worthy to stand before you to preach God's word, then I must trust that He has better for me."

Stiles sat back, holding Mya's hand, a broad smile on his face, listening to his brother's testimony. He felt proud and

grateful to see his prayers being answered for his family, especially his brother.

"Lastly, as I look over at my father. Pastor, I know you may
not comprehend the words I speak. But I carry the burden of
our strained relationship and extend a hand of love and understanding. I hope the spirit of forgiveness and reconciliation
permeates our family.

"This Thanksgiving, I am reminded of one of my favorite
Bible verses. John chapter eight verse thirty-six says, 'Whom
the son sets free is free indeed.' This means that when God sets
us free, we are indeed free. I've done a lot of wrong, but I thank
God I can boldly proclaim that I am free. I don't have to keep
going around in circles of guilt, sin, and struggle. So, I say this
to you: let us celebrate our blessings and the potential for healing, renewal, redemption, and reconciliation. May we find the
strength to forgive, the courage to mend, and the wisdom to
cherish our moments together. Happy Thanksgiving, and may
love guide our journey forward."

He wiped the tears forming and went toward his seat, only
to be greeted by Stiles, who embraced him, followed by a
weeping Fancy, who came up. He gathered her into his arms
and clung to her. The three embraced briefly before Stiles
approached the podium to offer a short closing prayer.

Suddenly, out of nowhere, screams and loud gasps filled
the room. Guests jumped up and looked around. Stiles dashed
from the podium, followed by Hezekiah and Khalil, along with
other guests.

"Let me through," Stiles insisted, clawing through the
crowd gathered around Pastor's table. He saw Josie bent over
an unconscious Pastor.

"Someone call 9-1-1," Stiles shouted. "Is there a doctor or
nurse here?"

"I'm a nurse," one of the guests said, dashing up and

kneeling beside an unconscious Pastor. Dribbles of slobber appeared from the side of his mouth. She checked his pulse, listened to his heartbeat, and rechecked his pulse.

The EMTs arrived within minutes and picked up where the nurse left off. After what seemed like a lifetime, one of the EMTs looked toward Josie and said, "I'm so sorry—"

47
LAST DANCE

"The song is ended, but the melody lingers on." Irving Berlin

Stiles delivered an eloquent eulogy. It was evident by the hundreds in attendance that Pastor had left an indelible mark on many.

"The legacy he leaves behind will be lived through the ministry, or should I say ministries he created and founded. Holy Rock grew from a handful of members to a membership of thousands under his leadership. This past year, our family has experienced devastating loss and indescribable pain. Many of you may know that my family laid to rest my brother's son, young Xavier McCoy, earlier this year. We are still reeling from that loss. But through it all, God is still good. Every day was not a dark day. We had some good days, some happy times, and some mighty good blessings."

"Amen," many in attendance praised.

"Now, again, our grief has been awakened, though it barely

had time to sleep, and here we are bidding farewell to our family patriarch, Pastor Chauncey Graham. God said it's time to come home, Pastor," Stiles said, his voice strong despite his pain. "God said, 'You've paid your dues.' So, dear Josie, Pastor is at rest."

Josie nodded and wiped her tears with a white lace handkerchief.

"Yes, my father is now with his Lord and Savior..."

Hezekiah sat on the front row, holding Josie's hand. He replayed the only visit he'd had with Pastor when he told Pastor he had forgiven him, but had he? Or were the words he said that day empty and self-serving? Whether he was sincere or not, it was too late now. Just like that, in an instant, time had slipped away. Pastor was no longer among the living.

Hezekiah felt empty. Where was the grief, the heartache, and the tears? He had wept so much for Xavier that he had nothing left to give his father. He released Josie's hand and placed his arm around her in comfort. He felt more compassion for her than sadness over Pastor's death.

Fancy sat on the other side of Josie, holding her other hand. Hezekiah caught a whiff of her sweet cologne, inhaled the fragrance, and began reminiscing about the good times. He wanted those days again. He understood he could never go back, but he prayed he could one day gain her trust again.

Khalil and Eliana were seated next to Fancy.

Missing was Pepper. She had told Eliana the day before the funeral, *'I am not going to Pastor or anybody's funeral. I don't want to hear preaching, crying, none of it. Anyway, that man was probably hitting ninety years old. He lived a very long life, unlike Xavier. I barely knew him. So it won't matter if I'm sitting on a pew staring at a casket or not. You go right ahead. I'll keep Khaliyah for you.'*

Victoria came over and offered Pepper a hand with the kids. She was concerned about her daughter, and rightfully so.

Pepper seemed to rely more on popping anti-anxiety pills rather than face the world and her grief head-on. The more she talked to Pepper about it, the more defensive Pepper became. She prayed that in due time, God would deliver her daughter from what was beginning to look like more of an addiction.

†

After the funeral, the family and others gathered in Holy Rock's gym for the repast. Mya remained by her fiancé, ensuring Stiles was not bombarded with an overflow of people offering condolences. She understood people's good intentions, but she wanted him to be able to sit down in peace and have a bit to eat. It had been a long day, more than that, a long week for it to culminate to this—the final farewell.

Hezekiah brought Josie a plate of food and sat down to enjoy his meal. He sipped his drink and dug into the hearty plate of deliciousness prepared by Holy Rock's kitchen ministry.

When he heard that familiar, irritating voice talking right in his ear but loud enough for the table to hear, Hezekiah started coughing, almost choking on a chunk of meat he'd just put into his mouth.

"I was sorry to hear about Pastor, my uhh, ex-daddy-in-law. You, uh, have my condolences. I mean that with all my heart," Rianna cooed, bending over, exposing her cleavage, and holding a white Styrofoam *to-go* container stuffed with food. As she talked, bits of juice or gravy started dripping from it and onto the floor.

Fancy looked up, frowning, as did Khalil and Eliana.

"Excuse you?" Khalil said, taken aback by Rianna's boldness.

"Oh, I'm sorry. Pastor Khalil, you have my sympathy too," Rianna purred, rolled her eyes, and focused her attention back to Hezekiah. "Now, remember, Hezekiah, if there's anything—and I do mean *anything*—I can do to help you during this difficult time, please....you know where to find me." She turned and swished off.

Hezekiah swiped his mouth with a cloth napkin and pounced up from the table, following Rianna.

Outside the gym, he caught up to her, grabbed her by the elbow, and jerked her around, causing her to lose her balance, but he caught her before she fell, planting his face so close to hers that bits of spit landed on her cheeks.

"As long as you live, don't you ever, and I mean ever, disrespect me like that again." His anger was apparent in his threatening tone and the deep creases on his face.

"You're hurting me, fool! What's wrong with you?" she screamed, looking around like she was hoping somebody, anybody, was out there and saw what was unfolding. For a split second, she wished someone was videoing their encounter. She imagined it going viral. But she saw no one in sight. "All I did was wish you my sympathy!"

"Do you understand what I said?" Hezekiah tightened his hold until he saw tears pouring from her eyes. He released her, and she stumbled backward, again almost falling had it not been for a truck parked behind her that stopped her fall.

He looked at her and started walking away but stopped, turned around, and spat, "You are messing with the wrong guy, Rianna. You, of all people, should know I'm not one to be played with."

He saw the container of food on the ground close to where she was standing. He squashed it with the tip of his shoes, grinding it until it was flat and the food was smushed and pouring out the side.

.

†

Back inside the gym, Luna and Christian mingled with some of the other people there to support the family.

"Pastor Graham, God bless you," a man with a noticeable but unfamiliar accent walked up to the table and said in a low tone.

"Thank you," Stiles responded, looking at the man who patted him on the shoulder.

At the sound of the man's voice, Luna, standing nearby talking to Christian, swiftly turned and looked over her shoulder. At the same time, for a second, she thought she smelled something, an unpleasant yet strangely familiar scent that, combined with that voice, made her heart race as if she was having an anxiety attack.

"I'm ready to leave," she announced without warning.

Christian looked at her strangely but took hold of her hand when he saw how flushed she was. "Uh, sure, but are you okay? What's wrong?"

She whispered to him, quickly explaining about the man. When Christian looked in the direction where she said the man was, he was no longer there.

She scanned the room and caught the back of who she thought was him exiting the gym.

"Take me home. Now, Christian."

Christian, still holding her hand, led her out of the gym without protest. When they arrived at the car, he comforted her, holding her in his arms.

"Christian, I'm telling you, it was him. That voice. That strange smell." She was shaking like a leaf.

Resting her back against the seat, she closed her eyes, "All this time, I've been so mad at myself for not remembering. And all it takes is walking into a dang repast of someone I don't even know, and boom, there it is, that voice, that smell. Oh, God. What's happening?"

"Come on, Luna. Don't do this, sweetheart."

"Who is he?" she kept asking aloud, ignoring Christian's pleas for her to calm down. "And what was he doing at Pastor Graham's repast? Oh, my gosh, Christian," she cried. "Did he follow me? Is he planning to kidnap me again?"

"*Shhh*, nooo, whoever he is, he won't hurt you again, Luna. I won't let anything happen to you ever again." He reached across the console, took hold of one of her hands, pulled it to his lips, and kissed it. "We're going to figure this out. I promise."

More to come in this addictive series!

WORDS FROM THE AUTHOR

"For I know that nothing good dwells in me, that is, in my flesh. For I have the desire to do what is right but not the ability to carry it out." Romans 7:18 ESV

Whom the son sets free is free—Indeed. Hezekiah is a free man in every sense of the word, but is he a *changed* free man? How can he live with himself after some of the devilish, under-handed things he did as recently as the day before he was released?

And Khalil, he's young, handsome, successful, supposedly walking with God, but will he be able to change his ways and save his marriage? Or is it already too late? I wouldn't blame Eliana if she were done with him once and for all. Then again, Love *is* Blind.

Luna and Christian face a whole fresh set of problems, the result of old trauma and the pressure of raising two little ones. Christian can't seem to make that connection with Laiyah Rose, but he has a special relationship with Dax. Will that ever change? Will he open his heart and accept Laiyah?

Again, here we are, reading about the infamous, charis-matic, drama-fueled, church-going families, *aka* the Grahams and the McCoys.

You may ask why I write about such flawed, imperfect people like these intertwined families. Well, I write about them because they represent life and living. They represent us, you and me, imperfect humans who are flawed in our flesh and in our thoughts. How can these folks I write about who stand in a pulpit and fill church pews proclaim God's love and forgiveness but then go home and commit sins of the flesh and more? Because they are human, they have a sinful nature. People are accountable for themselves. They must come to their own personal "this is enough for me" point in their lives. And no matter what it looks like through the lens of those looking from the outside, I believe it is God, and only God, who knows our hearts.

Well, that's enough of me 'babbling.' I'll let you get back to reading and following the Grahams and McCoys and their messed up, jumbled-up lives.

Thanks for riding with me on this literary journey. More perfect stories about imperfect people like you...and me are coming!

Shelia
    God's Amazing Girl

MORE PERFECT STORIES ABOUT IMPERFECT PEOPLE LIKE YOU... AND ME

If Your Price Is Right

Love Shoulda Brought You Home

Adverse City Series

The Real Housewives of Adverse City 1

The Real Housewives of Adverse City 2

The Real Housewives of Adverse City 3

The Real Housewives of Adverse City 4

Beautiful Ugly 2-book series

Beautiful Ugly

True Beauty

Young Adult Titles

House of Cars

The Life of Payne

The Lollipop Girl

Standalone Novels

Always Now and Forever Love Hurts

Into Each Life

Sinsatiable

What's Blood Got To Do With It?

Only In My Dreams

The House Husband

Cross Road

Forever Ain't Enough

Anthologies

Bended Knees

Weary to Will

Learning to Love Me

Show A Little Love (1)

Show A Little Love (2)

Nonfiction

A Christian's Perspective: Journey Through Grief

How to Live Your Life Like It's Golden

Journals

Journal Your Way Through It

Sister Sister Book Log Journal

If you enjoyed this book or any of my books, please go to your favorite review site and leave a positive review!

Other links to my books
bit.ly/sheliabell
bit.ly/sheliaebell
bit.ly/sheliabn

Join my mailing list for literary updates and new book release information
www.sheliawritesbooks.com

#iwriteforfilmandtv
#iwritebestsellers
#iwritepageturners
#iamgodsamazinggirl

Perfect Stories About Imperfect People Like You ...and Me!

VISIT ME ONLINE

www.sheliaebell.net
www.sheliawritesbooks.com
sheliawritesbooks@yahoo.com

facebook.com/sheliawritesbooks
x.com/sheliaebell
instagram.com/sheliabell
tiktok.com/@sheliaebell